ACCLAIM FOR AMY

"Clipston brings this engaging series to an [e]... reunions, a prodigal son parable, a sweet but... happy ending for characters readers have grown to love. Once again, she gives us all we could possibly want from a talented storyteller."

—*RT Book Reviews*, 4¹/₂ stars, TOP
PICK! on *A Simple Prayer*

". . . will leave readers craving more."

—*RT Book Reviews*, 4¹/₂ stars, TOP
PICK! on *A Mother's Secret*

"Clipston's series starter has a compelling drama involving faith, family and romance . . . [an] absorbing series."

—*RT Book Reviews*, 4¹/₂ stars, TOP
PICK! on *A Hopeful Heart*

"Authentic characters, delectable recipes and faith abound in Clipston's second Kauffman Amish Bakery story."

—*RT Book Reviews*, 4 stars on *A Promise of Hope*

". . . an entertaining story of Amish life, loss, love and family."

—*RT Book Reviews*, 4 stars on *A Place of Peace*

"This fifth and final installment in the 'Kauffman Amish Bakery' series is sure to please fans who have waited for Katie's story."

—*Library Journal* on *A Season of Love*

"[The Kauffman Amish Bakery] series' wide popularity is sure to attract readers to this novella, and they won't be disappointed by the excellent writing and the story's wholesome goodness."

—*Library Journal* on *A Plain and Simple Christmas*

"[*A Plain and Simple Christmas*] is inspiring and a perfect fit for the holiday season."

—*RT Book Reviews*, 4 stars

The Forgotten Recipe

ALSO BY AMY CLIPSTON

a read by the
Heath
Homestead novel

THE FORGOTTEN RECIPE

an
amish
heirloom

AMY CLIPSTON

ZONDERVAN®

ZONDERVAN

The Forgotten Recipe
Copyright © 2015 by Amy Clipston

This title is also available as a Zondervan e-book.
Visit www.zondervan.com.

This title is also available as a Zondervan audiobook.
Visit www.zondervan.com.

Requests for information should be addressed to:

Zondervan, *Grand Rapids, Michigan 49546*

Clipston, Amy.
The forgotten recipe / Amy Clipston.
pages ; cm
ISBN 978-0-310-34199-4 (trade paper)
I. Title.
PS3603.L58F67 2015
813'.6--dc23
2015023696
ISBN: 978–0–310–341994

Printed in the United States of America

15 16 17 18 19 20 21/ RRD / 20 19 18 17 16 15 14 13 12 11 10 9 8 7 6 5 4 3 2

In loving memory of my father,
Ludwig "Bob" Goebelbecker,
who taught me how to skip stones at Schroon Lake, New York

GLOSSARY

ach: oh

aenti: aunt

appeditlich: delicious

Ausbund: Amish hymnal

bedauerlich: sad

boppli: baby

brieder: brothers

brot: bread

bruder: brother

bruderskinner: nieces/nephews

bu: boy

buwe: boys

daadi: granddad

daadihaus: grandfather's house

daed: father

danki: thank you

dat: dad

Dietsch: Pennsylvania Dutch, the Amish language
   (a German dialect)

dochder: daughter

dochdern: daughters

Dummle!: Hurry!

Englisher: a non-Amish person

fraa: wife

freind: friend

freinden: friends

froh: happy

gegisch: silly

gern gschehne: you're welcome

grossdaadi: grandfather

grossdochder: granddaughter

grossdochdern: granddaughters

grossmammi: grandmother

Gude mariye: Good morning

gut: good

Gut nacht: Good night

haus: house

Ich liebe dich: I love you

kaffi: coffee

kapp: prayer covering or cap

kichli: cookie

kichlin: cookies

kind: child

kinner: children

kumm: come

liewe: love, a term of endearment

maed: young women, girls

maedel: young woman

mamm: mom

mammi: grandma

mei: my

mutter: mother

naerfich: nervous

narrisch: crazy

onkel: uncle

Ordnung: The oral tradition of practices required and forbidden
  in the Amish faith.

schee: pretty

schmaert: smart

schtupp: family room

schweschder: sister

schweschdere: sisters

Was iss letz?: What's wrong?

willkumm: welcome

Wie geht's: How do you do? or Good day!

wunderbaar: wonderful

ya: yes

AMISH HEIRLOOM FAMILY TREES

Martha "Mattie" m. Leroy Fisher

Veronica   Rachel   Emily

Annie m. Elam Huyard

Jason   Stephen

Tillie m. Henry (Hank) Ebersol

Margaret m. Abner *(Deceased)* **Lapp**

Seth (Deceased)   Ellie

Fannie Mae m. Titus Dienner *(Bishop)*

Lindann

Susannah m. Timothy Beiler

David   Irma Rose Beiler Smucker

Irma Rose m. Melvin Smucker

Sarah

A NOTE TO THE READER

WHILE THIS NOVEL IS SET AGAINST THE REAL BACKDROP OF Lancaster County, Pennsylvania, the characters are fictional. There is no intended resemblance between the characters in this book and any real members of the Amish or Mennonite communities. As with any work of fiction, I've taken license in some areas of research as a means of creating the necessary circumstances for my characters. My research was thorough; however, it would be impossible to be completely accurate in details and description because each community differs. Therefore, any inaccuracies in the Amish and Mennonite lifestyles portrayed in this book are completely due to fictional license.

PROLOGUE

JASON HUYARD HAD TO BE DREAMING. THE WHOLE SCENE playing out in front of him was surreal as he stood in the Lapp family's kitchen doorway and peered into their large family room. People, mostly strangers from other church districts, paraded in and out of the house, seemingly in slow motion. They walked through the family room, shaking hands with other visitors before expressing their condolences to his friend Seth's mother, Margaret, and his younger sister, Ellie.

Seth's body lay motionless in the coffin behind his family, and Jason's stomach twisted and bile rose in his throat as he looked at his best friend.

No, it wasn't a dream; it was a nightmare, one of the worst nightmares imaginable. It couldn't be possible that only two days ago he and Seth were talking as they built a shed together for the Lancaster Shed Company. Jason's world came to a screeching halt when a board broke, causing Seth to fall from the rafters, breaking his neck when he plummeted to the concrete floor.

In an instant, Seth was gone.

If only I hadn't walked away to grab those bottles of water . . .

Jason tried to push the thought to the back of his mind and moved into the family room to join his family. But he couldn't take his eyes away from Seth's mother. She was sobbing in the arms of a woman with graying hair peeking out of her prayer covering. Ellie, standing nearby, wiped tears from her rosy cheeks.

Jason must have told them a dozen times that he longed to go back in time and break Seth's fall.

It's my fault Seth is gone and his family is devastated.

Watching them cry was too much for him. The depth of their grief was palpable even from across the large room. Jason's chest constricted, and he felt as if he couldn't breathe. The heat in the room closed in on him, stealing the air from his lungs. He had to get out of there before he was sick or passed out.

He turned and weaved through the knot of people on his way back to the kitchen and mudroom, excusing himself whenever he bumped into someone.

"Jay?" his younger brother, Stephen, asked as Jason pushed past him. "Jason. Where are you going?"

"I need some air," Jason breathed out, pushing on the old, wooden back door, which moaned in protest as it opened.

"Wait," Stephen called after him.

Jason stepped out onto the wide, covered back porch, and the cool April air hit his face like a wall.

Finally! I can breathe! He moved to the railing and leaned over it. Staring down at the wet grass below, he took long, gasping breaths in an attempt to settle his violent stomach. He was glad no one else was there.

"Jay?" Stephen's brow furrowed with concern. "You're as white as a sheet."

Jason lifted his hat and raked his fingers through his hair. "I'll be all right. Just give me a minute."

Stephen pointed toward a group of people talking just inside open barn doors. "I see a couple of guys from work out there. I'm going to talk to them. Do you want to come with me?"

"No, *danki.*" Jason shook his head. "I'm going to stay here for a few minutes and enjoy the quiet."

"Okay. I'll be back in a minute." Stephen headed down the porch steps and dashed across the yard.

Jason turned and leaned back against the railing, crossing his arms over his chest as the cool wind seeped in through his black jacket. He moved his gaze upward. Puffy gray clouds strangled the sky, and the mist that had threatened all day finally transformed into steady raindrops. The weather was a fitting complement to the hundreds of community members who had journeyed to the Lapp home to say good-bye to Seth.

The back door creaked open, and a choked sob followed. Two women stepped out onto the porch as they supported a third woman, who seemed to be holding on to them with all her strength. They all shared similar facial features and looked to be in their twenties. The woman crying was dressed in black with wisps of blonde hair escaping her prayer covering. Her beautiful face crumpled with anguish and her ice-blue eyes, rimmed with dark circles, were clouded with tears.

The sobs grew louder as her legs seemed to buckled, causing the other two women to grasp her more tightly. Jason started to move across the porch to help them, but they successfully steered her toward a nearby bench and ordered her to sit down. The woman obeyed, and the other two young ladies sat on either side of her, cooing softly while holding her hands.

The door banged open, and a middle-aged couple rushed out and hovered over the three women.

"Veronica?" The older woman addressed the crying woman.

Jason's eyes widened as he whispered, "Veronica." *Seth's fiancée!* Seth had spoken of her so often that Jason felt as if he knew her.

"Veronica? Please take a deep breath. You need to calm

down or you're going to pass out again." The woman bent down to meet her eyes. "Do you want to leave?"

Veronica shook her head and dabbed her wet eyes with a tissue. "No, I promised Margaret I would stay."

"She would understand if you left," the young woman with light-brown hair said. "You've been here all day."

"Rachel is right," the one with blonde hair chimed in. "You've been here since the crack of dawn, and I heard you pacing last night. You haven't slept since . . ." Her voice trailed off and she cleared her throat. "*Mamm*'s right. You're going to pass out again if you don't calm down. And you need to sleep."

"I can't sleep." Veronica's voice was gravelly. "I need to be here. I *have* to be here for him. I can't leave him." Her voice broke, and sobs racked her body anew.

The agony in her eyes fueled his guilt. Why hadn't he saved Seth? Why wasn't he there when Seth fell? He could've broken his fall or warned him if he'd heard the board start to give way.

Now the blonde was rubbing Veronica's back. Tears still streamed from Veronica's eyes, and Jason gripped the railing behind him. He needed to apologize, tell her he was so sorry for her loss. He knew how much Seth loved Veronica. Seth talked about her incessantly. Seth acted as if Veronica was all he ever thought about.

Stephen sidled up to him. "Do you know them?"

"No, but I feel like I do."

"What do you mean?"

"Stephen, Jason." *Mamm* stepped out the door and onto the porch with *Dat* in tow. "I didn't realize you were out here." She turned toward the sound of crying, and a look of compassion crossed her face.

"I needed some air," Jason said.

"Are you ready to go?" *Dat* asked.

"*Ya*," Stephen said. "Jason looks like he needs to go home and rest." He patted his brother's shoulder. "Let's go."

His parents walked toward the porch steps, but Jason lingered behind. He turned back to Veronica, who was speaking softly with the women he now assumed were her mother and sisters. He couldn't stop watching her. He longed to take away her pain. He felt responsible for her suffering.

"Jay?" Stephen asked. "It's time to go. We've been here nearly all afternoon."

Jason nodded. "I'm coming."

"No, you're not, actually. You're still standing here." Stephen leaned closer. "Why are you staring at that *maedel?*"

"She was Seth's fiancée. They were supposed to be married in the fall."

"That's Veronica?" Stephen blew out a breath. "Oh no."

Veronica's eyes met Jason's for a quick moment, and his breath caught. No matter how much he needed to talk to her, he couldn't do it now, not when her emotions—*his* emotions—were so raw. He was sure he'd fall apart if he tried to speak. He had to wait until he was strong enough to tell her he felt responsible for Seth's death, that he would never forgive himself.

"Jason?" Stephen nudged him. "*Mamm* and *Dat* are ready."

He nodded and followed his brother down the squeaky porch steps. When he reached the bottom, he looked over his shoulder one last time and took in the sight of Seth's beautiful fiancée and her obvious grief. He was going to find a way to talk to her soon, and he would tell her just how sorry he was for not being able to save her future with Seth.

CHAPTER 1

"THE WINDOWS ARE DONE." VERONICA WIPED HER HANDS on her black apron as she stepped into the kitchen from the mudroom. "They're actually sparkling in the sunlight."

"Veronica, I told you. You didn't have to worry about the windows yet. We're not having church here until late August." *Mamm* shook her head while standing in front of the kitchen sink. Bubbles from the frothy water danced in the warm June sunlight that spilled in through the window above her.

Veronica spotted a smudge on the window and scooped a dishrag from the counter. "Don't move. I missed that one." She crossed the room, reached up behind her mother, and rubbed the spot. She smiled when the window pane looked perfect. "There. *Now* they're all done."

Her mother eyed her a moment, and her smile disappeared. Veronica sucked in a breath, preparing herself for the fervent advice her mother had repeated over and over during the two months since she'd lost Seth.

"Veronica." *Mamm* wiped her hands on a dish towel and then touched the short sleeve of Veronica's blue dress. "I know you're doing all of this cleaning to distract yourself, but you need to slow down. You need to allow yourself time to grieve."

"I'm fine." Veronica forced a smile. "I just enjoy helping out around the *haus*. You know I love to clean." She hoped she sounded convincing. The truth was, if she allowed herself to slow down, her memories crashed down on her, just like the waves she'd enjoyed at the beach last summer when she and her sisters traveled to the Maryland shore with the girls in youth group.

She couldn't allow the memories to drown her. She tried not to think of Seth, and his light-green eyes, blond hair, and radiant smile. She pushed away the memories of how he loved to tell silly jokes just to see his friends and family members laugh. She bit the inside of her lip and willed herself not to cry. She'd cried herself to sleep for so long, and she was tired of crying. In fact, she was surprised she had any tears left to shed.

"I understand how you feel, Veronica." *Mamm's* eyes glistened with sadness. "I know you feel like you can't get through this, but God will help your heart heal. You can't rush your grief. It's a process."

Veronica tried to listen to her mother's supportive words, but her mind checked off a list of what projects she'd completed—painting the bedrooms upstairs, cleaning up the garden, planting flowers, helping her mother and sister make quilts to sell at local stores and auctions, organizing the cabinets in the kitchen, and doing inventory for her father's harness shop. What hadn't she done?

The attic!

"*Mamm*," she said, cutting off her mother's lecture about accepting God's plan for her life and holding on to her faith. "I'm sorry for interrupting, but would it be okay if I cleaned the attic? I know you once mentioned it probably needs it, but you've never had the time."

Her mother gave her a blank expression and blinked her eyes. "You want to clean the attic?"

Veronica nodded. "*Ya*, I'd love to."

"But, Veronica, you can't continue to ignore your feelings. You have to work through this, *mei liewe*."

"I'm not ignoring my feelings." She knew it was a sin to lie, but today wasn't the day to work through her emotions or allow herself to fully accept that the love of her life was gone forever.

No, today wasn't the day. The sun was so bright and the sky was so blue, just like the day she and Seth had gone for a walk and he asked her to marry him. It was an unusually warm March day, and the birds were singing. His hair took on a golden hue in the sunlight. His seafoam-green eyes sparkled with nervousness because, as he'd admitted to her later, he wasn't certain she would say yes.

Veronica, however, had known she'd loved him since he'd first offered to give her a ride home from a youth group singing four years earlier. She'd had a crush on him since she was ten years old, staring at him at church and in school. He hadn't seemed to notice her until they were both eighteen. That was when everything changed, and she'd finally had a chance to be Seth Lapp's girlfriend. He wasn't only the love of her life; he was also her best friend. Of course she wanted to marry him.

Veronica pushed the thoughts away and willed her eyes not to well up with tears. She couldn't let herself dwell on those memories. Today had been a good day. In fact, it was her first good day since the accident had stolen her future.

"Veronica," her mother was saying, "you don't need to worry about that attic. We'll deal with it when we get the winter clothes out in the fall. Instead of worrying about cleaning, why don't you have a cup of tea with your *schweschdere* and me?"

"Really, I want to clean the attic." When her mother frowned, she quickly added, "I'll have tea with you, Rachel, and Emily later. Okay?" She forced another smile, but she was sure her mother could see right through her desperate attempt to have some time alone while doing something mindless like cleaning.

"Fine." Her mother sighed with defeat. "Call me if you need me."

Veronica grabbed a few rags, a dustpan, and a broom and moved up the spiral staircase in the old farmhouse that had been in her father's family for four generations. She continued up the stairs, passing the second floor, where her bedroom, her two younger sisters' rooms, and the sewing room were. When she reached the third floor, she pulled open the old door, which creaked loudly in protest, revealing the large, open attic that spanned the top floor of the large, white clapboard house.

The heavy scent of dust mixed with stale air permeated her lungs as she surveyed the sea of boxes, old oil lamps, furniture, and toys. She placed the cleaning supplies on the floor and then crossed to the small window. She unlocked it and pushed with all of her strength until the window slowly moved up in the track. She rubbed the sweat from her brow with the back of her hand and breathed in the warm, fresh air seeping in from the outside.

Veronica grasped the broom and began to push it across the floor, weaving past boxes and accumulating a pile of dust on her way across the large room. She stopped and forced open the small window on the far end of the attic, thankful for a light cross breeze. She wondered for a moment if this project was a silly idea, as her mother had implied, but the busy work was a welcome distraction from her emotional turmoil. She pushed the broom and hummed a hymn as she moved back to the other side of the room. She spotted a box marked "Dolls," and she wondered if her favorite baby doll was packed in it along with her sisters' favorites. She climbed over a box marked "Books," tripped on a loose book, and stubbed her toe on a large wooden chest. Sucking in a breath, Veronica lowered herself onto the chest and rubbed her throbbing toe.

Once the pain subsided, she stood and examined the large chest, running her fingers over the smooth wood. She didn't remember ever seeing the chest before. Where had it come from? Had it belonged to her mother or, from the look of it, possibly to her grandmother? It was well made, even beautiful. Why didn't her mother keep it in her bedroom? She tried to lift the lid, but it didn't budge. She bent and spotted a brass key sitting inside the lock. She turned it, and the lock clicked. She pushed the heavy lid up and breathed in the sweet aroma of cedar.

Her eyes widened with surprise when she found the large chest filled with linens, a quilt, and a few small boxes. She picked up the box on top and opened it, revealing yellow cards with frayed edges. The top card had a recipe for raspberry pie, written in beautiful, slanted handwriting. The handwriting was familiar. It must have belonged to her maternal grandmother, who had passed away when Veronica was little. Had this box belonged to her? If so, why was it stowed away, forgotten in this large, beautiful chest? Who had put it there? Had this chest also belonged to her *mamm*? Why would her mother hide something so beautiful and special up in the musty attic?

Veronica pondered the old card, taking in the instructions detailed in faded pencil. She swallowed a gasp as she gripped it. She could finally do something special with all those raspberries ripening in her mother's garden. Every summer the garden yielded rows and rows of raspberries, and every summer Veronica and her youngest sister, Emily, made jars and jars of jam to sell at the Bird-in-Hand Farmers Market. They froze the rest of the raspberries and rarely did anything more with them.

She felt a tingle of excitement. This recipe would give her

the chance to stay busy with another project—making pies. *I have to tell Mamm!*

Veronica slipped the card back into the box, closed the chest, and hurried down the steps. She crossed the second-floor hallway and stopped at the top of the staircase as voices floated up from downstairs. Veronica knew she shouldn't eavesdrop, but her body went rigid and her feet stopped moving forward when she heard her name.

"Where's Veronica?" It was Rachel.

"She's cleaning the attic," *Mamm* said.

"She's cleaning the attic?" Her sister sounded confused. "Why would she do that?"

"I told her it wasn't necessary, but she insisted." *Mamm* sounded weary. "You know how she is lately. She can't sit still. I've almost given up trying to convince her to let herself slow down and go through the grieving process."

"*Ya*, I know." Veronica thought she recognized a sigh. "I feel so bad when I hear her crying. I've tried talking to her, but she just tells me to leave her room. She wants to cry alone, and I can't stand seeing her so unhappy. I pray and pray, asking God to take away her pain. I can't imagine how difficult this is for her. I can't even imagine how difficult it would be to lose David like that. It would just crush me."

"We have to be supportive of her. If she wants to clean the attic, then I have to let her. I just want to see her *froh* again."

"*Ya*, I know. I keep asking God to bring someone else special into Veronica's life. Maybe she'll meet a *bu* and fall in love again."

Veronica straightened her shoulders. She didn't want her family's pity, and she didn't need a new boyfriend. She couldn't imagine finding anyone she'd love as much as she loved Seth, and she would never dream of betraying his memory that way.

She'd promised to love him and only him when he asked her to marry him, and she intended to keep that promise. No one could ever take his place.

"We can't force her, Rachel," *Mamm* warned. "You know that, right? Just be there for her when she needs you."

"*Ya*, I know."

"Rachel!" Emily's voice rang out from somewhere downstairs. "I didn't realize you were home from the market. How was your day?"

Veronica was grateful Emily had steered the subject away from her grief. She took a deep breath and started down the stairs toward the kitchen, where Rachel was detailing her day working at the Philadelphia Farmers Market with her friends and her boyfriend, David.

Before the accident, Veronica had worked with Rachel at the Philadelphia market three days a week—on Monday, Wednesday, and Thursday. Afterward, she couldn't bring herself to face the constant questions and pity she knew she'd receive from friends and acquaintances. Instead, she begged her parents to allow her to stay home and help her mother and sister make quilts and work around the house. She promised to go back to the market someday, but instead, she hoped to stay home and enjoy the security of her family.

"*Mamm!*" Veronica walked down the stairs and held up the box as she entered the kitchen. "Look what I found in the attic in a big cedar chest."

Mamm spun around, facing Veronica with her eyes wide with shock. "Oh? What did you find?" Her mother was no doubt afraid she might have overheard her and Rachel talking, but Veronica had no intention of letting on that she had.

"Look at this box!" Veronica shoved it toward her mother as her sisters crowded around her.

"What's that?" Emily asked, tilting her head to the side. At nineteen, she was the shortest in the Fisher family, six inches under Veronica's five ten. But she had the same blue eyes Veronica inherited from their mother.

Veronica opened the box, and Rachel blew out an excited breath. "Are those recipe cards?" At twenty-one, Rachel was tall like Veronica, only a mere two inches shorter. Unlike her sisters, she'd inherited their father's light-brown hair and deep-brown eyes.

"*Ya*. I think they were *Mammi*'s." Veronica handed the box to her mother, who only stared at it.

"Where did you find this?" *Mamm* asked.

"I told you. There's a large cedar hope chest in the attic. I unlocked it and found the box on top of an old quilt." Veronica took in the concern in her mother's blue eyes. "Did I do something wrong? Should I put it back?"

"No, no." *Mamm* cleared her throat as she sifted through the yellowed cards. "I had forgotten about that old chest. *Ya*, these were your *mammi*'s recipes."

"*Ach*, I miss *Mammi*'s cooking," Emily said with a sad smile.

"I do too," Veronica said, turning toward her younger sister. "Remember—"

"Grilled cheese!" the sisters yelled at the same time, laughing.

"We all loved her grilled cheese," Rachel said, wiping her eyes.

"Oh, *ya*," Emily agreed. "We had so much fun eating her *appeditlich* grilled cheese sandwiches, drinking chocolate milk, and talking with her."

"*Ya*, we sure did," Veronica said with a sigh. "I miss her."

"I do too," Emily agreed.

"Look at this raspberry pie recipe," *Mamm* said, studying the card Veronica had pulled out.

"I decided upstairs that I want to try to make it. It sounds *appeditlich.*"

"Raspberry pie?" Emily stood up on her tiptoes and craned her neck to read the recipe in *Mamm's* hand.

"Oh, *ya.*" Rachel grinned. "That does sound delicious. You should try to make it, Veronica."

"Did *Mammi* make these?" Veronica asked.

"She did." *Mamm* had a faraway look in her eyes. "My *dat* loved them. In fact, your *mammi* started making them for him when they were dating, and then it became a tradition every spring. I remember her taking care of the raspberries in the garden, and she always made and sold the pies."

"Where did she sell them?" Rachel asked.

"At the farmers' market in Bird-in-Hand," *Mamm* said as she continued looking through the recipes. "Oh my. There's her recipe for relish. *Mei mamm* made the most fantastic relish and pickles too."

Renewed excitement sparked within Veronica. These old recipes were just what her soul craved. "I want to make that too. I've never tried to make relish before."

"*Ya!*" Emily agreed.

Mamm held up a recipe card as a grin spread on her face. "Here's one for her peach salsa. We will have to make this too."

"Oh, yes." Veronica nodded with excitement. "I would love to try the salsa." She gnawed her lower lip as she examined the raspberry pie recipe. "I want to try this raspberry pie recipe first, though, and I don't know if I can do it."

"You're a *gut* cook, and I can help you," Emily chimed in. "I can't wait to try it. I've never had raspberry pie."

"I haven't either." Veronica smiled the first true smile since that horrible day in April. "I can't wait to get started."

VERONICA LOOKED UP AT THE CEILING THROUGH THE DARK while a chorus of crickets sang to her through the open window. She used to quickly fall asleep and dream of her future. She and Seth had chosen November 27, the day after Thanksgiving, for their wedding. She'd decided on purple for her wedding dress and the dresses of her attendants, who, of course, would be her sisters. Seth had planned to build a house on his parents' farm, and they had already talked about names for their future children.

All those plans were dashed when Seth had his accident.

Now she dreaded this time of night with every fiber of her being as her mind replayed that day. She still remembered the sound of the phone ringing in the barn as she weeded the garden. She recalled Ellie's distraught voice as she told Veronica to get to Seth's house right away. When Veronica asked her what had happened, Ellie began to sob, and Veronica's blood ran cold as her stomach twisted. Somehow she sensed that something had happened to Seth.

When she and her father arrived, she'd found Seth's mother sobbing in a friend's arms. She listened in disbelief as someone—she never could recall who—told her what had happened. Her knees buckled, sending her toward the floor before her father grabbed her arms. It felt as if she'd been living someone else's life. She wasn't supposed to lose the love of her life before their life together had even started. It didn't make sense. Why had God taken Seth before he had a chance to live?

Veronica rolled onto her side and faced the window while hugging her arms to her middle. The days after Seth's death had passed in a blur. She hardly remembered the visitation or the funeral, except for the sound of Margaret's and Ellie's sobs. Or had they been her own sobs? She recalled a nonstop parade of faceless people stopping by their house to visit and deliver food—food she couldn't eat because her appetite had evaporated the day Seth died. She'd lost enough weight that her dresses hung from her already slim body.

Her mother tried to encourage her to eat, but all she wanted to do was work. If she kept busy, then she didn't have to face the fact that her life was forever changed. She'd lost all of the plans and dreams she'd enjoyed since March. The fabric she'd bought for the wedding dresses sat in a pile in the sewing room. It was as if time had stood still and she didn't know how to make it move forward again. Until today.

Finding those recipes had awakened something deep inside her. The idea of baking something new, something that was all hers, took hold of her. And not only was it hers, but the recipe was a link to her grandmother. The link to her family history was a balm for her grieving soul. After she'd given the recipe box to her mother, Veronica had rushed back to the attic to close the windows and retrieve her cleaning supplies, deciding the attic could be cleaned another day. She asked her sisters to help her pick raspberries until it was time to help her mother cook supper, and then she continued picking berries after supper until bedtime. Tomorrow she would go to the grocery store to buy supplies so she could start baking.

Veronica rolled onto her back and closed her eyes. She hoped baking the pies would help fill the hole in her life. Her thoughts moved to her sister Rachel's confession of praying for Veronica to fall in love again. Veronica couldn't fathom finding another man to love. Her emotions hadn't recovered from losing the love of her life. Instead of looking for love, she'd look for relief, and right now, that relief was found in her kitchen. She was grateful her *mammi* had given those recipes to her *mamm*. She couldn't wait to get started.

CHAPTER 2

Jason placed his hammer on the workbench and wiped his sweaty brow with a red shop rag as the familiar aroma of wood and stain permeated his nostrils. He scanned the large, noisy shop. Hammers, saws, and nail guns blasted and voices boomed in Pennsylvania Dutch as the workers built sheds. And since it was an Amish-owned business, the air compressors powering the machinery ran off diesel generators. Lancaster Shed Company was co-owned by Jason's father, Elam, and uncle, Rufus.

He spotted Stephen talking to another worker as they nailed plywood sheeting to form the floor of a large shed. Although Stephen was twenty-one, three years younger than Jason, he was constantly mistaken for his older brother because he stood at six two, two inches taller than Jason's six-foot-even stature, and shared the same light-brown hair and brown eyes.

Both Stephen and Jason had grown up in this shop, handing workers tools and, when they were old enough, assisting with the creation of the sheds. His uncle and father had inherited the business from their father, who now was retired and lived in the *daadihaus* on his uncle's farm in Gordonville.

Jason looked at the large clock on the wall above the door

leading to the showroom, and he was relieved that it was noon. His stomach had been growling for nearly an hour, and he was ready for a break. He turned back to his brother, who raised his eyebrows as he pointed toward the clock. Stephen nodded and placed his hammer on the floor.

"Are you hungry or something?" Stephen joked as he approached.

Jason shrugged. "*Ya*, I am. I need a break too."

"Sounds *gut* to me," Stephen said as they crossed the shop and entered the large break room.

After washing their hands, they found their lunch pails and took their usual spot in the corner, farthest from the door. A line of employees filed into the room, and soon a hum of conversation filled the air. Jason glanced at the door, expecting Seth to walk in and take his usual spot at the table, next to Stephen. Even though it had been two months since the accident, Jason still found himself looking for Seth, who would burst into the room, ready to share another joke that was so stupid Jason couldn't help but laugh.

Seth had been a member of a different church district, so they hadn't gone to school together, and they had also been members of different youth groups. But the two had instantly become friends when Seth started working there six months ago. Because they were the same age, Jason's father asked him to train Seth, and the two fell into an easy conversation about their lives and families. Jason's best friend, Peter, had recently moved away, and Jason didn't have many close friends. He was grateful to forge a new friendship with Seth.

Jason enjoyed hearing about Seth's family, and especially about his girlfriend, Veronica. He'd known what she looked like and that she worked at the market in Philadelphia three days a week with her sister and friends. She loved to work in her garden and she enjoyed homemade pretzels. And Jason knew when Seth had proposed and how much his friend had worried that Veronica might say no. But she didn't say no. They'd picked a date to be married, and he was excitedly counting down the days. Jason had never met Veronica or Seth's mother and sister and had been looking forward to meeting them. He even wondered if Seth might ask him to stand up for him at the wedding.

That all ended when Seth tumbled to the hard, concrete floor.

Jason hadn't stopped thinking about Veronica since the visitation at Margaret Lapp's house. The sound of her sobs and the thud of Seth's body hitting the floor both haunted him when he climbed into bed at night.

"Jay?" Jason looked up to see Stephen watching him, holding his turkey sandwich in mid-air. "You're in another world."

"Sorry." Jason lifted a potato chip to his lips. "I was just thinking about Seth."

Stephen blew out a sigh. "I was thinking about him earlier too. I can't get used to not seeing him here. It's been two months, but it feels like it was only yesterday that the ambulance was parked out behind the shop."

He said just what I'd been thinking. Can my brother read my thoughts? Jason sipped his drink. Constant reminders surrounded him. Every time he heard the wail of an ambulance, he thought of that day. Each time he saw one of his coworkers perched up on the rafters, he stood beneath them, ready to catch them if they fell, even if another worker was there to spot them.

"It's not just Seth. I also can't stop thinking about Veronica," Jason admitted while running his fingers down his cool bottle of water. "I told you, I feel like I know her. Seth talked about her all the time. You have to remember the stories he told us."

Stephen raised an eyebrow. "But you've never even met her."

"True, but I've seen her. I know you remember her from the porch at the visitation at Seth's mother's *haus*."

Stephen shook his head. "You didn't even talk to her. You figured out who she was because someone said her name. That's not exactly the same thing as knowing someone."

"It wasn't the most appropriate time to approach her and tell her I was there when Seth died, not when we had never even met. I'm not even sure how much Seth might have mentioned me to her." He paused for a moment. "Do you think it would be all right if I went to visit Veronica?"

Stephen furrowed his brow. "No. You shouldn't go see her."

"Why not?"

"Jay, that would be weird." Stephen placed his sandwich on his napkin. "Think about this for a minute. Our *freind* died, and you're thinking about his girlfriend. Let's pretend you go see her out of the blue, tell her you feel like you know her because her deceased fiancé talked about her constantly, and you tell her you're there because you think about her all the time. It's just not done."

"Why not?" Jason challenged him. "She and I had a mutual *freind*. Isn't that how people meet all the time?"

Stephen sighed, sounding a bit exasperated. "Okay, let me put it to you this way. What if I were killed in an accident?"

Jason shook his head. "Don't even—"

Stephen held up a finger to silence him, and Jason complied. "This is hypothetical, so hear me out."

"Fine," Jason muttered with a frown before taking another sip of his water.

"Let's just pretend for argument's sake that I'm killed in an accident. One of my *freinden*, let's say Danny, was there when it happened. Danny can't stop thinking about me and how sad Leah was at my funeral. He goes to see Leah to tell her how

21

much he misses me too. He tells her he thinks about her constantly and worries about her. He wants to comfort her so they can both commiserate over my sudden death." He paused for emphasis. "Doesn't that sound a bit weird?"

Jason huffed. He couldn't stand it when his younger brother was right. "No, not really."

"I wouldn't want someone else consoling my girlfriend, not even one of my close *freinden*."

"Are you saying you'd rather she suffer alone? Remember, you're dead, right?"

After taking the last bite of his sandwich, Stephen wiped his mouth. "Jason, she has family and her church district to support her, and probably *freinden* too. I still think it's wrong. You don't even know her."

But I'd like to know her. The thought caught him off guard. Was Stephen right? Was it inappropriate to want to meet Veronica?

"You should come to youth group with Leah and me Sunday night," Stephen said while pulling a storage bag full of *Mamm*'s homemade peanut butter cookies from his lunch bag. "Her *schweschder* has been asking about you. She tried to talk to you at church last week, and you ignored her. She told Leah she was really disappointed."

Jason stole a cookie from Stephen's bag. "Mary tried to talk to me?" He didn't remember seeing her at church or after the service.

"You really didn't notice her?" Stephen's eyes were full of disbelief.

"No, I didn't. When did she talk to me?"

"She told Leah she asked you how you were doing while she filled your *kaffi* cup, but you just turned and spoke to *Dat*." Stephen shook his head. "Maybe you just didn't hear her, but I get the feeling you're so worried about Seth's girlfriend that you haven't even noticed the *maed* in our district." He leaned forward and lowered his voice. "I miss Seth, too, but you have to move on. There was nothing you could do when he fell. Stop feeling like he died because you weren't there. He knew you were step-ping away; you told him you were. He shouldn't have stayed up on the rafters like he was without someone nearby. He broke the rules, Jay."

Jason gripped his sandwich. His brother was wrong. Jason had no business going for water at all while his friend was sitting on the rafters. He should have made sure Seth had moved to a safer place or had come down to take a break with him.

"After church on Sunday we're going to play volleyball," Stephen continued. "You should come. Mary would enjoy your company."

"I'm too old," Jason said quickly. "How old is Mary? Nineteen?"

"No, she's twenty." Stephen rolled his eyes. "That's only a four-year difference. What's the big deal? *Mamm* and *Dat* are six years apart."

As usual, Stephen had a point, but Jason still wasn't inter-ested. "I'd be the oldest one at the youth group."

"No, you wouldn't. You know we have some members around your age in our youth group. You're not too old. Besides, Mary likes you. Why don't you come and talk to her? Give her a chance. Age is only a number, right?"

"Why are you so determined to set me up with Mary?" Jason regarded Stephen with suspicion.

Stephen shrugged. "I think it's time you dated. It's been a long time since Arie broke up with you. It's time for you to move on."

Where's Dat when I need him? Jason glanced across the break room. He longed to change the subject. He didn't want to dis-cuss the girl who had broken off their engagement, shattering his spirit in the process.

"Are you going to help me finish building the floor on that shed after lunch?"

Jason's shoulders relaxed. He could easily talk about work all day long. "*Ya,* I will." He took another cookie.

"Why didn't you pack your own cookies?" Stephen asked. "The jar was on the counter."

"I don't need to pack my own when you already packed enough for both of us." Jason grinned.

Dat appeared and sat down beside Stephen. "How is your day going? I haven't had a chance to come back and check on you two." Jason and Stephen had inherited their light-brown hair and brown eyes from their father. The gray threaded through his hair revealed he was growing older, closing in on fifty-five.

"It's been busy," Stephen said, wiping his hands on a napkin. "The usual. Building sheds and getting splinters."

"*Ya,*" Jason agreed with a nod between bites of one of his mother's delicious peanut butter cookies. "And you need to wear your work gloves."

"It's going to get busier. We had four more orders this morning." *Dat* unpacked his lunch, pulling out a sandwich, an apple, and a bag of cookies.

"See?" Stephen pointed toward *Dat*'s bag of cookies. "Even *Dat* brought his own."

Jason shrugged and opened the bag. "More for me."

Dat chuckled. "Your *mamm* makes those *kichlin* for me. They've always been my favorite. In fact, she won my heart with those *kichlin.*"

"I thought she made them for me." Stephen feigned disappointment, wiping away invisible tears for dramatic effect. "Now I'll cry myself to sleep tonight knowing I'm not *Mamm*'s favorite."

With a laugh, Jason shook his head and took a cookie from

his father's bag. He could count on his brother to lighten the mood, and he was thankful for that.

Jason bowed his head in silent prayer after he finished eating that evening. Soon he heard his father push back his chair, the sign that the after-supper prayer was complete.

Dat stood and kissed his mother's cheek. "Supper was *appeditlich* as usual, Annie. The best meat loaf you've made so far."

Mamm smiled. "*Danki*, Elam."

Dat started toward the mudroom, then looked back toward Jason and Stephen. "Aren't you *buwe* coming? Let's go take care of the animals."

Stephen rose and stretched, thanked *Mamm* for supper, and followed *Dat* to the mudroom, where Jason knew they would pull on their work boots. Jason remained seated. He'd spent all afternoon considering his lunchtime conversation with his brother. Was Stephen right when he told Jason not to go see Veronica? Then why did Jason still think about her constantly? He couldn't let go of the notion that he needed to see her—if not for her sake, then for his.

He needed his mother's advice, but he wanted to speak with her in private. Waiting until his brother and father went out to take care of the animals would be the best chance.

Jason stood up slowly, placed another plate on top of his, piled on some utensils, then carried the stack toward the sink. His mother had filled one side of the sink with warm, frothy water and dropped in the dirty pots and pans.

Stephen craned his long neck into the kitchen. "Are you coming, Jay?"

"I'll be there in a minute," Jason promised before gathering up his parents' plates and utensils and carrying them to the counter as well.

"You can go with your *bruder* and *dat*," Mamm said. "I'll get that."

"I don't mind helping." Jason brought two platters and a bowl to the counter while he worked up the courage to ask his mother her opinion of his feelings for Veronica Fisher. Did he have feelings for her? Was this some misguided crush or obsession if he'd never even talked to her, just as Stephen had insinuated?

Mamm faced him, leaning her slight body against the sink behind her. She was shorter than all the men in the family and still had no gray in her brown hair. As she crossed her arms over her black apron and smiled at Jason, he thought he saw a questioning look in her hazel eyes. "It's not every day that you stay inside to help with dishes instead of going outside to take care of the animals."

Jason shrugged and gathered up the glasses. "Why should you do all of this alone?" He placed the glasses next to the plates.

"Because it's my job, that's why." *Mamm* touched his arm. "Is something wrong?" She looked up at him. "Jason, you were quiet during supper. I can tell there's something on your mind. You can talk to me."

He hesitated, suddenly feeling ridiculous for wanting to discuss this with her. What was wrong with him? Why couldn't he let this go, like Stephen said he should?

Mamm motioned toward the table. "Do you want to sit?"

He nodded and sat down across from her. She gave him an encouraging smile, and he cleared his throat.

"I can't stop thinking about Seth and the accident."

"I understand." She nodded and patted his hand. "You miss your *freind*."

"It's not just that." Jason pushed a crumb with his finger. "I also can't stop worrying about Seth's fiancée, Veronica."

"Oh." *Mamm*'s expression transformed from concern to surprise. "You knew his fiancée?"

"No, that's the problem." Jason paused, thinking about the visitation at Seth's mother's house. "Do you remember when we were leaving Seth's mother's house when we went to visitation?"

"*Ya*." *Mamm* shrugged.

"You saw her. She was on the porch when we were leaving. She was crying, and her parents and sisters were consoling her."

Mamm nodded slowly, recognition flickering in her eyes. "*Ya*, I do remember. It was so tragic to see her grief. The poor *maedel*."

"Seth talked about her all the time. They were going to be married in November." Jason rested his chin on the palm of his hand. "I feel like I need to go see her. I want to talk to her."

"I see." *Mamm* studied him. "I can tell it means a lot to you."

"It does." His shoulders relaxed. *Mamm* understood, just as he knew she would. "Do you think it would be okay if I went to see her?"

"Why wouldn't it?"

"Stephen thinks it would be inappropriate for me to visit a *freind*'s fiancée." He couldn't bring himself to use the word *weird* as his brother had. "He said he wouldn't want one of his *freinden* to see Leah if something had happened to him."

Mamm paused, considering this. "I don't think there's anything wrong with it. You want to express your condolences, right?"

"*Ya*, that's right." He nodded. "And I want to make sure she's okay."

"I think that would be nice." *Mamm* squeezed his hand. "I think Seth would appreciate it. You were *gut freinden*."

"*Ya*, we were. I keep expecting him to walk into the shop or sit down at the lunch table with Stephen and me. It's been two months, but it feels like it was only yesterday that he was joking around with us."

"It's tough when you lose someone close to you. I still miss my *schweschder*, and she's been gone nearly twenty years. The ache gets easier, but it takes time."

Jason nodded. "*Danki, Mamm*. I knew I could talk to you." He pushed his chair back. "Would you like me to clean off the table?"

"I can handle the kitchen. You go help your *dat* and *bruder* before they come looking for you." She stood and waved him off.

Jason walked to the mudroom, pulled on his work boots, and grabbed his hat before heading out the door toward the barn. His mother's encouraging words resonated with him. Since he'd been close to Seth, he was only doing what any good friend would do. Now all he had to do was find out where Veronica Fisher lived.

CHAPTER 3

VERONICA AND HER SISTERS GATHERED AROUND THEIR father as he sat at the head of the table the following afternoon. She served him the first piece of raspberry pie and then held her breath as his fork sliced through the flaky crust. A sweet aroma permeated the kitchen as he raised the fork up to his mouth. Veronica gnawed her lower lip, hoping the pie would taste as good as it looked and smelled.

"Mmmm." *Dat* nodded his head and looked up at her. "Veronica, you've outdone yourself." His gaze slid to *Mamm*. "I'm sorry, Mattie, but I think this pie is better than your *mamm's*. It's positively mouthwatering. I think I may keep this whole pie for myself."

Veronica blew out a breath while her sisters clapped. She did it! She found something she was good at other than cleaning.

"I want a piece!" Emily announced, grabbing the knife.

"Cut one for me," Rachel insisted as she grabbed a plate and fork from the center of the table.

Mamm draped her arm over Veronica's shoulder. "I find it hard to believe that it's better than my *mamm's*, so I'll have to see for myself."

Veronica smiled. "Let's find out."

Emily slid four pieces onto plates and distributed them as Veronica, her mother, and Rachel took their seats around the table. Veronica held up her fork and then waited while the rest of her family took bites of their dessert. Like a choir, they all moaned and sighed their approval of the pie, and a smile turned up Veronica's lips. It was a sin to be prideful, but satisfaction swelled within her.

"Veronica," *Mamm* told her, "your *dat* was right. I think this *is* better than your *mammi*'s raspberry pies. *Mei mamm*'s pies were fantastic, but this crust is flakier and buttery, not at all dry. And the raspberries seem sweeter. I think your filling is a little better."

"This is scrumptious," Rachel chimed in. "I've never had anything so sweet and tart at the same time."

"Where's the vanilla ice cream?" Emily popped up from her chair and raced to the freezer. "I bet that would make it even better."

"You need to make this for the *Englishers* Saturday," *Mamm* added between bites. "I was trying to think of something different to serve for dessert, and this would be perfect."

"*Ya!*" Rachel agreed. "They will love it."

Emily returned to the table with a tub of vanilla ice cream and dropped a scoop onto the pie. She took a bite and made a little moaning noise. "Veronica, you need to sell these pies."

"You think so?" Veronica took a bite and nodded. "It is *gut, ya*?"

"*Ya*," *Mamm* said with a little laugh. "It's *appeditlich*."

Dat pushed his empty plate toward Emily. "Would you please cut me another piece?"

Veronica set her fork on the plate and smiled. "I guess I'll make another one."

"No," Emily said, shaking her head. "Make a dozen. I'll help."

THE THREE SISTERS HELPED MAMM SERVE A HOMEMADE SUPPER to the group of two dozen *Englishers* Saturday night. While answering questions about their culture, they served fruit salad, green beans and pickles made with cucumbers—both from their garden—barbecue meat loaf, chicken and noodles, and boiled potatoes.

"For dessert," *Mamm* said when most of the guests looked ready, "we have shoo-fly pie, chocolate cake, and raspberry pie."

Emily brought two shoo-fly pies to the table, and Rachel delivered two chocolate cakes.

"Did you say raspberry pie?" a rotund woman with a wide smile asked. "I haven't had that in years."

Mamm smiled at Veronica and pointed toward the three pies sitting on the counter. "Since you made them, you can bring them to the tables."

Veronica hesitated. What if the visitors hated them? What if her family had said they were good just to encourage her? Veronica wasn't naive; she was certain her family had been handling her with kid gloves since she'd lost Seth. They were so concerned about her feelings that they would say or do anything just to see her happy again. These visitors, however, were paying for the meal, and they had no reason to worry about Veronica's fragile feelings.

"Veronica?" *Mamm*'s eyes held concern as she lowered her voice. "The guests would like to try your pies. Would you please bring them to the table?"

"Oh, of course." Veronica carried two of the pies to the table, placing one in front of the woman who had expressed interest.

"Isn't that gorgeous?" the woman said. "You made these, dear?"

Veronica nodded while fingering the edge of her black

apron. *"Ya*, I did. I found a few of my grandmother's recipes, and I thought this looked like a good one."

"It smells divine, doesn't it, Judy?" she asked a woman with flaming red hair sitting across from her.

"Absolutely. Would you please cut me a piece?" Judy pushed her plate toward Veronica.

Veronica and Emily gathered empty platters, bowls, and dishes and took them to the sink, where *Mamm* was already filling one side with hot, soapy water. Then they sliced and served the pies as well as the cake.

"Oh my," Judy said after her first bite of the raspberry pie. "This is heavenly. I've never tasted anything like it, Harriett."

"I agree," Harriett chimed in before insisting the other folks at the table try the raspberry pie too.

Veronica watched in awe as all three pies disappeared and the guests showered her with compliments about her baking abilities.

"You need to try my sister's relishes and jams too," Emily announced. "She's very talented with those also."

"Really?" Harriett asked. "Do you have them for sale?"

"Ya, we do." Emily disappeared into the pantry and returned with a jar of raspberry jam and a jar of sweet relish.

Harriett examined them. "I'll take two of each if you have more. I need to take something home to my sister, but I also want to keep one of each for myself."

"I'll take three of each," Judy said. "But would you also sell me a couple of pies?"

Veronica blinked. "You want to buy one of my raspberry pies?"

"No, dear," Judy said with a grin. "I want to buy two of them."

"Oh." Veronica glanced at her mother, who nodded as if giving permission. "I do have six more." She didn't say she only made that many to share with some of their neighbors.

"Oh good," Judy chimed in. "I'll take two then."

By the time the guests left, she had sold six jars of relish, eight jars of jam, and all six of her pies.

"You need to make more pies," Rachel said while wiping off the long table. "Now you know for sure you can sell them, especially once someone has tasted them."

Veronica nodded while drying a dish. "I'll get back to baking on Monday."

"They went quickly," Emily said, placing glasses in the cabinets. "I'm glad you found those recipes."

"I am too." Veronica glanced at her mother, who returned her smile.

Would Seth have liked my raspberry pie? The question caused her smile to collapse and her mood to sink. Just when she was convinced she was moving through her grief, a thought would catch her off guard and send her plummeting back into the painful memories that tore at her soul. She placed the dry dish in the cabinet and picked up another one from the drying rack.

"Veronica?" *Mamm's* hand touched her shoulder. "Are you all right?"

"I think I need to lie down," Veronica whispered. "My stomach is upset." It wasn't a fib. As soon as her thoughts turned to Seth, her stomach roiled with renewed agony over his death.

"Go on." *Mamm* gestured toward the stairs. "We'll take care of this."

"*Danki.*"

Her sisters told her to feel better as she left the kitchen for the privacy of her room. She flopped onto her bed without even taking off her apron and examined the ceiling, as she'd done time and time again since that day in April. Her vision blurred with tears, and she sniffed. She needed to find a way to cope with this overwhelming bereavement. Closing her eyes, she silently asked God to bring joy back into her life.

JASON SAT ON THE PORCH SWING WHEN HE ARRIVED HOME from church Sunday afternoon. He looked out across the pasture toward the pond at the far end of his parents' property. His father had once promised he'd help him build a house beyond the pond. When he was engaged to Arie, he had drawn up plans for that little house, and he was ready to pay a local contractor to pour the foundation. After she'd broken off the engagement, Jason had toyed with the idea of building the house anyway, but the thought of living in the house alone seemed dismal at the time.

Sometimes he sat on the porch and tried to imagine the house with its two stories, wraparound porch, and three bedrooms. Would he ever build the house? Eventually he would be expected to move out and live his own life, but he hoped it wouldn't be to live alone. He wanted a family. He'd always imagined he'd be married by twenty-five, but his next birthday was approaching quickly, and he wasn't any closer to that goal now than he was last year.

The screen door opened and slammed with a loud bang as Stephen rushed out.

"Why haven't you changed your clothes?" Stephen asked, standing before Jason. "Aren't you coming to the youth gathering?"

Jason rubbed his clean-shaven chin. "I already told you no. I think I'm too old to—"

"Oh, cut it out," Stephen snapped with a grimace. "Quit feeling sorry for yourself and go get changed. You need to get out and do something fun. I promised Leah I'd be there in thirty minutes, so we have to leave soon. Since it's at her farm she might need my help. We're going to be late."

Forty-five minutes later, Stephen guided the horse into the rock driveway leading to the Esh farm. Three volleyball nets were assembled in the grass behind the white, two-story clapboard house. Teams of young people played at each homemade court, leaping, jumping, and laughing while the volleyballs sailed through the air. Small groups of young people sat nearby, some cheering on the teams and others oblivious to the games while they talked.

Jason's memories flashed to five years earlier when he attended a similar youth gathering and met Arie, the *maedel* he was sure he was going to marry. She was petite and pretty with dark-brown hair and gray-blue eyes. They had been on the same volleyball team and met by literally running into each other. When the ball sailed toward him, he and Arie both ran for it, crashing into each other and landing on the trampled grass in a heap of laughter. Jason pulled himself up and held out his hand.

She took his hand, stood, brushed herself off, and said, "Thanks for the help, but that was my ball."

"No, actually, it was mine," he insisted.

Arie crossed her arms over her chest in defiance. "No, it was mine. It was coming toward me."

He raised an eyebrow, stunned by her stubbornness. "I'm Jason."

"I'm Arie, and next time, go after your own ball." She gave him a devious grin before serving the ball with a perfect flourish of her thin arms.

And at that moment, he was smitten with the short, outspoken brunette. It took him a month to work up the courage to ask her to be his girlfriend, and he worked up the courage to ask her to marry him two years later.

AMY CLIPSTON

It was a cold night in mid-October, only a month before their wedding date, when Arie knocked on the back door of his parents' house. Jason had been alone in the kitchen, and when he pulled open the door, he immediately saw the worry wrinkling her pretty face. He asked her what was wrong, and a single tear trickled down her pink cheek.

"I'm sorry, Jason," she whispered, her voice quaking. "I can't marry you."

"What?" He felt as if he'd been punched in the stomach. At first he hoped it was a cruel joke and she'd laugh before telling him she was kidding. But she never smiled.

More tears ran down her cheeks as she explained that she didn't love him enough to spend the rest of her life with him. He begged her to change her mind, but she insisted she had already made the decision. He visited her every day for a week, dropping off notes and even talking to her parents, but nothing changed her mind. He heard a couple of months ago that Arie married a man from western Pennsylvania and moved out there with him.

Despite his heartbreak and disappointment, Jason hoped Arie had a happy life. After all, he didn't want to marry someone who wouldn't love him completely. Still, Jason never understood why Arie had changed her mind so abruptly. He craved a more thorough explanation. Sometimes he wondered if she'd met her future husband while she was still dating Jason and decided she would have a better life with him.

"Jay?" Stephen's voice broke through his memories. "Are you going to get out of the buggy?"

"*Ya.*" Jason pushed open the door.

"Are you all right?" Stephen asked. "You're lost in your thoughts again."

"I'm fine." Jason climbed down and followed Stephen to the

36

volleyball courts. He recognized some of the faces in the sea of young people, but he still had the feeling he was the oldest member of the group, no matter what Stephen said. Why had he allowed his brother to convince him to come here? He knew the answer to that question. It was because he *was* tired of being home alone. Maybe it was time for him to try to date again. Two years was a long time to be alone.

Or maybe he would meet someone who could tell him where Veronica Fisher lived. He knew some people socialized with other church districts more than he did.

Leah Esh emerged from a group of young women sitting near one of the volleyball courts. A *maedel* who resembled Leah with the same light-brown hair and brown eyes sidled up to her and gave Jason a sweet smile, revealing dimples in her pink cheeks. This was Mary, the girl who, according to Stephen, was eager to spend time with him. She *was* pretty, and about average height for a *maedel*, like her sister Leah.

As Leah and Stephen fell into conversation with each other, Mary and Jason exchanged awkward nods and smiles. Jason tried to think of something to say to her, anything at all that would break the ice, but nothing came to his lips.

Finally, Mary pointed toward the volleyball courts. "Do you want to play?"

He shrugged. "Sure, if you do."

She shook her head and smiled, flashing those cute dimples again. "Not really. I'm not very *gut*, so I don't get picked."

He smiled. Mary was honest, and that was a good quality.

"Would you like to go for a walk instead?" she offered, taking a step closer to him.

"Okay." He shrugged again.

"We're going for a walk," Mary told Leah.

Her excited tone sent worry through him. Both Stephen and

Leah grinned at Mary, and Jason fought the urge to bolt back to the buggy. Jason didn't want to give any of them the false hope that he was going to fall in love with Mary. She seemed like a nice girl, but he really wasn't looking for anything serious right now. He still hadn't fully recovered from Arie's rejection.

"Let's walk toward the horse pasture," Mary said as they started down the rock driveway.

"Your *dat* sells horses, right?" he asked, slowing his gait so she could keep up.

"*Ya*, that's right. And yours owns a shed business where you work." She smiled up at him.

"*Ya*, he does."

"Do you enjoy working there?" she pressed.

"*Ya*," Jason said, jamming his hands into his pockets. "I like building things and working with my hands."

"I work at the hardware store over in Ronks two days a week," Mary offered. "I enjoy talking to the customers."

"Oh." Jason scanned the pastures peppered with beautiful horses and tried to think of something to say. Why couldn't he relate to this pretty *maedel*? Had Arie stolen his ability to talk to women? Would he even know what to say to Veronica if he did have the opportunity to meet her?

They stopped at the fence, and Jason leaned against it.

"Do you like working with the horses?" he asked.

She nodded. "*Ya*, I do. My *dat* and my six *brieder* mostly handle the training, but sometimes Leah and I get to help."

He kept his attention trained on the animals. "I always wondered what it would be like to live on a farm, working with a lot of animals instead of going to a shop every day."

"*Ya*, I suppose it would be different for you." She stood close to him. "Leah told me you lost your *freind* in an accident a couple of months ago."

Jason blanched. He hadn't expected her to mention Seth. He kept his focus on the horses in an attempt not to get emotional. "*Ya*, that's true. My *freind* Seth was killed when he fell from the rafters in a shed we were building."

"That had to be difficult for you and Stephen. Leah said you were very close to him." Mary touched his arm, and he flinched with surprise. "If you ever need someone to talk to, I'm *froh* to listen."

"*Danki*." He took a slight step away from her. He wasn't ready to get close to her. After all, he hardly knew her, but she seemed eager to know him better.

"So, how long have you worked at the shed store?" Mary asked, taking a step closer to him.

He looked down at her, and he imagined he might suffocate in the brightness of her smile. He tried to smile, but it felt more like a grimace.

"I started going to work with my *dat* on Saturdays when I was twelve. By thirteen I was assisting the other workers."

"Wow." She leaned her arm on the fence. "That's really *wunderbaar*. I bet you're a great shed builder. Probably the best."

"I suppose I do okay," he said, wondering what Stephen would think about that remark. "After all, *mei dat* hasn't fired me yet."

His lame joke caused her to laugh a little too loudly for a little too long. Actually, she seemed to be *more* than eager to know him. She acted like she had a big crush on him, and he felt unworthy. Why would she want to date him? What could he possibly offer her that was more special than anyone else in the youth group?

"How about you? How long have you been working at the hardware store?"

"Three years," she began, then launched into talking on and on about her job, telling him about the other employees and what she liked to do for fun in the evenings. He was relieved he didn't have to carry the conversation, but he also struggled to focus on what she was saying. Instead of listening to her stories about her family and friends, his thoughts turned to Veronica. Was she also at a youth gathering tonight? Did she like to play volleyball, or was she more introverted, like he was?

He was thankful when Stephen and Leah found them and invited them to come into the house for a snack. Gathering in a group to eat lessened the pressure on Jason to keep the conversation going if talkative Mary ran out of things to say.

When it was time to go home, Jason, Stephen, and the sisters all walked to the buggy. Stephen and Leah moved behind the buggy to talk in private, and Jason and Mary looked at each other awkwardly.

"I had a nice time," she said, her cheeks flushing bright pink. "I hope we can spend more time together."

"*Ya*, I'm sure we will," Jason said. He smiled politely, but he longed to take the words back. *Why did I say that?* He'd said it because he didn't want to reject and hurt her the way Arie had rejected and hurt him—even if they had been engaged and he and Mary weren't anywhere close to a relationship.

"We better go," Stephen said, climbing into the driver's seat. "*Gut nacht.*"

The sisters echoed the words as Jason got into the buggy.

"Did you have a *gut* time with Mary?" Stephen asked with a sideways glance as he guided the buggy down the rock driveway.

"*Ya*," Jason said, lifting one shoulder up and down. "She's a nice *maedel*."

"So you like her?" Stephen actually grinned.

"Are you a matchmaker now?" Jason asked. "You're my younger *bruder*, remember? You shouldn't be trying to take care of me. It should be the other way around."

"Leah and I were just trying to help. You seem so unhappy lately, and Mary really likes you. Why not try to get to know her?"

Jason looked out the window and sighed. Maybe his brother was right and it was time for him to start dating again. Mary seemed nice enough, but he couldn't stop thinking about Veronica Fisher. He wished he'd been free at the gathering to find someone who might have known her. He knew he wouldn't stop thinking about her until he had a chance to talk to her. Perhaps after he had the opportunity to apologize to her he would be able to concentrate on getting to know Mary.

CHAPTER 4

On Wednesday morning, Veronica balanced a pie plate in her hands as she stood between *Mamm* and Emily on Bishop Dienner's front porch. His wife, Fannie Mae, was recovering from pneumonia, and when Emily knocked on their door, it was the couple's daughter, Lindann, who swung it open.

"Hello," Lindann said, motioning for them to come in. *"Danki* for coming by. *Mei mamm* will be thrilled to see you."

They followed Lindann into the kitchen, where Fannie sat at the table.

"Hi, Fannie Mae," *Mamm* said. "How are you feeling?"

"Much better, *danki*," Fannie Mae said before giving a little cough.

"We brought you one of Veronica's raspberry pies to cheer you up."

"I hope you like raspberries," Veronica said as she pulled the foil off the pie and placed it in front of Fannie Mae.

"Oh!" Fannie Mae's tired face lit up with delight. "This looks *wunderbaar.*" She looked at Veronica. "You made this?"

Veronica nodded. "I found *mei mammi*'s recipes in the attic. We've always been blessed with a generous amount of raspberries in the summer, so I thought I would try out the recipe."

"I can't wait to taste it," Fannie Mae said.

Veronica cut five slices and placed them on plates while Lindann poured mugs of coffee. When Fannie Mae and Lindann tasted the pie, their eyes widened, just as the *Englishers'* had done last week.

"Veronica," Fannie Mae offered after her first bite, "this is more than *wunderbaar*. It's positively fantastic!"

"Oh, Veronica," Lindann gushed, "you must let me take a pie to my cousin Amanda. She owns the Ronks Bakery, and I think she would love to sell these."

"*Ya*," Fannie Mae agreed. "These would be perfect for Amanda's bakery. You have to give her a pie to try. She'll take orders."

"Would it be all right if I called my cousin and told her to contact you?" Lindann asked.

Veronica dabbed her mouth with a napkin and nodded. "*Ya. Danki.*"

Her cheeks flushed with embarrassment. She'd only made the pies as a coping mechanism. Baking helped her avoid the suffocating grief that threatened to grip her every morning when she woke up and every night before she fell asleep. She never meant for baking the pies to be anything other than a hobby. Now two more people had told her she should sell the pies, more than occasionally as she had to the *Englishers* visiting her home. Veronica turned to her mother, who smiled with pride. She took that as a sign that she should allow her friend to try to sell the pies for her at the Ronks Bakery.

LATE THAT AFTERNOON, VERONICA WAS PULLING A PIE OUT of the oven when Rachel rushed through the door after her day working at the market.

"Let's go see Irma Rose and her *boppli* tonight," Rachel urged, dropping her tote bag on the floor.

"That's a *wunderbaar* idea!" Emily gushed while wiping her hands on a dish towel. "She had a girl, right?"

"That's right, and she's two weeks old now, so it's all right for us to visit." Rachel snatched an apple from the fruit bowl on the counter. "They named her Sarah. I can't wait to meet her."

"David must be so excited," Emily said. "He's an *onkel*."

"*Ya*, he is, and when we're married, I'll be the *aenti*." Rachel blew out a dramatic sigh.

"That will be nice," Veronica said. "We'll have to go get a gift before we visit, though."

"I stopped at the grocery store on the way home and picked up a package of diapers and some wipes," Rachel said, waving off her comment. She pointed toward the four pies cooling on the rack. "You can share one of your famous pies, Veronica."

"I wouldn't call them famous yet," Veronica said. "Let's see if Lindann's cousin really thinks anyone will buy them at her bakery first."

The bottom step of the stairs squeaked, announcing *Mamm*'s return from the sewing room on the second floor. "Rachel," she said as she stepped into the kitchen, "I didn't hear the van drop you off. How was market today?"

"*Gut*." She beamed. "Let's go see David's *schweschder*'s new *boppli* tonight. I've already picked up a gift. We should go right after supper." Rachel sighed. "I can't wait to hold her. David said he'll be there too."

Mamm paused, seeming to debate this. "All right. But we don't want to be a burden. We'll only visit for a few minutes."

"Yay." Rachel clapped her hands. "Just think, I have a niece."

"Be careful, *mei liewe*," *Mamm* warned, placing a hand on

Rachel's shoulder. "You and David aren't officially engaged yet, let alone married."

Veronica frowned, not even hearing Rachel's reply. *She's closer to marriage than I'll ever be.* She wanted to kick herself for feeling jealous, which was another sin, but the feeling crept up on her. She was happy for her sister, who had been dating David for more than three years, but she also longed to have the same joy back in her life.

"I'll start supper," Veronica said, thankful for the distraction. "How about fried chicken, corn, and green beans?"

"Sounds perfect," *Mamm* said, sidling up to Veronica by the counter. "I'll help you."

AFTER SUPPER, VERONICA AND EMILY EACH CARRIED A PIE as they walked to Irma Rose's house at the end of their street. They lagged behind Rachel and their mother, who nodded in response as Rachel talked on and on about how she couldn't wait to get married and have children.

"*Was iss letz?*" Emily asked.

"Nothing." Veronica forced a smile. "I'm just tired today."

"Did you have a difficult time sleeping last night?" Emily's pretty face was full of concern.

"I slept fine, but it took me a long time to fall asleep." It was the truth. Thoughts of Seth had overtaken her mind, and she cried as softly as possible into her pillow while once again mourning all their dashed plans.

"I can't imagine how difficult this is for you." Emily placed her hand on Veronica's shoulder. "Remember Psalm 46? The Lord said, 'Be still, and know that I am God.' He's with us always, even in our times of trouble. I'm always here too. If you ever can't sleep, you can come in with me. I'll always listen, even if it's two in the morning."

Veronica nodded as tears drenched her eyes. She was so thankful for her wonderful sisters. She had girlfriends in their community, but over the last couple of years Rachel and Emily had become her best friends. She did not want to hurt her closer friends, so many of whom offered to walk beside her in her grief, by confessing it was the comfort of her sisters she most craved among the young of their community.

"*Danki*, Emily."

Their shoes crunched up the rocky path leading to the front door of Irma Rose's small house, which was on the same property as her parents' large farmhouse. Rachel knocked, and Susannah, Irma Rose's mother, answered the door.

"Hello," Susannah said as she gestured for them to come in. "It's so nice to see you all."

"Hi, Susannah," Rachel said as she stepped inside with their mother. She was holding a pink gift bag containing the disposable diapers and package of wipes. "I can't wait to see the *boppli*."

Veronica followed Emily through the door, and they handed the pies to Susannah. "Hi, Susannah," Veronica said. "We brought two raspberry pies. Please feel free to save them for later."

"Oh, *danki*, Veronica." Susannah inhaled the sweet aroma. "I haven't had a raspberry pie in years. We will enjoy this."

"*Gern gschehne*," Veronica said before following Emily into the family room. Rachel was already seated in a rocking chair and holding the tiny baby wrapped in a pink blanket. *Mamm* stood behind her, smiling down at the infant, and Irma Rose's husband, Melvin, sat nearby.

Veronica and Emily took seats on a sofa near Rachel, who

smiled at David, sitting next to her in a chair. "David, I can't wait until we have our own *kinner.*"

Veronica noticed David briefly nodded but did not return Rachel's smile. Was something bothering him tonight?

"May I hold her?" Emily asked. "She's so *schee.*" Rachel handed her the baby, and Emily looked down at little Sarah as she touched her tiny fingers.

"*Ya,*" Veronica agreed. "She is." Then her delight dissipated as she admired the newborn's tiny face. *Would I have had a boppli with Seth? Would the boppli have looked like Seth or me? Or would the kind have had a mixture—his green eyes and my nose?* She bit her lip in an effort to keep her emotions at bay.

"Where's Irma Rose?" *Mamm* asked.

"She's taking a nap," Melvin explained. "She's been really worn out."

"We shouldn't stay long," *Mamm* said. "Irma Rose needs her rest. I don't want her to hear our voices and think she has to join us."

Rachel sighed. "*Mamm*'s right, but I just couldn't wait to see little Sarah." She touched David's hand. "I know you're excited to be an *onkel, ya?*"

David nodded but kept staring at his lap. Veronica wondered again what could be going on with him, especially when she saw the delight in Rachel's eyes fade a bit. She felt a pang of concern, but she'd leave it to her sister. She shouldn't get involved unless Rachel asked her to.

"David, would you please make sure Irma Rose gets the gift bag?" Rachel nodded toward the bag now sitting on the coffee table.

"*Ya,*" David mumbled.

"Veronica," Susannah said as she stood in the doorway

leading to the small kitchen. She held up a dish with a piece of the raspberry pie on it. "I couldn't wait to try this. It's *appeditlich*. Do you take orders?" She pushed her fork through her piece, ready to eat another chunk.

Veronica shrugged. "*Ya*, I could."

"I'd like to order six from you," Susannah said. "I'm going to a family reunion next week, and I'd love to take them."

"Six?" Veronica asked.

"*Ya*. I'll need them next Monday. Do you think you can have them ready by then?" Susannah asked.

"*Ya*, I'll have them ready for you."

"*Danki*. I can't wait for my *aenti* to try this. She'll love it!"

WHEN THEY ARRIVED HOME FROM IRMA ROSE'S HOUSE, Emily and Rachel made their way upstairs and Veronica stayed in the kitchen with *Mamm*.

"I better get baking again tomorrow. I'm surprised Susannah ordered six pies." Veronica peered inside the pantry, searching for ingredients.

"I'm *froh* for you." *Mamm* walked up behind her. "I know you enjoy making the pies. And if Lindann's cousin decides to take orders at her bakery—or even for the bakery—then you'll be very busy."

"*Ya*, that's true. I'll be very busy." *So busy that I won't have time to think about Seth.*

"Veronica," *Mamm* said.

She turned and found her mother watching her, her eyes showing concern. "You were awfully quiet at Irma Rose's *haus*. Are you feeling okay?"

Veronica leaned on the counter beside her. "I feel fine." She paused. *Should I tell* Mamm *the truth? Will she think I'm terrible?*

"You can talk to me," *Mamm* said as if reading her thoughts. "I can tell something is bothering you. Sometimes it helps to say it aloud instead of letting the emotions build up inside."

"I had a difficult time seeing Irma Rose's *boppli*." Tears overtook Veronica's eyes, and her voice was thin. "When I looked at her, all I could think about was Seth and the *kinner* we'll never have." Her voice broke on the last word, and she dissolved into sobs.

"Oh, Veronica." *Mamm* hugged her, and Veronica rested her cheek on her shoulder like a child. "I know it's difficult, *mei liewe*. It's okay to cry. Go ahead."

As her mother patted her back, Veronica rubbed her eyes and sniffed. "I have a difficult time seeing Rachel and David together, and I can't help feeling jealous when she talks about their plans. I know it's a sin to feel this way. I'll never find anyone I'll love as much as I loved Seth. I'm going to be alone while my sisters both are married and have *kinner*."

"That's not true." *Mamm* gently touched Veronica's shoulder. "You will love again. You just need to give yourself time to heal. Right now you feel like you've lost everything, but you'll find someone. Trust me."

Veronica shook her head as more tears threatened her eyes. "No, Seth was the love of my life. We fit so well together. He was everything to me, and now he's gone." Her bottom lip quivered.

"Seth will always have a very special place in your heart, but you will love again. You deserve to have a family. You'll meet someone special, get married, and have *kinner*, just like your *schweschdere* will." She smiled. "Maybe you should go to a singles group, or you could go to youth group with your *schweschdere*. Just go out and meet people. You don't have to date yet, but you do need to talk to young folks your age."

Veronica nodded, but she couldn't imagine herself at a singles group or her sisters' youth group. She only wanted to bake and avoid the pity and stares she would encounter at those gatherings. "I'm going to go to bed. I have a lot of baking to do tomorrow."

"Okay." *Mamm* yawned. "I think I'm ready for bed too. I'll see you in the morning."

As she climbed the stairs, Veronica thought about her mother's words. Would she ever find a man who would love her as much as Seth had? Could she possibly love someone else? *If I did find someone else, I would betray Seth's precious memory. Right now I just need to make pies and try to forget my heartache.*

AT THE GROCERY STORE ON SATURDAY MORNING, JASON leaned on a cart as his mother consulted her shopping list, then examined a display of lettuce.

"Jason?"

He turned to see Mary and Leah approaching them.

"Hi, Mary," he said. "Leah. *Wie geht's?*"

"I didn't expect to see you here," Mary said with a wide smile that revealed her dimples.

"Hi, Annie," Leah said.

"It's nice to see you," *Mamm* said. "I guess it's everyone's day to visit the grocery store."

"*Ya,*" Mary said. "I suppose so."

"Where's Stephen?" Leah asked, resting a full shopping basket on her small hip.

"He's working on a project at home with *Dat.*" Feeling self-conscious about it in front of these young women, he had to explain why he wasn't helping the two men. "*Mamm* asked me to take her shopping to help with the heavy lifting."

"Are you coming to the youth gathering tomorrow?" Mary sounded eager. "We can be on the same volleyball team."

"I thought you didn't like to play," Jason said.

Mary shrugged. "I suppose I could give it a try."

"You don't want her on your team if you want to win," Leah teased. Mary blushed. "She's better at cheering from the sidelines than she is playing."

"Everyone deserves a chance, though, right?" *Mamm* asked. "Maybe you can teach her how to play, Jason."

"Sure." *Please don't encourage them, Mamm!* He had to get his mother out of there before she invited them over for supper.

"That's a deal then," Mary said from under her lashes. "You can teach me how to play and then *mei schweschder* won't say I'm not a helpful team member."

"I'll do my best." He turned to his mother. "Well, we'd better keep moving, *Mamm*."

Mamm gave him a confused expression. "Okay." She smiled at the younger women. "It was nice seeing you. Tell your *mamm* hello for me." She chose a leafy green lettuce and a romaine lettuce and dropped them into the basket as Jason said his good-byes to Mary and Leah.

"Why were you in such a hurry?" *Mamm* asked when they were alone. "They're nice *maed*."

"I told *Dat* I'd help him and Stephen with the fence when we got back. I want to get home before they finish." He pushed the cart and she walked beside him, moving toward the dairy cases.

"You weren't in a hurry earlier." *Mamm* gave him a sideways glance. "Mary likes you."

He fought the urge to roll his eyes. *Is it that obvious?*

"Jason." She stopped walking. "I'm glad to see you going to youth gatherings. It's time you started dating again."

"Don't get too excited." He pressed his lips together. "Mary is only my *freind*. I really don't know her that well. We spent some time talking the other night, but we don't have much in common really." *And I don't have any feelings for her.*

"That's a *gut* start." She patted his arm. "Your *dat* and I started out as *freinden*. You never know where that might lead." She walked toward the milk case, and he pushed the cart behind her.

"I know." He sighed. He didn't want to be pressured into dating anyone.

"You should go tomorrow. I always loved playing volleyball. It's a lot of fun." She grinned at him. "It seems like Mary is eager for you to teach her how to play."

"Like I said, I'll do my best—as a *freind*." He leaned forward on the cart as his mother examined the milk expiration dates before making her choice. He had to think of an excuse to avoid tomorrow's youth gathering. Someone else could teach Mary how to play volleyball. He didn't want to give her the impression he was interested.

What he really needed was to find someone who knew where Veronica Fisher lived, without looking for a needle in a haystack at a youth gathering. Margaret and Ellie Lapp would know, of course, but like Stephen, they might think it awkward that he wanted to see Seth's fiancée.

It was time he asked around. He knew what church district Seth's family had been in, and Seth had always made it sound like Veronica's family was in the same one. Perhaps he could start there.

CHAPTER 5

VERONICA WAS PULLING A PIE OUT OF THE OVEN WHEN Emily entered the kitchen through the mudroom.

"You had three messages on voice mail." Emily placed a piece of paper on the counter. "Lindann's cousin Amanda wants to talk to you about ordering pies for her bakery. Fannie Mae wants another pie, and Susannah also left a message reminding you about the six pies she's going to pick up around eleven today for her family reunion."

Veronica gasped. "Oh my goodness. I'm way behind already. Would you help me?"

"Of course I will. I don't have much to do for *Dat* on Saturdays, and we're all set for the next *Englisher* group dinner tonight." Emily grinned. "You're becoming famous."

"No, my pies are the famous ones." Veronica laughed. "We'd better get to baking."

"I NOTICED SUSANNAH CAME TO PICK UP HER PIES," MAMM said while they ate lunch later that day.

"*Ya*, she did." Veronica wiped her mouth with a paper napkin.

"I spoke to Lindann's cousin Amanda. She wants to order six pies and pick them up Friday. I'm so surprised by the interest in the pies. It seems like it's not going to stop until the season is over." She paused as an idea came to her. "*Dat*, would you build me a bake stand by the road? I could sell my pies, relishes, and jams out there once a week. Maybe on Saturdays."

Dat placed his sandwich on the plate and turned to *Mamm*, who tilted her head with curiosity.

"If you want to build a bake stand, does this mean you're not going to go back to work at the market?" *Mamm* asked.

Veronica shook her head. "I really don't want to go back to the market. I'd rather stay here and help you and Emily with chores and sell my pies and relishes. Also, I can sell the jars of jam here and not have to take them to the Bird-in-Hand Farmers Market anymore." She met her father's concerned expression. "Would that be all right, *Dat*? I'm already making money by selling the pies, and if I had a bake stand, I would make even more money."

"It's fine with me." *Dat* turned to *Mamm*. "How do you feel about it, Mattie?"

"I think you can stay home from the Philadelphia market for now since baking the raspberry pies will keep you busy for at least the rest of the summer. The bake stand is a *wunderbaar* idea," *Mamm* said. "Anyone who tastes them is definitely interested in the pies, and baking them is something you enjoy."

"*Ya*, I agree," Emily chimed in as she lifted a pretzel from her plate. "Word will really get around about your *appeditlich* pies if you have the stand. Living on busy Gibbons Road has its advantages."

"*Danki*." Veronica smiled. She felt excited as she considered the possibility of selling even more pies. It seemed she really did have something of her own now.

Veronica looked over toward the house and smiled when she saw her mother carrying two glasses of tea to where she and *Dat* were applying the last coat of white paint on the bake stand. It had only taken *Dat* and their neighbor, Hank Ebersol, two weeks of spare time to build the stand, which resembled a medium-sized shed with a counter and several shelves for her to display her items for sale. She would keep the pies cold with the help of large coolers.

A sign sitting in front of the stand and matching the one they'd made for Gibbons Road advertised Fishers' Foods, and once the last coat of paint dried, Veronica would be ready to sell her pies, relishes, and jams. The customers coming up the driveway to her father's harness shop would pass right by her new business too.

"You two must be thirsty." *Mamm* held out the glasses of iced tea as she admired their work. "It looks *schee*."

"*Danki*." Veronica moved her hand across her brow. "I'm so *froh* with it. *Danki, Dat*. It's even more wonderful than I imagined it would be."

Veronica smiled up at her father. She was grateful for his generosity.

"*Gern gschehne*," he said. "Now you have to bake."

"*Ya*." She nodded. "I have to put a few more pies in the oven if I want to have enough to sell tomorrow."

"You go and get started," *Dat* told her. "I can finish up the painting, and I'll hang the sign above the shelves. I'm also going to buy an awning to help keep the food in the shade, and I'll put the other sign out by the road too."

"*Danki*." Veronica kissed his cheek, then hurried toward the house, excitement bubbling up inside of her. She couldn't wait to start selling her pies, jams, and relishes from her very own stand!

JASON FOLDED THE LIST AND PLACED IT IN HIS POCKET BEFORE climbing into the buggy.

"Are you going to the hardware store?" Stephen called as he descended the back porch steps and moved toward him.

"*Ya, Dat* gave me a list of supplies to get so we can fix the barn door. Do you want to come?"

"Yes." Stephen came to the other side of the buggy. "*Mamm* asked me to run out to Bird-in-Hand for her, and we might as well do both errands together. She wants me to pick up something on Gibbons Road. It's not far from the hardware store. We can visit the hardware store first and then go out there."

"What does she need?" Jason guided the horse down the rock driveway toward the main road.

"She said a *maedel* is selling raspberry pies at a bake stand on Gibbons Road. *Mamm* heard about it in her quilting circle yesterday. The pies are supposed to be amazing. The girl's last name is Fisher, but she couldn't remember her first name."

Jason's hands gripped the reins tighter. *Her last name is Fisher and she lives on Gibbons Road?* That wasn't far from where Seth lived. Could this *maedel* be Veronica Fisher or maybe one of her sisters? After having a hard time working up the courage to ask his parents who they knew in Seth's church district, was it going to be this simple to find her?

After picking up the supplies at the hardware store, Jason guided the buggy toward Gibbons Road. When he spotted a Fishers' Foods sign, anticipation fluttered through him. *What if this is Veronica's stand?* He pushed the thought away, convincing himself it would never be so easy to find her.

"The way *Mamm* said one of the women raved about the pies, they must be *gut*," Stephen said, pulling Jason back to the present.

"*Ya*, they must be." Jason guided the horse halfway up the rock driveway to the stand. His gaze moved around the property, taking in the row of barns and the two-story white house. He spotted a store with a large sign that said Bird-in-Hand Harness Shop at the far end of the property, and his mouth dried. Seth had said Veronica's father owned a harness shop.

This has to be it!

"May I help you?" A short, pretty blonde approached the buggy, and Jason recognized her as one of the sisters who had consoled Veronica at Seth's visitation.

"We want to buy a pie," Stephen said as he pushed the buggy door open.

"Oh, *wunderbaar,*" the blonde said. "I'll go inside and get *mei schweschder.* I'll be right back. You may go over to the stand if you'd like. There are jars of jam, pickles, and relish for sale too."

Jason climbed from the buggy and walked toward the stand as the *maedel* rushed toward the front porch. She climbed the steps, opened the door, and called, "Veronica! You have customers!"

Veronica! I've finally found her. Jason felt as if he were cemented in place. The door creaked open, and Veronica stepped out. She glanced over at Jason and Stephen and smiled before walking down the stairs with her sister in tow.

Jason couldn't take his eyes off her. She was even more beautiful than he remembered. As she came closer, he took in how her blue dress complemented her ice-blue eyes—they were so much brighter than they'd been as she'd cried at the visitation. He took in her gorgeous eyes and still found sadness there. Her smile was shy, as if she wasn't comfortable talking to strangers.

As she approached, Jason realized he was tongue-tied. Everything he'd longed to say to her was carried away on the warm July breeze. He could only look at her, taking in her sweet face.

"*Wie geht's?*" Stephen asked, smiling. "Our *mamm* sent us out to find your raspberry pies. Apparently they are legendary around here."

Veronica's cheeks flushed, and she shook her head, staring down at a blue cooler rather than meeting Stephen's eyes. "I wouldn't say they're legendary, but I've been getting quite a few orders." She pulled a pie out of the cooler. "Did you say one?"

"Make it two," Stephen said. "If they're that *gut* I'm sure we'll eat more than one." He gave Jason a sideways glance as if to ask him why he was staring, not talking.

Veronica placed the pies on the counter, and Stephen slid his wallet out of his back pocket. "How long have you had this stand?"

"I just opened last Saturday," she said. "That's the day I'll be open all summer."

"That's great." Stephen grinned at her, and Jason actually felt a pang of jealousy. Why should he be jealous of Stephen, who was madly in love with Leah? That was preposterous! Perhaps what he truly envied was Stephen's outgoing personality. He was never shy or tongue-tied. It was as if he'd never met a stranger.

"Do you need anything else?" She pointed toward the sign on the counter. "I also have relish and a few different kinds of jam."

Jason studied her, wanting to speak but not finding any words. She looked at him, and their stares locked. Stephen said nothing, apparently deciding to leave him hanging dry.

"Do you need anything else?" she repeated.

"Relish," Jason said. "Please," he added quickly.

Her eyes flickered in question before she lifted a jar of relish and placed it next to the pies. "There you go. Anything else?"

"Would you like some jam?" Jason asked Stephen.

Stephen shrugged. "Sure. *Dat* likes it. Which kind?"

"One of each," Jason said. He spotted Stephen staring at him in his peripheral vision, but he kept his own eyes focused on Veronica as she placed their items in a large bag.

"There you go," Veronica said. She quoted the price, and

Stephen paid her. "*Danki* for your business. I hope you enjoy the pies."

"I'm sure we will." Stephen started toward the buggy. "Have a *gut* day."

Jason lingered at the stand, not wanting to leave. "It's a *schee* day."

The confusion was back in her eyes. "*Ya*, it is."

"It won't rain until Wednesday." *Did I really just comment on the weather?* Jason felt like a buffoon, but it was the only thing he could think of to say. He just wanted to be near her. He wanted to hear her voice again.

"Really? I hadn't heard that." She paused, blinking as if he were an intricate puzzle. "Well, have a *gut* day. *Danki* again for your business."

"I hope to see you again soon," he said. "Uh, to buy more pies, I mean."

Her pink lips formed a scowl. "Good-bye." She started toward the house, and he slowly moved toward the buggy.

Great. I managed to scare her off by sounding like a stalker. He longed to hide his face in his hands. As he walked, he glanced toward the porch, just as Veronica disappeared into the house. He climbed into the buggy, and Stephen raised his eyebrows.

"Why were you acting so weird?" Stephen asked.

"Do you realize who that is?" Jason guided the horse toward the road. He looked at the house one last time and spotted Veronica watching them from the window.

"No, who is she?"

"Didn't you hear her sister call her name? Veronica. *Veronica Fisher*," Jason said with emphasis. "She was Seth's fiancée."

"She was?" Stephen sounded shocked. "Are you sure that's her?"

"I'm positive. Seth lived less than a mile from here. I thought she probably didn't live far from him, but I didn't know who to ask exactly where." Jason guided the horse onto Gibbons Road. "I wanted to talk to her just now, but I couldn't form the words."

"So that's why you just stared at her like a statue?" Stephen shook his head.

He swallowed a groan. "Was it that bad?"

Stephen snorted. "*Ya*, it was."

"Great." Jason huffed. "I messed up. I really wanted to talk to her."

"Go back," Stephen suggested simply, as if it would be the easiest task ever. "Just turn the buggy around and explain that you were nervous but you really need to talk to her."

Jason shook his head. "No, I can't possibly do that."

"Why not?"

"I want to talk to her alone. It has to be the right moment." *It has to be perfect.*

"All right," Stephen said. "Go get another pie next Saturday then. But remember to go easy. She seems a little shy, and she's probably still grieving. Don't come on too strong."

"You're right." Jason sighed. Why was his young brother so intuitive?

"And don't act so strange." Stephen chuckled. "You need to relax."

"Relax," Jason repeated, but that would be impossible. He wasn't only nervous about what he needed to tell Veronica. She was the most beautiful *maedel* he'd ever seen. How could he possibly relax around her? He considered asking Stephen how he managed to relax around attractive *maed*, but he couldn't bring himself to solicit any more advice from his younger brother. He didn't want to feel like an even bigger buffoon.

What was he thinking? He had to remember *why* he needed to talk to this beautiful woman. He gripped the reins and took a deep breath. He'd finally located Veronica, but now he had to find the best time and place for their talk. He still didn't know how she would react to what he had to say about Seth.

Maybe Stephen was right. Maybe next Saturday would be his perfect opportunity.

VERONICA PEERED OUT THE KITCHEN WINDOW AS THE buggy tires crunched down the rock driveway toward the road. When the driver looked up toward the window, she took a step back, out of his line of sight. Who was this man? He was tall, taller than Seth, and he had light-brown hair instead of Seth's sun-kissed blond. The man had eyed her with such intensity in his deep-brown eyes that he made her self-conscious. She couldn't wait for him to leave, but he lingered as if he wanted to ask her out on a date. She was thankful when his brother climbed into the buggy to leave. She wondered if he would've stayed if his brother hadn't been with him.

The back door opened and closed with a bang as Emily entered the kitchen through the mudroom. "What did they buy?" she asked.

Veronica leaned back against the sink. "Two pies, one jar of relish, and four jars of jam."

"Wow!" Emily clapped her hands. "Only two Saturdays and the bake stand is already a great success."

"*Ya.*" Veronica peered through the window again to make sure those odd customers were truly gone. She would have to run and get her father for protection if they came back.

"Those men were handsome." Emily's voice was full of excitement. "They were so tall."

Veronica frowned. Emily was right. The one who had stared at her had the most attractive brown eyes she'd ever seen. They were the color of caramel. Although he was handsome, he seemed too interested in her—almost infatuated. The thought made her bristle.

"Don't you agree?" Emily looked confused. "What's wrong? You look concerned about something."

"One of them was a little odd." Veronica hugged her arms to her chest as she remembered how he had assessed her with his eyes. "The shorter one stared at me, and it made me feel uncomfortable. He hung around as if he wanted to ask me out."

"Really?" Emily's eyes were wide. "But he didn't?"

"No," Veronica said.

"Would you have said yes if he had asked you out?" Emily asked. "He was really handsome."

"No," Veronica said with disenchantment in her tone. "I don't even know him."

"You could've invited him to youth group," Emily suggested. "Actually, you could have invited both of them." She blushed. "I wouldn't mind getting to know them."

"I'm not ready for that," Veronica said quickly.

"I am," Emily said with a sigh.

"Don't worry." Veronica smiled as her shoulders relaxed. "You'll meet the right guy someday, Em. You're *schee* and sweet."

Emily's smile was encouraging. "And you will meet someone too. I'm sure of it." She jammed a thumb toward the door. "Want to help me sort quilting squares until your next customer?"

"Sure." Veronica followed her sister out through the mudroom as she wondered again who the stranger had been. Would he come back to the bake stand? And if he did, would she have enough courage to ask him for his name?

CHAPTER 6

"WAS THE STAND BUSY AGAIN TODAY?" MAMM ASKED WHILE she washed the dishes and Veronica dried them that evening. Her sisters had gone outside with *Dat* to help him with the animals.

"*Ya*, it was." She told her mother how many pies, jars of relish, and jars of jam she sold. "I'm going to have to get busy baking again on Monday after we finish the laundry." She finished drying a plate and added it to the stack while her thoughts moved to the mysterious visitor at the bake stand. "These two young men stopped by to buy pies for their mother. One of them was sort of odd."

"What do you mean by odd?" *Mamm* stopped scrubbing a pot and looked over at her.

"He stared at me, and his eyes were really intense." Veronica paused for a moment while trying to choose the words to describe it. "I felt really self-conscious, like he was maybe thinking something inappropriate while he was looking at me, or at least wanted to ask me out, even though we've never met."

Mamm's eyes widened with concern.

"Wait." Veronica held up her hands. "Just let me finish. I thought about him all afternoon, and another thought occurred to me. It was more like he wanted to tell me something, but he didn't know how to say it. There was something in his eyes. I can't explain it."

"Maybe you shouldn't be out there alone," *Mamm* said.

"I don't think he wanted to hurt me," Veronica continued. "I just got this feeling." She wished she could put it into words.

Mamm shook her head as she returned to scrubbing the pot. "I want Emily to stay out there with you."

"It's okay, *Mamm*, really. I'm almost twenty-three. I can take care of myself."

"No, not if a strong man tries to hurt you." She shivered. "I don't even want to think about that." She rinsed off the pot in the side of the sink with the plain hot water and handed it to Veronica.

"*Mamm*, do you think we could make a quick trip to see Margaret and Ellie tonight?" Veronica asked, absently moving her dish towel over the pot.

Mamm looked surprised. "It's Saturday and we have church tomorrow. We need to go to bed early."

"I know, but I promise it won't be a long visit. I just want to give Margaret a pie and see how she's doing. I'm really worried about Ellie. She and Seth were close."

Mamm was silent for a moment. "This means a lot to you."

"*Ya*, it does." Veronica nodded. "I promise to make it quick. It will be difficult to talk to them alone at church. If we go to their *haus*, we'll have more privacy."

"Fine." *Mamm* nodded toward the table. "Let's finish the dishes, and then we'll walk over there."

VERONICA AND *MAMM* WALKED UP THE FRONT STEPS OF Seth's mother's house, and Veronica knocked on the door. She scanned the porch, and memories assaulted her mind—sitting with Seth and Ellie while watching a thunderstorm last summer; snuggling together on the swing while the first snowflakes fell last winter; rushing out the door and holding back tears after their first argument. So many wonderful, though heart-wrenching, memories. She prayed none of them would ever fade. Seth would always live on in her memories.

Ellie opened the door, and her lips formed a smile. At nineteen, Ellie had the same blonde hair and light-green eyes her older brother had. Shorter than Veronica, she looked up into her eyes. "Hi, Veronica."

"Who's here?" Margaret appeared behind her in the doorway. "Oh, hi, Mattie, Veronica. I didn't expect you."

"Hi, Margaret," *Mamm* said. "Veronica especially wanted to stop by for a quick visit."

"I know we have church tomorrow, but I want to give you one of my raspberry pies," Veronica explained. "I've been selling them at my bake stand, and I thought you might enjoy one."

"Oh. *Danki.* Please come in." Margaret opened the door and motioned for them to follow her to the kitchen, inviting them to sit down at the table.

Veronica cut the pie, and they each had a piece. As they ate, she glanced around the kitchen, where more memories teased her mind—sharing lunches and dinners with Seth's family, playing board games, laughing when he told another silly joke, teaching Ellie how to make pumpkin spice kiss cookies . . .

"This is *wunderbaar,* Veronica," Margaret said. "You are a talented baker."

"*Ya,*" Ellie agreed. "Where did you get the recipe?"

"*Mei mamm* used to make these pies for *mei dat,*" Mamm explained

"So you have a bake stand now, Veronica," Margaret said. "I

noticed the sign the other day when I was coming home from running errands. How is it going?"

"It's been busy." Veronica wiped her mouth with a napkin. "I'm enjoying it."

"I bet you're selling a lot of pies. This is fantastic." Ellie took a drink of water. "Veronica, I want to show you something upstairs when we're done here."

Veronica and Ellie washed and dried the dishes while their mothers visited on the porch, then made their way upstairs. Ellie walked quickly down the long hallway, but Veronica's steps slowed. She felt as if she were walking through quicksand as they came closer to Seth's room.

She'd been in his room only once when he asked her to run upstairs and get him a clean shirt and trousers after he'd fallen into the pond while chasing one of his pigs that had escaped its pen. Veronica laughed until she couldn't breathe when he walked back up to the porch, covered in mud from head to toe. He feigned a glare and then asked her to go get him the clean clothes. She'd walked gingerly into his room, feeling as if she were invading his most personal space.

Taking her time, she first ran her fingers over the quilt folded at the bottom of his double bed and then found one of his green shirts, the color she loved most on him, in the bottom drawer of his dresser. She located his trousers hanging in the closet before rushing down to meet him in the mudroom.

When she saw him, still covered in mud, she started laughing again. Seth had grabbed a rag and cleaned only his face, but he pulled her to him. He flashed his amazing smile and then kissed her until she was breathless.

"Are you all right?" Ellie asked. She was standing in the doorway leading to Seth's room.

Veronica nodded as a lump swelled in her throat.

"If this is too difficult for you, I can just bring it to you in the hallway."

"No, I'm okay." Veronica cleared her throat. "I'm fine."

"I want to give you something. I asked *mei mamm*, and she said it was okay if I did." Ellie stepped into the room.

Veronica stood in the doorway, and she was astounded to see that the room was exactly as she'd remembered it. Seth's family hadn't touched anything. His dresser stood in the corner with his favorite trinkets lined up on top of it, including the wooden sign spelling Love that she'd given him on Valentine's Day. The pegs on the wall held his jackets, and with the door cracked open, she spotted his trousers hanging in the closet.

"It looks the same." Veronica said the words before she could stop herself.

Ellie nodded and her eyes glistened. "*Mamm* won't let me change anything."

"I think that's nice." Veronica crossed the room and stood beside the double bed. "May I sit on it?"

"Of course." Ellie sat down on the bed and patted a place next to her.

Veronica lowered herself onto the edge of the bed and touched one of the pillows, trying to imagine Seth lying there asleep the night before he died. Had he slept well? Had he dreamed of her and their future together?

She remembered Ellie was sitting beside her. "How have you been?"

Ellie shrugged. "I have *gut* days and bad days. Some mornings I'm sure he's going to run into the kitchen and grab a banana on his way out the door because he's late for work again." She looked down at her hands. "Sometimes I hear *mei mamm* crying at night." She looked up at Veronica. "I can't stand hearing her cry. It just hurts so much." A single tear trickled down her cheek.

"I understand." She squeezed Ellie's hand. "I miss him too. All the time."

Ellie nodded. "I know you do. He loved you so much, Veronica. He talked about you all the time."

Veronica's lip quivered. *Don't cry in front of Ellie! If you start, you won't be able to stop.*

"That's why *mei mamm* and I want you to have this." She picked up the quilt at the bottom of the bed, folded it in half, and handed it to Veronica. "*Mei mammi* made this for Seth when he was twelve. It's been on his bed since then. We want you to have it."

Veronica couldn't stop the tears from escaping her eyes as she hugged the quilt to her chest. She lifted it to her face and breathed in his scent—soap mixed with earth and wood—and her tears continued to spill, dripping onto the quilt. She closed her eyes and imagined Seth smiling down at her while they walked hand in hand toward the back pasture on his mother's farm. It seemed like it was only yesterday that he was whispering how much he loved her into her ear.

She felt a hand on her shoulder and turned toward Ellie, who was wiping tears away from her own eyes.

"*Danki*, Ellie," Veronica whispered. "I will treasure this."

"I know, Veronica." Ellie nodded. "He would want you to have it."

There were no words to describe the emotions roaring through her. Veronica placed the quilt on her lap, leaned over, and hugged Ellie.

"This pie is fantastic," Jason's mother said as they sat around the table that evening. "It's just as *gut* as Anna Mary said at the quilting bee."

Jason took a bite of the raspberry pie and closed his eyes,

savoring the sweet and tart taste. It was amazingly more delicious than he'd ever imagined!

"*Ya*, it is," *Dat* agreed. "It's the perfect dessert."

"You must go get me another pie next Saturday so I can take it to my quilting circle the following week," *Mamm* said.

"I can do that." Jason smiled, and Stephen raised his eyebrows.

After dessert, Jason and Stephen strode out to the barn to check on the horses.

"That pie was *appeditlich*," Jason said as they stepped into the barn. "I definitely need to go buy a few more."

"So you can see Veronica," Stephen said. "I'm not stupid. I know you want to talk to her again, and I think there's more to it than wanting to tell her you knew Seth and feel guilty about his accident."

"*Ya*, that's the truth." He might as well admit it. He couldn't wait to see her again. In fact, he couldn't get her off his mind.

"When you do talk to her, you have to be confident. Just pretend you're talking to me," Stephen encouraged.

Jason chuckled. "I don't mean any offense, but you're not nearly as attractive as she is." He stopped and faced his brother. "I hate asking your advice, but I have to."

"You need some help with *maed*?" Stephen leaned against a stall and smirked. Jason knew his younger brother was enjoying having the upper hand yet again.

"*Ya*." Jason sighed. "How did you find the courage to talk to Leah?"

Stephen shrugged. "I just talked." He tilted his head. "Did you have problems talking to Arie?"

"No," Jason insisted. "She never intimidated me the way Veronica does. I looked into Veronica's eyes and turned to Jell-O."

"Jell-O?" Stephen snickered, and Jason regretted being so honest with him.

"Never mind." Jason started toward the back of the barn. "I can figure it out myself."

"Wait, wait. I'm sorry." Stephen trotted after him. "I didn't mean to laugh. I just never expected you to ask me for advice. I figured you had it all under control since you dated Arie—even if you had trouble today. Just be yourself. Pretend you're talking to Leah or Mary. She's only a person."

"Right." Jason repeated the advice in his mind but knew that he'd turn to gelatin when he saw her again. Something in her ice-blue eyes melted him to the core. He'd never felt such a strong attraction to anyone, and he hoped someday she might feel the same way about him—just as soon as he straightened things out with her about Seth.

Stephen also suggested he go slow because Veronica was probably still grieving. He couldn't forget that.

VERONICA CURLED UP ON HER BED LATER THAT EVENING. Despite the hot, humid July air coming through the open window, she hugged the quilt to her body, breathing in Seth's smell while contemplating her favorite memories of him. She hoped his scent would never fade from the blanket, even though she knew someday it would. Veronica missed him so much that her soul ached for him, but she was thankful for this special gift that could help her hold on to him for a little bit longer.

VERONICA CARRIED TWO PIES TO THE STAND THE FOLLOW-ing Saturday morning. She looked toward the road and saw a horse and buggy heading toward her. She stowed the pies in the cooler and then smoothed her hands over her apron as the horse halted in front of the stand. When she spotted the mysterious man from last week climbing from the buggy, her stomach tightened. She recalled her mother's worries about her safety, and she considered calling for Emily, who was working in the garden.

When the man met her gaze and smiled, however, all her worries faded away. There was something genuine in his light-brown eyes.

He nodded. *"Gude mariye."*

"Gude mariye," she said. "Did you enjoy your purchases last week?"

"Ya." He pointed toward the coolers. "I'm hoping you have more pies. My family ate the first two quickly, and *mei mamm* sent me back to get more."

"Oh, *gut*. I'm glad you liked them."

"What's your secret?"

"It's an old family recipe." She lifted two pies from the cooler. "How many do you want?"

"Three." He pulled out his wallet and paid her. "Do you grow the raspberries in your garden?"

"Ya," she said. "My *mammi* planted them many years ago, and they come back every season. We have an abundance of raspberries. There are so many that my *schweschder* has to help me pick them and freeze them."

"That's amazing." His smile was warm and genuine.

Veronica looked up at his face twice as she placed the pies in a bag, first taking in his chiseled cheekbones, then his perfectly proportioned nose. He was handsome, just as Emily had said, but she wasn't interested. No one could ever fill the hole Seth had left in her heart.

"Here you go." He handed her the money and then picked up the pies. "I know we'll enjoy these. My *mamm* is taking one to her quilting circle."

"Danki." She slipped the money into a pocket in her apron and recalled their brief conversation last week. "Your weather report was right, by the way."

"What?" He raised his eyebrows in question.

"Last week you told me it wasn't supposed to rain until Wednesday, and you were right. In fact, it poured on Wednesday. Have you heard a weather report for this week?"

The corners of his lips twitched with amusement. "Let me think." He looked up at the cloudless sky, and she knew he was going to fabricate a weather report. "I heard it isn't supposed to rain until Tuesday."

"Tuesday." She folded her arms over her apron. "I'll make a note of that and be prepared when I go to buy groceries."

"That's a *gut* idea." He looked at her for a moment, and the nervous expression she'd seen last week returned to his face. Was he afraid to really talk to her?

"What's your name?" She felt outspoken and bold after asking the question, but the words had slipped from her lips before she could stop them.

"Jason." He gave her a hesitant smile. "Jason . . . Huyard."

"Well, Jason Huyard, I hope you enjoy your pies, and I'll be sure to find my umbrella for Tuesday."

"Gut." He nodded. "Stay dry."

"You too."

He climbed into the buggy and gave her a little wave before guiding the horse back down the driveway.

"Jason Huyard," she whispered. Why was that name so familiar? Was there another Jason Huyard in their community? She doubted it since Huyard was a rare Amish last name, unlike Fisher. She stared after his buggy and wondered if he would come back for more pies next Saturday. And if he did, would he have another make-believe weather report to share?

She smiled. He seemed like a nice person, but she wasn't looking for a boyfriend. He might, however, eventually become a friend, and maybe she could use a brotherly friend right now.

JASON PLACED THE PIES ON THE KITCHEN COUNTER. HE smiled as he contemplated his short conversation with Veronica at the bake stand. She'd seemed happy to see him, and she even teased him about his weather report. She was stunningly beautiful in her rose-colored dress. He'd had a difficult time pulling his focus away from her. And he was glad she hadn't recognized his name. He still wasn't ready for the talk he knew would have to come.

"You went by the bake stand again?" Stephen stepped into the kitchen and reached for a bottle of iced tea from the refrigerator.

"*Ya, Mamm* wanted three more pies, so I stopped at Veronica's bake stand after going to the hardware store."

"Oh." Stephen poured two glasses of tea and handed one to Jason. "And? How did it go? Did you actually talk to her this time?"

"*Ya*, I did." Jason frowned before taking a sip. "We joked about the weather, and she asked me what my name is."

"Did you tell her you worked with Seth?"

Jason sighed and placed the glass on the counter. "No, I didn't. I couldn't bring myself to say it. I'm afraid I'll scare her away if she finds out I knew Seth."

Stephen gave him a look of disbelief. "I thought you wanted to express your condolences to her and tell her you miss Seth too. What about your plan to grieve with her?"

"I chickened out." Jason couldn't admit that he was so taken by her beauty that he was afraid of saying something that would ruin the moment. When she joked about his weather report, he felt as if it was an invitation to be friendly and get to know her better. He feared that bringing up the subject of Seth might have turned a fun conversation into something depressing.

"You have to tell her the truth if you're going to keep seeing her," Stephen insisted.

"I will tell her," Jason promised. "I'll tell her the next time I'm there."

"*Gut.*" Stephen took a long drink. "Are you coming to the youth gathering tomorrow night?"

"I don't know." Jason shrugged.

"You should come." Stephen placed his glass on the counter. "Mary has been asking about you. It seemed like you two got along when you went to their farm. You should see her again. Give her a fair chance, especially since you can't be sure how your talk with Veronica will go." He started for the back door. "See you later."

Jason placed the pies in the refrigerator and contemplated Mary. She was sweet and pretty, but he didn't feel the spark with Mary he felt with Veronica. When Veronica smiled today, his elation had thrummed through his whole body. He had never felt such an overwhelming yearning to get to know someone. He knew his brother was right; he had to tell Veronica he had been friends with Seth and was there when he died. He'd find a way to tell her the truth, but he also wanted to find a way to spend more time with her—and that was what made following Stephen's advice so hard.

CHAPTER 7

Veronica looked up at the foreboding gray clouds and chuckled to herself as she and Emily walked into the grocery store Tuesday morning. From the look of the sky, Jason was right again, and it was going to rain on the day he had predicted. She wondered if he'd noticed the clouds yet.

"What's so funny?" Emily asked as she pulled a shopping cart from the rack.

"Nothing." Veronica consulted her list. "We need to get flour and sugar. Should we go to the baking aisle first?"

"That sounds like a *gut* plan." Emily pushed the cart toward the aisle. "We need to get back to baking as soon as we get home."

"*Ya*, I know." Veronica glanced toward the deli as they passed, and her breath hitched when she saw Jason Huyard ordering at the counter. Was he there because she mentioned grocery shopping today?

"What's wrong?" Emily turned toward the deli. "Oh, look! There's that guy who bought those pies from you."

"His name is Jason Huyard," Veronica said softly. "He told me Saturday when he came for more pies."

"Jason," Emily sighed with a dreamy expression. "He's so handsome."

"Shh. Don't be so loud." Veronica nudged her sister toward the baking supplies aisle. "Go."

"Why don't you want to talk to him?" Emily looked surprised.

"I don't know what I'd say, and I don't want to appear overly eager to see him," Veronica whispered. "He probably won't even recognize me since we've only spoken twice. He doesn't even know my name. I asked his but he didn't ask mine."

"Veronica!"

She turned toward Jason, and her eyes widened as he waved and started toward them.

"Apparently he does know your name," Emily said between gritted teeth. "He probably heard me calling you the first time he came to the stand." She waved at Jason just as Veronica felt the tips of her ears burning with embarrassment.

"Hi, Jason! How are you? I'm Emily. I saw you and your *bruder* at Veronica's stand."

"Hi." Jason had two packages of lunch meat in his hands, and after nodding at Emily, he looked directly at Veronica. "I didn't expect to see you here—though I think you did mention possibly going grocery shopping today."

Just look at that cute, crooked grin.

"We're here for baking supplies," Emily said. "You?"

Veronica's eyes were frozen on Jason, but she caught the curiosity in her sister's voice.

"That's great. Me? Uh, lunch meat. Are you making more pies, Veronica?" Jason had replied to Emily, but he hadn't taken his eyes off Veronica.

How red are my ears now?

"*Ya*," Veronica said, gripping her list. "We're out of flour and sugar. We can't make more pies without them."

"That's very true." He shifted both of his packages to one hand and rested his free hand on their cart. "My *bruder* and

I finished one of your pies last night. I need to get a few more from you."

How many raspberry pies can one family eat?

"You should come by the house," Emily offered. "We have some already made."

"Oh." Jason smiled. "That would be great. I may have to stop by." His eyes seemed to search Veronica's as if asking for permission to visit again.

"*Ya*, you should come by again soon," Veronica agreed, finally relaxing a little. "In fact, I'll need a new weather report from you." She gestured toward a window. "It seems you were right again."

He grinned, and she noticed he looked even more handsome. "You saw those threatening clouds."

"Of course I did." *And you noticed them too.* "You definitely have a future in weather forecasting."

Jason laughed, and she relished the warm sound. She pushed the thought away, reminding herself that she wasn't interested in finding a boyfriend. She didn't even know this man.

"What are you talking about?" Emily looked at each of them with a confused expression. "What's so interesting about the clouds? And why would—"

"It's nothing," Veronica told her sister. "We just were talking about the weather when Jason stopped by the bake stand on Saturday."

"Oh." Emily shook her head and frowned with disappointment. "I guess I had to be there to understand it."

"I have to get back to work, and I'd better let you *maed* do your shopping," Jason said. "It was nice seeing you."

"*Ya*, you too," Emily said.

Jason smiled at Veronica.

"Have a *gut* day," Veronica told him. Now she could feel her cheeks heating. Why was she acting like a teenager around him? He was just a nice man who bought pies from her, and that was it. And of course he would have no idea exactly when she would do her shopping today. What did she think he'd done? Come first thing in the morning and waited for her?

"He likes you," Emily sang as Jason moved toward the cashier.

"Shh," Veronica muttered.

"He can't hear me." Emily pushed the cart down the aisle. "I think it's sweet. Actually, I'm a little jealous because he's so attractive, but he does have a nice-looking *bruder*. Maybe we can invite both of them to a youth group meeting."

Veronica searched the shelf for sugar while trying to ignore her sister.

"Did you hear me?" Emily leaned closer to her. "Why don't we invite them to youth group?"

"You can invite them. I'm not interested." She jerked a large bag of sugar from the shelf and dropped it into the cart with a thump.

"What do you mean you're not interested? Are you talking about Jason or youth group?"

"Both." Veronica moved to the display of flour and picked up a large bag.

Emily touched Veronica's arm. "Why aren't you interested in getting to know Jason better?"

Veronica shrugged. "He's nice, but I'm just not interested."

"You're not interested in him or in dating at all?"

Her youngest sister certainly knew how to get to the heart of issues. Veronica turned toward her. "I'm not ready to date." *And I never will be.*

"Veronica." Emily's expression was serious. "Seth would want you to be *froh*. He wouldn't want you to stop living your life because he can't live his anymore."

A lump began to swell in Veronica's throat and her eyes stung with tears. How could she have felt an attraction to Jason? She didn't want to get emotional here, in the middle of the grocery store, while other shoppers watched with curiosity and pity.

"I will not have this conversation with you now," she whispered. "Let's get the rest of our groceries and go home." Veronica glanced at the shopping list in her hand and then stalked down the aisle.

"Veronica, wait." Emily trotted to catch up with her. "I didn't mean to upset you. I just want you to be *froh*."

"Emily, please." Veronica faced her. "Drop it now."

"Fine." Emily frowned, and Veronica couldn't stand the hurt in her sister's eyes. Emily only wanted what was best for her, but Veronica was content to take care of herself.

"How was your trip to the store?" Mamm sat at the kitchen table peeling peaches.

"It was *gut*," Veronica said as she and Emily dropped their grocery bags onto the counter. "What are you making?"

"Peach salsa," *Mamm* said. "Want to help?"

"Sure." Veronica stepped over to the stove and checked the pot of boiling tomatoes. "Is this *Mammi's* recipe?"

"*Ya*," *Mamm* said. "*Dat* loved this salsa. *Mamm* would can at least two dozen jars of it when peaches were in season and then store it in the pantry in the basement so *Dat* could have his chips and salsa after supper at night."

"He ate chips and salsa every night?" Veronica asked as she began to put away the groceries.

Mamm nodded. "Just about every night. *Mamm* enjoyed

making the salsa for him. I always helped her too. She once told me she loved cooking for *Dat* because he told her she was the best cook in Lancaster County." She chuckled. "*Mamm* loved it when *Dat* complimented her."

"Everyone likes to be complimented, I suppose," Veronica said, setting the lettuce in the drawer inside the refrigerator.

"That's true," *Mamm* agreed with a smile. "I enjoy it when your *dat* tells me he enjoys my cooking."

"I'll help you peel peaches." Emily fetched a paring knife from the block on the counter, sat down at the table, and picked a peach from the pile.

Veronica finished putting away the groceries and then pushed the grocery bags into the cloth bag saver hanging on the back of the pantry door before returning to the stove.

"We ran into Veronica's *freind* at the market," Emily said.

Veronica stiffened just as she began to remove the tomatoes from the boiling water.

"Which *freind* did you see?" *Mamm* asked. She dropped a peach into the vegetable chopper and began turning the handle.

"Jason Huyard," Emily gushed. "He's so handsome, and he likes Veronica."

"Veronica likes a *bu*?" Rachel walked into the kitchen from the hallway. "Why didn't anyone tell me?"

"I don't like him," Veronica insisted as she brought a bowl of tomatoes to the table.

"What does he look like?" Rachel asked. She grabbed another knife, sat at the table, and started peeling peaches.

Emily described Jason while Rachel grinned with approval.

"He sounds amazing." Rachel looked over her shoulder at Veronica.

"Just stop it, okay?" Veronica pleaded as she dropped more

tomatoes into the boiling water. "He's just a *bu* who comes to the bake stand to buy pies for his *mamm*. That's it. I don't like him, and I really don't even know him."

"Is he the one who made you uncomfortable?" *Mamm* looked concerned.

Veronica nodded as her temper boiled like the water on the stove. Why couldn't her sisters stay out of her private life? She didn't want to discuss this anymore.

"Why would he make you feel uncomfortable? He's nice," Emily continued. "I think he's sweet."

"Really?" Rachel smiled. "I think this is just what you need, Veronica. It's time you met someone."

"I told her to invite him to a youth gathering," Emily said as she started peeling a second peach. "He has a handsome *bruder* too. I'd like to talk to him."

"*Ach*, that's a *wunderbaar* idea!" Rachel gushed while peeling a tomato. "Do you have his number? You can call him and ask him and his *bruder* to come this Sunday."

"No," Veronica seethed. "I am not interested."

"Veronica, I told you already that Seth wouldn't want you to stay home alone. He'd want you to live your life," Emily insisted.

"Oh, *ya*," Rachel chimed in with a concerned frown. "You're not hurting anyone by seeing someone else." She handed another peeled tomato to *Mamm*, who put it in the hand chopper and then dropped it into the large plastic pan with the rest of the chopped peaches and tomatoes.

"I'm not seeing him!" Veronica hadn't meant to yell so loudly. Her sisters and mother stopped working and stared at her with wide eyes. "Just stop, okay? I'm not dating him, and I don't want to. Stop pressuring me."

"We're not pressuring you," Rachel said softly. "We just want you to be *froh* again. We don't want you to cry anymore. Maybe if you give Jason a chance, you'll find joy again and the pain won't hurt as much."

"Rachel is right," Emily agreed with an emphatic nod. "Jason might help you with your grief."

Veronica's hands trembled. "I don't need you or anyone else telling me how to deal with my grief. You have no idea how I feel, so just leave me alone!" She rushed out of the kitchen and up the stairs as her sisters called after her. She hurried into her room and sat down on the edge of her bed. She ran her fingers over Seth's quilt as tears trickled down her hot cheeks.

Why couldn't her sisters understand that she didn't want their advice? All she wanted was their love and support.

A knock sounded on her doorframe, and she looked up at her mother standing there.

"May I come in?" *Mamm* asked with worry in her eyes.

"*Ya.*" Veronica wiped away her tears and cleared her throat.

Mamm sat beside her on the bed and touched the quilt. "I know you cherish this quilt. It was nice of Ellie to give it to you."

"It still smells like him," Veronica whispered. "Some nights I hug it and just breathe in his scent." She almost felt silly admitting it out loud, but she knew her mother would understand.

Mamm was silent while she turned her attention to the dark-blue and maroon material. "I know you're in pain, and you want to protect his memory." She looked into Veronica's eyes. "But you have to remember that your *schweschdere* are worried about you. I'm worried about you too."

"I'm fine," Veronica whispered, her voice thin. "I just need some time."

"Your *schweschdere* love you."

Veronica nodded and stared at the quilt.

"I've told them to stop pressuring you, but I have to admit, I think they're right."

Veronica looked up at her mother. "What do you mean? You've told me you understand how I feel. Now you're taking their side?"

Mamm smiled. "There are no sides in this. We all love you, and we're worried about you. I just agree that maybe you should go to a youth gathering with them. I've told you that before. You don't have to invite Jason, but maybe you should go on Sunday. You don't have to talk to any *buwe*, Veronica. You can talk to the other young women there. Just go with them so you can get out of the *haus* for a while and be around other young people. It will be *gut* for you."

Veronica sighed. "Maybe I'll go." She hoped the weak promise would satisfy her mother.

"*Gut.*" *Mamm* hugged her. "Now, I really need your help with this peach salsa. There are probably a hundred peaches yet to peel."

Veronica nodded. "I'll be down in a minute."

"All right." *Mamm* touched Veronica's cheek and then stood. "Take your time coming downstairs."

"*Danki.*" Veronica waited until her mother had left before she hugged the quilt to her chest. She breathed in the faint scent of Seth and sighed.

A light tapping sound caught her attention, and when she glanced toward the window, she spotted raindrops hitting the panes. A laugh escaped her lips. Jason had been right about the weather again.

She knew her sisters only meant well, but she didn't want them to pressure her about Jason. No one would ever replace her

Seth—not even a handsome amateur weatherman. Next time she saw Jason Huyard, she'd be a friend. Nothing more.

"*GUDE MARIYE!*" JASON CLIMBED OUT OF THE BUGGY SATURDAY morning and walked over to the bake stand. Veronica stood smiling behind the counter, dressed in an emerald-green dress and black apron. "How are you? I wanted to stop by sooner this week, but it's been really busy at work."

"*Gude mariye!* I'm fine. It's *gut* to see you." She pointed toward the sky. "I was hoping you'd come and share your weather forecast for this week since you were correct about Tuesday's rain."

He chuckled, and her smile widened. "I can't take any credit for that prediction. It was just a *gut* guess."

"But you were right." She tapped her chin as a smile played at the corners of her mouth. "I wonder if you could get a job writing a weather column for the newspaper. Have you considered that as a profession?"

"No, I can't say that I have." He stood in front of the bake stand and silently admired how the emerald dress complemented her blue eyes. Did she have any idea how beautiful she was?

"What do you do for a living?" she asked.

He hesitated. Now was his chance to tell her where he worked and how sorry he was for Seth's death. All he had to do was open his mouth and tell her everything. "I work in construction."

"Oh." She smiled. "Do you build homes?"

"Sometimes." Why couldn't he tell her the whole truth? Why couldn't he simply say he knew she missed Seth because he did too?

"That's nice. Where do you live?"

"About five miles away from here in Gordonville."

"Oh." She pointed toward a blue cooler. "So, are you here for more pies, or are you tired of them yet?"

I could never get tired of seeing you. "Ya, I'm here for more pies. My *mamm* wants to take a couple to her quilting circle this week."

"Your *mamm* makes quilts?" she asked, and he nodded. "My *mamm* and Emily do too. I help them sometimes, but I'm not the best quilter. *Mamm* says I don't have the patience for it." She shrugged, and she was adorable. "I suppose she's right."

"I would imagine you do just fine." He smiled and she blushed. "Your *schweschder* seems nice. Do you have any other siblings?" He knew she did, but he didn't want to raise questions he wasn't ready to answer.

"Ya, I have another *schweschder* named Rachel. Emily is the youngest and then Rachel. I'm the oldest. How about you? Do you have any other siblings?"

"Just my *bruder*, Stephen, the one who was with me the first day I came to buy a pie." He felt happiness swell inside of him. He was finally getting to know her. Maybe she'd consider him a friend. Then a pang of guilt overtook him. Friends were honest with each other. He should tell her the truth, but he couldn't bring himself to form the words.

She opened one of the coolers. "So you wanted two pies for your *mamm* this week?"

"That would be fantastic," he told her while pulling out the money he'd tucked in his pocket.

"What about the weather report?" she asked. "I can't give you the pies unless you tell me when it's going to rain." Her pink lips formed a feigned frown. "You know I depend on this weather report to plan my week."

"Is that so?" He rubbed his clean-shaven chin. "Let me

think." He took in the large, fluffy clouds in the sky. "I predict rain on Friday." He met her smile, and his pulse raced.

"Friday, huh?" She smoothed her hands over her apron. "I will be sure to have my umbrella handy."

"That's a *gut* plan. And if it doesn't rain, then at least you can say you were prepared."

"Do you like rain?" she asked. "I mean, do you like to listen to it or watch it?"

He nodded. "*Ya*, I like listening to it at night when I'm trying to fall asleep. It's sort of soothing."

"I like storms too." She had a faraway look in her eyes as she looked toward the road. "I used to sit on the porch and watch them with . . . a *freind*."

That friend was Seth; Jason was certain of it. He recalled Seth talking about sitting on his parents' porch and holding Veronica's hand last summer during a loud and bright thunderstorm. "I like storms too." *And I would love to watch them with you.*

Veronica's smile returned. "Well, come back and see me when you run out of pies again. At this point, I feel like I should give them to you free as a payment for the weather reports."

Jason chuckled. "I don't think my weather guesses are worth free pies. I wouldn't feel right about that."

She smiled, and he again considered telling her he had known Seth. But he was sure her smile would disappear if he mentioned her fiancé's name.

"Well, if it rains on Friday, next week's pie is free." Her smile suddenly faded, and pink stained her cheeks. "Only if you need a pie next week. I didn't mean that you should feel pressured to come back next week."

Was she embarrassed, afraid she'd been too bold to assume he wanted to visit with her? She had no idea just how much he enjoyed their conversation.

"I'm certain I'll be back next week, and there's no pressure."
He lifted the pies. "And if it rains on Friday, I'll be surprised, but
I'll still pay for my pies. Have a *gut* week."

"You too."

Jason started for the buggy and glanced back once to look at
Veronica. His smile deepened as she waved.

"Veronica?" Rachel stood in the doorway of her sister's room later that evening.

"*Ya?*" Veronica looked up from the Christian memoir she
was reading.

"I was wondering if you were still angry with me for talking about Jason the other day." Rachel ran her fingers over the
doorframe.

"No, I'm not." She patted the bed beside her. "You can
come in."

"*Danki.*" Rachel sat down on the edge of the bed. "I'm sorry
for upsetting you. We're all just worried about you."

"I know." Veronica sighed and closed the book. "I realize
that, but I don't like to be pressured."

"I know." Rachel picked at lint on her white nightgown.
"Emily and I want you to come to the youth gathering tomorrow."

Veronica opened her mouth to protest, and Rachel held up
her finger to silence her.

"Just wait one minute and hear what I have to say," Rachel
added. "We're combining our youth group with another, so it
will be a bigger group than usual. We're going to play volleyball
and Ping-Pong, and there will be a lot of food. Just come and
have a *gut* time. There won't be any pressure to meet *buwe*. You
can just hang out with me and Emily and our *freinden.*"

It was tempting. She used to enjoy being with her sisters at the youth gatherings, but she stopped going when she started spending more time with Seth and his family.

"Please, Veronica." Rachel's brown eyes pleaded with her. "Just come and be with us. Emily and I miss you."

"I'll go." Veronica said the words when she realized just how much she missed being with her sisters and their friends. "It sounds fun."

"*Danki!*" Rachel leaned over and hugged her. "I promise you'll have a great time."

"I'm going to make sure you keep that promise," Veronica said, joking.

Before Rachel stepped into the hallway, she looked back over her shoulder at Veronica. "Did he come to buy another pie today?"

Veronica knew her sister was asking about Jason. "*Ya*, he bought two more."

"I think Emily is right about him." Rachel faced her and leaned against the doorframe. "It sounds like he really likes you."

"I know." Veronica sighed. *And I have no idea what to do about it.*

"*Gut nacht,*" Rachel said.

"*Gut nacht.*" Veronica smiled, thankful that her sister didn't say anything else about Jason. She'd spent all afternoon contemplating him. Talking to him seemed too easy and fun. She longed to see him again, but she couldn't allow herself to think about him too much. Yearning to know him felt so wrong.

Veronica pushed thoughts of Jason away and lifted the book off her bed. While trying to immerse herself in the story, a vision of Jason's smile crept back into her mind. He was handsome, fun, and sweet, but her heart belonged to someone else. She shouldn't even think about Jason, but she found herself wondering when she'd see him again.

CHAPTER 8

JASON GRIPPED A CUP OF WATER IN HIS HAND WHILE HE watched a young woman and a young man play Ping-Pong in a large barn the following evening. The aroma of animals and hay wafted over him as he scanned the large, open area. Mary stood close beside him and smiled up at him.

"So I was thinking maybe we could take a walk around the pond," Mary said. "I want to tell you all about my week. I had some interesting encounters at the hardware store."

She prattled on about the customers she'd seen, and Jason tried and failed to listen to her. Instead, he glanced toward the entrance to the barn and worked on coming up with an excuse to leave. Even though the barn was huge and full of dozens of young people, he felt as if the room were closing in on him. He longed to walk around the pond alone and enjoy his thoughts, which had been tied up with Veronica since he'd seen her yesterday. He knew a friendship was beginning to form between Veronica and him, and he'd contemplated going to visit her tonight instead of going to the youth gathering. His brother, however, started nagging him this morning and didn't relent until Jason had agreed to go. Stephen insisted that Jason had to see Mary tonight, even though Mary was the furthest person from his mind.

"Did you hear what I said?" Mary eyed him, frowning as she placed her hand on her small hip. "I was telling you about the farmer who wanted me to help him pick out a chicken coop. Have you ever built a chicken coop?"

He blinked at her in disbelief. Did she really want to discuss chicken coops? *I have to get out of here.* "I'll be right back."

"What?" she asked. "Where are you going?"

"Just wait here." Jason forced a smile as he placed his plastic cup on a chair. He walked toward the door, picking up a battery-operated lantern as he stepped outside into the sweltering July night. He looked up at the clear sky, taking in the bright stars. He walked toward the pond, passing groups of young people talking and laughing. Volleyball games lit by Coleman lanterns continued in a nearby pasture.

Jason took a deep, cleansing breath. His shoes crunched on the rock pathway as he neared the pond. He spotted the silhouette of a young woman sitting on a large rock and he slowed his pace. He didn't want to bother her.

She turned to look at him, and his breath caught in his throat.

"Veronica?" he asked. No, he had to be dreaming. Why would she be here?

"Jason?" She smiled. "Oh, it's such a relief to see a familiar face." She touched a flat rock beside her. "Do you have a minute to talk?"

"Absolutely." He sank down onto the rock and placed the lantern between them. The warm glow illuminated her pretty face and sparkling blue eyes. "I didn't expect to see you here."

"I didn't expect to be here." She shook her head. "My *schweschdere* insisted I get out of the *haus* and meet some people my own age. I haven't met anyone over the age of twenty-one."

"I'm twenty-four." He grinned.

"That's a relief. I'm twenty-two, almost twenty-three."

"When is your birthday?" he asked.

"October." She sighed and tossed a pebble toward the pond. It skipped twice before plopping into the water.

"If it's any consolation, my *bruder* forced me to come here too."

Her eyes widened. "He did?"

"Yeah." Jason tossed a pebble into the pond, and it landed with a plop. "You are much better at skipping stones than I am."

"It's one of my rare talents." She tossed another pebble, which skipped four times before sinking.

"You make *appeditlich* pies, relishes, and jams, and you can skip stones." He shook his head. "You are a multitalented *maedel*."

"*Danki*." She giggled, and the sound was a sweet melody to his ears. "So why didn't you want to come here?"

He sighed. "Stephen is trying to set me up with his girl-friend's *schweschder*."

"Oh, your *bruder* has a girlfriend?" Veronica frowned. "I didn't realize that."

Jason's stomach plummeted. *Oh no, please don't tell me you have a crush on Stephen!* He pushed on, hoping to shield the worry from his face. "*Ya*, he's been seeing Leah Esh for almost a year now."

"Emily will be very disappointed." She skipped another stone and then wiped her hands on her apron.

"Emily will be disappointed?" Jason's shoulders relaxed.

"*Ya*." Veronica gave him a shy smile. "She said she wanted to invite him and you to a youth gathering."

Jason rested his elbows on his knees. "Really? Why haven't you asked us?"

"I don't know." She shrugged and fingered a rock. "So why don't you like Leah's *schweschder*?"

She was dodging the question, and it was adorable.

"Mary is nice, but we don't have anything in common. I can tell she likes me, and I don't want to disappoint her. I keep trying to tell Stephen I'm not interested, but he won't listen." Jason took in Veronica's face as she skipped another pebble. "Why didn't you want to come here?"

"My reasons are very similar to yours." Veronica turned toward him, and her eyes were serious. "My *schweschdere* have been pressuring me to get out of the *haus* and meet some people. When they say meet some people, they really mean they want me to date again. They think if I fall in love, I'll get over my grief." She tossed a flat rock, and it skipped six times before sinking.

"You have to show me how you skip those stones," he said. "You're an expert."

Veronica's eyes glistened. "My fiancé taught me how. It's all in the wrist."

Jason's mouth dried.

"Watch this." She flicked her wrist three times and then skipped another stone. "See? It's the wrist."

"I see," he said softly. *I should tell her the truth. I need to tell her I knew Seth.* He opened his mouth, but no words came out.

"His name was Seth Lapp, and he died," she whispered so softly that he almost missed it because of the loud commotion coming from the makeshift volleyball courts. She skipped stones while she spoke. "He built sheds for a living, and he fell accidently. He died instantly."

"I'm sorry," Jason said softly. The grief in her eyes caused his chest to squeeze. He wanted to take away all the pain she felt. He wanted to apologize for not saving Seth, but he couldn't speak. He couldn't say the words he knew she needed to hear.

"Thanks." Her smile was sad. "It's been three months, but

some days it feels like it was only yesterday." She sighed. "My *schweschdere* think I'm going to fall in love and all the hurt will dissolve like some distant memory. The truth is, I don't think I could ever fall in love again." She suddenly stared at him. "Do you think God gives us more than one person to love?"

Jason paused, stunned by the question. Why was Veronica asking for his opinion on something so intimate? "I hope so," he said softly.

Veronica skipped another stone. "I don't know how I can ever forget him," she continued while keeping her eyes trained on the pond. "When I close my eyes, I see his face. I hear his voice. His *schweschder* gave me a quilt his *mammi* made him when he was twelve. I can still smell his scent on it, and I cuddle up with it at night." She skipped another stone. "Some nights I dream about his accident, and I'm actually at the shop and I save him. I catch him before he hits the floor, and he lives."

The blood drained from Jason's face. *I have the same dream!*

"It's so ridiculous because he was too heavy and muscular. I know I couldn't have saved him." She glanced at him and blushed. "Am I embarrassing you with all this personal information?"

"No." He shook his head with emphasis. "Not at all."

"For some reason I feel comfortable with you, but you must think I'm *narrisch*. Why would some *gegisch maedel* share her intimate thoughts with someone she doesn't even know?"

"You trust me because I'm your weatherman, and you can tell me anything."

She gave a bark of laughter and then covered her mouth. "I'm sorry. That was a really ugly laugh."

"No, it wasn't ugly at all. I think it was *wunderbaar*."

She smiled. "Now you have to tell me something personal, so I don't feel so embarrassed."

"Hmm." He lifted his hat and brushed his brown hair back

from his forehead. "All right. I actually came out here to hide from Mary. Do you think that's terrible?"

Veronica nodded. *"Ya,* I do." She bit her lower lip and then gave him a shy smile. "But I'm glad you did."

"I am too."

"What are you going to tell her when she finds you?" Veronica asked.

"I'm going to tell her you're giving me stone-skipping lessons," he quipped.

Veronica laughed again. "I hope she believes you."

"If she saw you skip stones, she would. You're an expert."

Her smile faltered. "When I told you I liked to sit on the porch and watch storms with someone, it was Seth."

I know. Jason nodded. "It must be difficult for you. I know you miss him." *I miss him too.*

"I miss him all the time. Some days are worse than others. Sometimes I'll see something that makes me think of him, and I fall into this pit of grief I can't get out of." She turned toward him. "Did you lose someone too? Is that why your *bruder* is pushing you to date Mary?"

"Ya." He tossed a stone, and it skipped three times before sinking.

"What happened?" she asked, her voice full of concern. *"Ach,* I'm sorry. It's none of my business."

"No, it's okay. I want to tell you. I was engaged once too." He looked out over the pond to avoid her sympathetic expression. "She changed her mind a month before we were supposed to marry."

"Ach, no." Veronica breathed the words. "I'm so sorry."

"Thanks." He lifted one of his shoulders in a lazy shrug, as if it were no big deal. "She moved on and married someone else, but I've been single ever since."

"What was her name?"

"Arie." He met her stare, and her expression was warm with empathy.

"We've both been hurt. Aren't we two peas in a pod?"

Jason raised his eyebrows with surprise. "I guess we are."

"The weatherman and the stone skipper, both broken-hearted and alone." Her smile was wide.

He grinned. "*Ya*, we are, but at least we have each other." He was falling for her, fast. His heartbeat leaped when she gave him another shy smile. Did she feel the same way? Did she feel a close connection to him? He had to tell her the truth before it would be too painful to admit.

"Jason?"

He spun around and found Mary staring at him with her eyebrows knitted together. "Oh, hi, Mary," he said, hoping to sound casual instead of nervous.

"I've been looking all over for you." Mary looked at Veronica for a long moment and then looked back at Jason. "I didn't realize you were meeting another *freind* tonight."

"He actually was helping me," Veronica said. "He was walking by, and I was sitting here alone. I was feeling down in the dumps, and I asked him to sit with me for a minute just to talk. Jason was really nice, but I could tell he wanted to go. I was selfish and kept talking. I didn't realize he was with you. I'm sorry."

Jason eyed her with surprise. *Why is Veronica protecting me?*

"Oh. That's very nice of you, Jason. I didn't realize you were helping someone else. I thought you were avoiding me." Mary's expression softened. "I'm sorry for being upset with you." She pointed toward the ground. "May I join you?"

"No, no." Veronica shook her head. "I don't want to intrude." She smiled at Jason. "*Danki* for listening to me. You may leave now."

His lips twitched, and her eyes sparkled with mischief. He

longed to grab her hand and take her on a long, private walk through the pasture. "I'm sure Mary won't mind sitting with us," he said. "I don't want to leave you alone if you're still upset."

"I'm fine now." Veronica faced Mary. "My *schweschder* is here with her boyfriend, and I'm embarrassed to admit I was jealous. They're *froh* together, and I'm alone. I was feeling sorry for myself."

Jason examined Veronica's expression and found truth there. *Is she truly jealous of her sister?*

"*Ach*, no." Mary touched her hand to her chest. "Don't be embarrassed. I actually know how you feel. My *schweschder* has a boyfriend, and sometimes I have a difficult time watching them together." She glanced toward Jason, and her cheeks were red with embarrassment. "I also am hoping to find someone special."

Jason shifted his weight on the rock. He suddenly felt self-conscious. He didn't want to hurt Mary's feelings, but he'd have to find a way to tell her the truth. He wasn't interested in her; instead, he was interested in the *maedel* sitting beside him.

Veronica looked at Jason and smiled. "I'm sure you will. There seems to be some nice *buwe* here today."

Jason hoped her smile meant she liked him as much as he liked her.

"I'm Veronica," she told Mary. "Where do you live?"

Mary and Veronica fell into an easy conversation, discussing where they worked and mutual friends. Soon it was ten o'clock and the young people were filing to their buggies to go home. Jason walked between the two women as they moved toward the buggies. He and Stephen had driven to the gathering with Mary and Leah, so they had to take them home. He longed to ask Veronica if he could take her home, but he knew it wouldn't be proper to leave Mary—even if he had a second horse and buggy here.

Veronica stopped short of a buggy where Emily and their brunette sister were waiting with a young man, whom he assumed was her sister's boyfriend. Veronica turned toward Jason, and her expression told him she wanted to talk to him alone.

Mary was oblivious to that as she prattled about her work schedule at the hardware store.

"Mary," he said, interrupting her, "I'm going to see Veronica to her buggy, but I'll be back in a minute. Why don't you go find Stephen and Leah?"

"Oh." Mary looked surprised. "Okay. *Gut nacht*, Veronica."

"*Gut nacht.*" Veronica flashed her bright smile and gave Mary a little wave.

As they walked together toward Veronica's sisters, Jason reached out to take Veronica's arm and then stopped, afraid of being too forward with her. "*Danki* for covering for me earlier," he said softly into her ear. The smell of her lavender shampoo overtook his senses, and his pulse quickened.

She smiled up at him. "It was no problem. I didn't want you to get into trouble on my account. I had a nice time."

"I did too." He didn't want to say good night to her. "*Danki* for the stone-skipping lessons."

"*Gern gschehne.* I'm looking forward to the rain on Friday. My garden can use it."

He laughed. "I can't really guarantee it."

"I'm going to hold you to it, though." Her smile was playful.

As they approached her buggy, Jason nodded a greeting to them.

"Jason! It's *gut* to see you." Emily grinned at Veronica, who blushed. "I didn't expect to see you here tonight. This is our sister, Rachel, and this is David."

"*Ya*, it was a nice coincidence," Jason said as he nodded hello to the others. He looked at Veronica. "I hope to see you soon."

"*Ya,*" she agreed and then lowered her voice. "I'll need another weather report next weekend."

"We'd better go," David said. "It's after ten."

Jason frowned. He didn't want Veronica to leave, but he had to let her go. For now. "*Gut nacht.*"

Veronica leaned toward him. "Stay dry on Friday." She smiled and then climbed into the back of the buggy.

He waved and then walked down the rock path toward Mary, who was standing by his buggy and watching him intently.

"I CAN'T BELIEVE JASON WAS HERE!" EMILY GUSHED TO Veronica, who sat next to her in the back of the buggy.

"*Ya,* I was surprised too."

Veronica suddenly wondered if Emily and Rachel knew the second youth group was Jason's and hoped he would be there. But Emily's surprise seemed genuine, and Rachel seemed to be paying little attention to anyone but David. No, she was sure her sisters hadn't insisted she come along just so she'd run into Jason.

Veronica peered out the back window toward Jason's buggy. Thanks to the light of their lanterns, she could see Jason talking to his brother before they both climbed into their buggy.

David and Rachel continued to speak to each other softly up front while David guided the buggy down the rock driveway toward the main road.

"I was wondering where you'd gone," Emily continued. "All of a sudden you'd disappeared."

"I wanted to get outside and get some air. It was hot in the kitchen. I was sitting at the pond, and Jason just happened to come along. It wasn't planned." Veronica fingered the hem on her apron while she thought about her conversation with Jason.

He was so handsome and funny, and she felt as if she could share every emotion and every secret with him.

In fact, she'd shared more with him than she'd ever told her mother or her sisters. Veronica hadn't told her mother or sisters about the nightmares she had about Seth's death, but when she started telling Jason about her grief, it all came out of her mouth as if she'd known him for years. She couldn't wait to see him again.

Veronica shook her head. How could she possibly think about another man when Seth had only been gone three months?

"I think he really likes you," Emily continued. "He looked at you as if you were the most important person in the world. It was as if Rachel, David, and I didn't exist."

"He's very nice," Veronica said, keeping her eyes focused on her apron.

"I know he's going to come visit you."

Veronica shrugged. "I guess we'll see. We're only *freinden*."

"Did you talk to his *bruder*?" Emily asked. "I never saw him either."

Veronica was thankful the focus of the conversation was taken off her. "No, I didn't, but Jason told me Stephen has a girlfriend. Her name is Leah Esh."

Emily frowned. "Oh."

"I'm sorry." Veronica touched her sister's hand.

"It's fine. I'm not in a hurry to meet someone special," Emily said with a shrug.

"You're always concerned about everyone else, but you never worry about yourself," Veronica said. "We need to find you someone nice."

Emily grimaced as she leaned back on the bench seat. "*Ya*, I agree, but it seems like all the *buwe* I like are either dating someone or very immature. I don't mean to sound picky, but I want

AMY CLIPSTON

to find someone who is easy to talk to and has depth, you know? I want someone who will let me share my feelings but will also share his."

Veronica nodded. "I understand. You want a boyfriend who is also a really *gut freind*."

"Exactly." Emily nodded with emphasis. "But I'm patient. I'll meet someone eventually. Until then I have plenty to do at the *haus* to keep me busy. I have my chores and my quilts to make."

"I know you'll find someone soon," Veronica said, touching Emily's hand. "Don't give up hope."

"I won't." Emily smiled. "Don't you give up hope either. Jason likes you."

I think so too. Veronica sighed. She was thankful that she and Emily could discuss things like this, but she was also nervous. Her sister was right when she said Jason liked Veronica, but she couldn't allow herself to fall for him. It was too soon. She needed to be strong and hold fast to Seth's precious memory.

JASON CLIMBED INTO BED LATER THAT NIGHT. AS HE looked up at the ceiling in the dark, he smiled. He hadn't wanted to go to the youth gathering, and yet it had turned out to be the most wonderful night he could have ever imagined. He had never expected to see Veronica, and he had never dreamed she would open up to him and share her most intimate feelings about losing Seth. Veronica had trusted him like a close friend would trust someone they had known for years. She'd opened up to him and poured out her deepest emotions, and Jason should have taken that opportunity to tell her the truth.

Rolling to his side, Jason rested his arm on his forehead. He had missed the perfect opportunity to tell Veronica he worked with Seth, but he was afraid of scaring her away. What would she say if she knew he had originally sought her out to share his grief with her, but then said nothing? Would she call him a stalker, just as Stephen had predicted?

Jason blew out a deep sigh. He was falling in love with Veronica, and he couldn't expect her to love him if he didn't tell her the truth. He had to find a way to break it to her without losing her trust. As he closed his eyes, he recalled her beautiful face and gorgeous arctic-blue eyes. He couldn't wait to see her again, and he hoped she felt the same way.

CHAPTER 9

VERONICA CLIMBED OUT OF THE BACK OF THE BUGGY ON Sunday morning and followed her mother and sisters. Since it was an off Sunday for her church district, her father decided it was a good time to visit his good friend's district for service today.

Veronica glanced down at her black dress and black apron as they walked toward the large farmhouse where the women gathered before the service. She had dressed in all black again this Sunday, just as she had for all the previous Sundays since she'd lost Seth. It was one way she could indicate she was still mourning him. No one from this church district would necessarily know whom she was mourning, but she knew.

Emily touched Veronica's hand. "Don't you want to come with us to see the youth before the service begins?"

Veronica shook her head. "I'm going to go into the kitchen with *Mamm*. I'm too old to be with the youth."

Rachel rolled her eyes. "No, you're not too old. Come with us."

"I want to be with *Mamm*," Veronica insisted. "I'll sit with you during the service." She ignored her sisters' frowns and stepped into the kitchen where the women stood in a circle and greeted each other.

As she smiled and shook hands with the other women,

Veronica's thoughts were stuck on Jason. Although they'd had a nice time at the youth gathering last week, he hadn't come to see her at the bake stand yesterday. All week she'd looked forward to seeing him on Saturday. She'd waited all day for his buggy to appear in the driveway so she could tease him about the weather and ask him why it didn't rain on Friday as he'd predicted. Had she shared too many of her private feelings and scared him away?

Veronica shook off her worries as the kitchen clock chimed nine. It was time to focus on the Lord and not worry about whether Jason Huyard liked her. After all, she *was* in mourning. Veronica exited the kitchen and found her sisters in the group of young people. She followed them into the barn, where they sat with the other unmarried young women. Veronica sank onto the backless bench between her two sisters and then glanced around, greeting a few acquaintances from the market and various other places members of the wider community gathered.

"Veronica," Emily whispered. "Look. Look!"

"*Was iss letz?*" Veronica leaned toward her sister.

"Look over at the young men." Emily tapped her arm. "Jason is here."

"What?" Veronica asked, a little too loudly. She turned toward the rows of young, unmarried men and found Jason sitting beside his brother. Delighted, she took in his handsome face. She had missed him yesterday more than she'd realized when he hadn't come to the bake stand. He was even more attractive than usual dressed in his Sunday clothes with his black trousers, crisp white shirt, and black vest. Veronica could watch him for hours, but she pulled her attention away from him and looked down at her apron. She had to find a way to remove these thoughts from her mind.

"*Was iss letz?*" Emily whispered in her ear.

"Nothing." Veronica sat up straight and lifted the hymnal

beside her from the bench. "I'm just preparing my mind for worship."

Emily lifted an eyebrow. "Aren't you *froh* to see Jason here?"

"*Ya*, it's *gut* that he's here." Veronica kept her eyes focused on the hymnal, turning to the opening hymn.

"I didn't know this was his church district."

"I didn't either. We never asked which district was at the youth gathering when we saw Jason there." Veronica wanted to look across the aisle toward the young men so she could admire Jason some more, but she knew it was too risky. She couldn't allow herself to get attached to him. She couldn't let go of Seth that quickly.

Rachel stopped talking to the young woman beside her and looked at Veronica.

"Are you okay, Veronica?" Rachel asked. "You look upset."

"I'm fine." Veronica forced a smile.

"Jason is here," Emily whispered, also a little too loudly. "He's sitting over there with his *bruder*." And, to Veronica's horror, she pointed.

Veronica yearned to crawl under the bench and hide as she felt embarrassment spread through her. Why did her sisters always have to make spectacles of themselves?

"Stop," Veronica hissed at Emily. "He'll see you."

"Don't you want him to see you?" Rachel asked while smiling toward Jason and Stephen.

"No, not right now," Veronica insisted. "I'll talk to him after the service."

Emily and Rachel turned back toward the front of the barn, and Veronica breathed a sigh of relief. She stole one last glance toward Jason and found him looking at his hymnal. *Thank goodness he hasn't seen me!*

She would do her best to avoid him until he confronted

her. As much as she yearned to see him, she also feared that he no longer wanted to be her friend. His rejection would hurt too much.

The service began with a hymn, and Veronica redirected her thoughts to the present. She joined in as the congregation slowly sang the opening hymn. A young man sitting across the barn served as the song leader. He began the first syllable of each line, and then the rest of the congregation joined in to finish the verse.

While the ministers met in another room for thirty minutes to choose who would preach that day, the congregation continued to sing. During the last verse of the second hymn, Veronica's gaze moved to the back of the barn just as the ministers returned. They placed their hats on two hay bales, indicating that the service was about to begin.

The chosen minister began the first sermon, and Veronica tried her best to concentrate on his holy words. She folded her hands in her lap and studied them, but her thoughts turned to Seth and then to Jason. She tried her best to keep her focus on the minister, but her stare moved toward the young men across the aisle. She contemplated Jason, who sat with his head bowed, focusing on his hands in his lap.

What was he thinking about? Was he thinking about Mary? Had he driven home with her last Sunday and realized he cared for her more than he originally thought? And why should Veronica be concerned if he had decided to date Mary?

While the minister continued to talk in German, Veronica lost herself in memories of the last year, of sitting with the young women in her congregation and thinking of what she and Seth would do when the service was over. Sometimes they would go for walks. Other times they would visit with his family or hers. She missed those days and relished the special memories. How long would the pain of his loss linger? When would the ache become less raw?

She redirected her thoughts to the sermon, taking in the message and concentrating on God. She wondered what God had in store for her. Did God want her to move on and find someone else to love? Was Veronica supposed to allow Jason to get close to her, or was he only a friend who would help her through her grief before he married someone else?

The first sermon ended, and Veronica knelt in silent prayer between her sisters. She closed her eyes and thanked God for her wonderful family and friends. She also prayed for Jason, asking God to watch over him and his family. After the prayers, the deacon read from the Scriptures, and then the hour-long main sermon began. Veronica willed herself to concentrate on the sermon, listening to the deacon discuss the book of Romans.

Relief flooded Veronica when the fifteen-minute kneeling prayer was over. The congregation stood for the benediction and sang the closing hymn. While she sang, her eyes moved to Jason. She wondered if he could feel her eyes watching him. She had to admit the truth. She hoped he would find her and want to talk after the service.

Rachel touched Emily's and Veronica's hands. "Let's go help serve the meal."

"*Ya*," Emily said.

Veronica glanced toward Jason and saw him talking to two other young men. She considered walking over to him after all, but she didn't want to seem too eager any more than she wanted him to ignore her. Instead, she followed her sisters out of the barn and toward the house.

"Are you going to talk to Jason?" Rachel asked as they climbed the back porch steps.

Veronica shrugged.

"You need to fill *kaffi* cups," Emily chimed in. "You can go to his table and fill his cup. That way he'll have to talk to you."

As Veronica considered that idea, she stepped into the kitchen and found Mary placing peanut butter spread and bread on trays. Her stomach sank. It made sense that if this was Jason's district, it would be Mary's too. But how could she talk to Jason if Mary was around?

"Veronica," Mary said in a bright voice, though her smile was phony. "I thought I saw you during the service."

"Hi, Mary." Veronica tried her best to sound happy to see her. "These are my *schweschdere*, Emily and Rachel."

"It's nice of you to join our church district for service today." Mary handed a tray of peanut butter spread to Rachel. "Would you like to help serve?"

"*Ya*, we're here to help," Emily said as she took another tray.

"I'll pour the *kaffi*." Veronica took the coffeepot and walked with her sisters back outside toward the barn. The July air was sweltering as the sun beat on her black dress and apron.

"Who's Mary?" Rachel asked.

"Remember I told you Leah Esh is dating Jason's *bruder*, Stephen? Well, Mary is Leah's *schweschder*. Leah and Stephen are trying to set Jason up with Mary."

"Oh," her sisters grumbled in unison.

"Well, he obviously likes you, so I wouldn't worry about it," Rachel said while balancing the tray in her hands.

"I'm not worried." Veronica knew she didn't sound convincing. Mary's phony smile was proof that Mary saw Veronica as competition, and it was silly. After all, Veronica wasn't interested in Jason. She sighed. Of course she was interested in Jason, but she wasn't ready to give up her heart yet.

Veronica carried the coffeepot into the barn and walked around the tables, filling cups. Her stomach fluttered when she came to the table where Jason sat surrounded by a group of men, including his brother. Her father was there, too, sitting at the far end beside the friend he had specifically wanted to visit today.

Jason looked up at her and his eyes widened as he smiled, causing butterflies to swirl in her stomach.

"Veronica! I didn't know you were coming to church in my district today," he said.

"My *dat* wanted us to visit his *gut freind*'s district today. I didn't realize it was your district either." Though her father was deep in conversation with his friend, she saw the other men near Jason staring at her and felt self-conscious. She kept her eyes on Jason and ignored their curiosity.

"How are you?" he asked.

"I'm fine." She held up the pot. *"Kaffi?"*

He nodded, and she filled his cup, her hands shaking slightly.

"I'm sorry it didn't rain Friday." His voice was soft and warm.

"I was going to discuss that with you."

She gave him a tentative smile and went on to fill the other cups nearby. Before long, her pot was empty. She was walking toward the house when she heard someone call her name. Turning, she found Jason approaching her with an anxious expression on his face.

"Jason," she said. "What are you doing?"

"I want to talk to you." He hurried over to her. "You didn't seem to want to talk to me in the barn."

"I didn't think it was appropriate to chat too much." She hesitated for a moment and then asked the question that had been haunting her since yesterday. "Why didn't you come to my bake stand yesterday?"

"I wanted to, but I had to help my *dat* with a project at the *haus*. One of our barn doors was hanging off the hinges, and

Stephen and I had to fix it before it fell on one of us or an animal." His expression went from anxious to hopeful. "Did you miss me?"

Yes! She held the coffeepot closer to her body as if to block her heart. "I was surprised you didn't stop by. I was hoping for another weather report."

"I'm sorry I couldn't share the weather report yesterday," he began, stepping closer to her, "but what if I stop by tonight and we'll talk about it?"

Veronica's breath caught in her throat. If he came by the house, he would want to start dating her. *Say no! I have to say no!* "Ya, that would be fine."

"Great." He grinned, and her cheeks warmed. "I'll check my sources and see if I can bring a more accurate report."

"*Gut.*" She smiled at him and then strode back to the house, her pulse leaping with every step. She should've told him not to come. It wasn't right to lead him on when she knew that she couldn't date him. But when she looked deeply into his eyes, she was nearly hypnotized.

Veronica shook away any thoughts of Jason and stepped into the kitchen.

"There she is!" Emily pointed at Veronica and then led an older woman over to her. "This is my *schweschder*, Veronica. This is Naomi. She was asking about your amazing raspberry pies."

"And you have a bake stand?"

"*Ya*, I do. On Gibbons Road." Veronica nodded as she set the empty coffeepot on the counter and acknowledged the woman's interest.

Another woman stepped toward them.

"My son has been bringing your pies home almost every Saturday for the past few weeks," the second woman said. Then she leaned in closer and lowered her voice. "Although I'm not sure if he goes to get the pies or to see you. I'm Annie Huyard. My family and I enjoy your pies very much."

"*Danki.*" Veronica blushed. Jason shared his mother's brown hair, but she had hazel eyes. Kind eyes.

"I have to send him over to get another pie soon," Annie said before lifting a tray filled with pieces of apple pie. "It was nice meeting you."

"*Ya*, it was nice meeting you too." As Annie walked toward the door, Veronica wondered how she was going to say no to Jason when he visited her tonight.

JASON GUIDED HIS BUGGY DOWN THE ROAD BEHIND HIS parents' buggy later that afternoon. Jason liked to have his own transportation, and generally Stephen rode with him.

He'd been so surprised to see Veronica at his district's church service. He had missed seeing her yesterday, but then she'd appeared before his eyes today. It was as if she was meant to be in his life. He couldn't escape the feeling that they belonged together.

"I saw you talking to Veronica earlier," Stephen said, breaking through Jason's trance while he sat beside Jason.

"*Ya*," Jason said. "I'm going to see her later tonight."

"You're going to visit her?" Stephen's tone was incredulous. "I thought you were going to the youth gathering with Mary, Leah, and me."

"You assumed I was going with you, but I never said I was going." Jason kept his eyes focused on the road. "I already have plans tonight."

"What about Mary?" Stephen asked. "She really likes you, and she'll be disappointed if you don't come with us."

Jason huffed. "Mary is nice, but I don't feel any spark with her. I don't see us being anything other than *freinden*. I'm not attracted to her."

"And you feel a spark with Veronica." Stephen finished the thought.

"*Ya*, I do." Jason nodded with emphasis.

"Have you told her the truth yet?" Stephen asked.

Jason pursed his lips. "I'm going to tell her tonight."

"So she still doesn't know you worked with Seth." Stephen shook his head. "You know she's going to be upset when she finds out the truth. It's going to seem like you've lied all along, which in a way you have."

"I realize that, Stephen. I'm not stupid." Jason took a deep breath. "Tonight I'm going to tell her I care about her and ask her to be my girlfriend. If she tells me she feels the same way, then I'll tell her the truth." *Hopefully she'll tell me she cares for me too!*

Stephen was quiet, and Jason turned toward him. "What?" he asked. "You obviously have something you want to say."

"Did you notice she was wearing all black today?" Stephen frowned. "You know what that means, right?"

"Of course I know what it means." Worry nipped at Jason's nerves.

"If she's still in mourning, then do you really believe she's going to want to date you?"

"Veronica and I have a connection," Jason insisted. "When I saw her at the youth gathering last week, we talked like old *freinden*. She shared really personal things with me. It was as if I'd known her for years. She's probably only wearing black in memory of Seth and out of respect for his parents."

Stephen shrugged. "If that's what you want to believe."

Jason gripped the reins tighter. Stephen had to be wrong. After all, why would Veronica have agreed to let him visit her if she wasn't interested in dating him?

"You should be careful," Stephen continued. "You may find yourself really let down. She might tell you she only wants to be *freinden*."

"If she says that, then I'll wait for her," Jason said. "I care about her enough to give her time."

"You don't want to be her rebound. You might wind up right back where you were with Arie."

Jason gritted his teeth. "Look, Stephen, you're entitled to your opinion, but it's my life. You're *froh* with Leah. You should worry about her and stay out of my business."

"Whoa. Calm down, Jay." Stephen held up his hands as if to stop Jason from talking. "I was only trying to help because I don't want to see you get hurt again."

Jason frowned as worry drenched him. He noticed the dark clouds gathering in the sky above and hoped his brother was wrong. Veronica had smiled when he saw her today, and she'd blushed when he'd asked if she missed him. Those were definite signs that she cared about him. If she cared about him, then certainly she'd want to date him. Wouldn't she?

Doubt nearly overcame him as he guided the horse toward their house. But he fought it. He refused to live in fear of rejection. He would go to Veronica's house tonight and tell her how he felt.

"ARE YOU COMING TO THE YOUTH GATHERING TONIGHT?" Rachel asked later that afternoon. She was standing in the doorway leading to Veronica's room.

"No, I'm not." Veronica shook her head.

"Why not?" Rachel stepped into the room. "I thought you had a nice time last week."

"I did have a nice time." Veronica sank into the chair in the corner by her window. "Jason is coming by to see me tonight."

"He is?" Rachel's voice pitched higher. "That's *wunderbaar!*"

Veronica smiled, but her stomach twisted with confusion. "*Ya, it is.*" *But I can't tell him I want to date him.*

"Are you nervous?" Rachel asked.

Veronica nodded. "*Ya,* I am."

"Don't be." Rachel touched her arm. "He really cares for you, and Emily told me she overheard his mother tell you he likes you. You have nothing to be nervous about."

"Right." Veronica smiled at her sister and wondered if she would ever find happiness again.

Emily stepped into the doorway. "Are you ready to go?"

"Veronica is staying home because Jason is coming to see her tonight," Rachel announced.

"That's great!" Emily clapped. "I can't wait to hear all about it when we get home."

Veronica nodded. "I hope you have fun tonight." *You'll be disappointed when you find out how my evening goes.*

"We'll see you later," Rachel said. "Have fun."

"Bye," Emily said as she waved.

Veronica sighed as her sisters walked down the stairs, their excited voices echoing through the house. She looked toward her bed, and her eyes focused on Seth's quilt. Sadness washed over her as she recalled the first time he came to visit her. She didn't have a doubt in her mind when Seth asked her to be his girlfriend. Would she ever feel that certain about anything in her life again?

CHAPTER 10

JASON'S HANDS TREMBLED AS HE CLIMBED OUT OF HIS BUGGY later that evening and walked up the front porch steps at Veronica's house. The small raindrops hitting his straw hat did little to cool the humid evening.

He took a deep breath and knocked on the storm door. Footsteps sounded inside the house, and then the front door opened with a squeak, revealing Veronica clad in a blue dress and black apron. He was relieved to see her wearing a brighter color. Perhaps Stephen was wrong when he said Veronica's black clothing that morning was a sure sign she wasn't ready to date.

"Hi," he said while drinking in her beautiful face.

"Hi." She leaned against the doorframe. "Would you like to visit out here?"

"*Ya*, that would be nice." He looked over his shoulder at the rain. "It's starting to rain harder, but it's not hitting the porch yet."

"I put together a snack for us. Do you like peach salsa?" She lifted a tray containing two glasses of iced tea, a small bowl of salsa, and a bag of chips.

"*Ya*. That sounds great." He held the storm door open as she

114

stepped out onto the porch. He followed her to the swing and sat beside her. His pulse sped up at their close proximity.

Veronica set the tray on the table beside the swing and then handed him a glass of tea. "I helped my *mamm* and *schweschdere* make the salsa the other day after our neighbor brought over the peaches. We used my *mammi*'s recipe. Apparently my *daadi* enjoyed chips and peach salsa every night after supper."

Jason dipped a chip into the salsa and took a bite. "I can see why he enjoyed it so much. It's *appeditlich*. This means you can make amazing pies, jams, and relish; you can make salsa; and you're an expert stone skipper. You become more and more talented every time I see you."

She smiled, but her smile didn't reach her eyes. Something was wrong. His stomach twisted with apprehension.

"It's a *schee* night, despite the rain." She looked toward the road and sipped from the glass.

"*Ya*, it is. I suppose this is the rain I predicted on Friday." When she didn't laugh, he gripped the glass as more worry threatened his resolve.

"I met your *mamm* today after church. She was very nice." Veronica took a chip and smothered it in salsa.

"I'm sure she was *froh* to meet the *maedel* who makes the amazing pies." He longed to see her smile. Just one genuine smile would calm his frayed nerves.

"*Ya*, she mentioned the pies." Veronica ate the chip.

"She asked me to bring one home tonight. Could I buy one from you?" he asked, and she nodded. "*Gut*. My *mamm* will be pleased."

"My *schweschdere* went with the youth group this evening." Veronica stared into his eyes as if she were trying to find an answer there. "They tried to convince me to go with them. I'm surprised you didn't go to yours with Mary."

"Did you really think I wanted to go with Mary?" he asked.

"I wasn't sure." She ran her fingers down the condensation on the glass.

Why is she avoiding eye contact with me? "You know I don't like Mary, right? She's a *freind*, but that's it."

"*Ya*, I know." Veronica nodded. "Church was nice."

He had to quit stalling. He wanted to ask her to be his girlfriend, but he was fearful of her rejection. Why was this so difficult? *It's difficult because I haven't told her the truth!*

He thought about their conversation at youth group last week and a question overtook his mind. "Do you remember when we were talking with Mary by the pond last Sunday?"

"*Ya*." She looked confused. "Why do you ask?"

"You told Mary you were sitting alone because you were feeling jealous after spending time with Rachel and her boyfriend. Was that true or did you only say that to Mary to cover for me?"

Veronica examined the hem on her apron. "It was true."

"Veronica?" He leaned down to get a better look at her face. "What's wrong?"

She sighed and met his gaze. "Nothing. I'm just tired." Her expression betrayed her, and there was something more than exhaustion in her eyes.

"I know you well enough to know when you're not telling the truth," he said gently. "You can talk to me. Remember what you said last week? We're two peas in a pod."

Her lip quivered, and his happiness withered like a plant desperate for water.

"*Was iss letz?*" He took her hand in his, and she pulled it away. "Please, Veronica. Please talk to me."

She sucked in a deep breath and swiped her hand across wet cheeks.

"Have I done something to upset you?" he asked, pleading with her to speak.

"No." She shook her head and took another sip of iced tea.

"I came over here tonight to tell you I care about you," he said. "I think about you all the time, and I want to get to know you better."

Veronica focused her attention on her glass, and his throat dried. This wasn't the reaction he'd hoped to see.

"Do you care about me?" Jason asked, his voice small and unsure.

She looked at him, and her expression was full of pain. "I can't do this," she whispered as more tears trickled down her cheeks.

"What do you mean?" he asked.

"I can't be with you. I'm not ready." She stood and placed the glass on the tray before lifting it. "I'm sorry, Jason." She opened the front door and stepped inside.

"Veronica, wait." He jumped up and rushed to the door. "Let's talk about this. I didn't mean to pressure you." His body trembled with anxiety.

"It's not you. It's me." She sniffed. "Wait here. I'll get your mother's pie." She disappeared into the house and returned a moment later with two pies wrapped in aluminum foil. She opened the door and handed them to him. "Give these to your *mamm*. I'm sorry, Jason. I have to go. *Gut nacht.*"

"Wait." Jason stuck his foot on the threshold to stop the closing screen door. "Please talk to me."

Veronica blinked and tried to swallow her emotion. "I'm not ready. I told you, every time I close my eyes, I see Seth. I can't date someone else while I'm still grieving for Seth. I'm sorry."

"I care about you, Veronica. Let me help you through your grief."

Her eyes narrowed. "No one can help me. You should go see Mary. She cares for you. I could see it in her eyes when she caught us talking last week, and I think I saw it again today. You should give her a chance." Her voice was shaky. "Don't waste your time on me." A sob broke in her throat, and she backed away from the door. "*Gut nacht.*"

As she disappeared into the house, Jason's emotions were once again destroyed, just as they had been when he saw the depth of grief Seth's mother and sister were experiencing at the visitation. He had felt Veronica's grief that day, too, but had hoped she would let him help her through it now that they were friends.

He didn't want to date Mary; he only wanted to see Veronica. How could he make Veronica see she should give their relationship a chance? Wouldn't Seth want her to be happy again?

VERONICA'S SOBS SOUNDED THROUGH THE HOUSE AS SHE raced up the stairs to her room. When she reached her bed, she flopped onto it and hugged Seth's quilt to her chest. The rain beat a loud cadence on the roof above her.

She'd wanted to tell Jason yes. In fact, she almost had said yes, but then she remembered the promise she'd made to Seth the day he'd proposed to her—that she'd love him for the rest of her life—and she couldn't move on just because his life had ended. Not yet.

At the same time, she couldn't stop thinking about Jason and the pain she'd seen in his eyes when she'd told him she couldn't see him. She'd not only hurt him, but she'd also caused more pain to herself as well. Veronica felt her own spirit break as she told him to see Mary. The idea of him with another girl caused her skin to crawl, but she couldn't bring herself to say yes to him.

Veronica cared about Jason more than she wanted to admit.

Her rejection had pained him deeply, and she'd never meant to hurt him. She didn't want to push him away, but she also couldn't lead him on. She couldn't be his girlfriend when her emotions were a jumbled mess of grief.

"Veronica?" *Mamm's* voice sounded from the hallway. "What happened?"

She sat up and wiped her eyes as *Mamm* crossed the room to her bed. "Jason came over tonight and told me he cares about me. He was about to ask me to be his girlfriend." Her voice quaked. "I told him no before he could even get out the words. I told him every time I close my eyes I see Seth's face. I can't date Jason when I'm still grieving for Seth." More tears trickled down her face. "He looked so hurt, *Mamm.* I couldn't stand it, so I ran away. I know I hurt him, but I can't let go of Seth yet. I just can't."

"*Ach, mei liewe.*" *Mamm* sat on the edge of the bed and touched Veronica's cheek. "I'm so sorry to see you hurt like this."

"I feel so lost, *Mamm.* Jason is funny and sweet. He's a *wunderbaar* man, but I'm a mess. Why would he want someone like me?"

"He sees the wonderful, sweet *maedel* you are. You'll get through this, *mei liewe.* Don't give up on yourself." *Mamm* pulled Veronica into a hug and rubbed her back. "I know how you feel, and you can't give up on love. You will love again. The pain will get easier, and you'll realize that you're allowed to love again. You won't see Seth every time you close your eyes, but you'll still cherish the *gut* memories."

Veronica looked up at *Mamm.* "But I don't want to forget Seth. I still love him."

Mamm touched her chin. "You'll always love him and remember him, but you'll move on. Let yourself grieve. Allow yourself time to feel the pain, and then move past it."

Veronica nodded. "Okay." She sniffed, trying to hold back more threatening tears.

"I think you need a cup of tea." *Mamm* held out her hand. "Come downstairs with me, and I'll make us some."

"No, thank you. I want to stay up here for a while and listen to the rain."

Mamm hesitated and then nodded. "All right. I'll give you some time alone, but I'm going to check on you later."

Veronica nodded before her mother disappeared from her room. Closing her eyes, Veronica prayed that Jason would recover from her rejection. Her emotions were in shambles for hurting him, and she hoped they both would recover soon.

JASON STOWED HIS BUGGY IN THE BARN AND THEN LED HIS horse, Maximus, to his stall. The aroma of rain mixed with dust, animals, and hay assaulted his senses as his body shook with a mixture of anger and despair. In a fit of utter agony, he kicked the barn wall with all his might. A loud *thwap!* echoed throughout the large barn, and he hollered as pain radiated through his foot.

Tears clouded his vision as his foot throbbed. He hopped on his good foot over to a bench and sank down before pulling off his shoe and rubbing the injured toes. Jason took long, deep gulps of air in an attempt to catch his breath and ease the soreness.

He had spent the long ride home pondering why Veronica had rejected him. Although he'd been nervous on his way to her house, he had never in his worst moments of doubt imagined that she would turn him down. Their attraction had been palpable at the youth gathering last week. Veronica had shared her secrets and intimate emotions with Jason, and they had laughed and joked like old friends. It seemed only natural that Veronica would want to take their relationship a step further and become more than friends.

Why had Veronica suddenly changed her demeanor toward him? Had he done something wrong? Had he pushed her? He'd gone over the conversation again and again during the ride home, and he couldn't come up with anything. He supposed she could tell he was about to ask her to be his girlfriend, and if she wasn't ready . . . But she was already upset when he got there. Had she decided before he'd even arrived to reject their friendship?

His attention moved to the stall where Maximus watched him with curious eyes. "What's gone wrong, Max?" Jason whispered, as if his horse might hold the answer to the mystery.

The horse whinnied and nodded his head.

"Jason?" *Dat* appeared in the doorway, holding a lantern. "I thought I heard a crash. What happened?" He craned his neck and looked at Jason's foot. "Are you hurt?"

"I kicked the wall. I think I may have broken a toe or maybe even my foot." Jason nodded toward the wall as his foot continued to throb.

Dat tilted his head in question. "Why would you do that? You know that hurts, right?" He smiled at his attempt to make a joke, but his amusement quickly disappeared. "Something is wrong." He sat down next to Jason on the bench. "What is it?"

"She said no." Jason's voice hitched on the last word.

Dat's eyebrows knitted together. "I'm sorry, but I'm not sure who *she* is. You have to be more specific. Who said no to you, and what was the question?"

Jason heaved a deep sigh and looked at his sock while massaging his injured toes. "I asked a *maedel* to be my girlfriend tonight, and she said no. I'm stumped. I really thought we had a special connection, but I guess I didn't read all of the signs correctly."

"*Ach,* I'm so sorry, son." *Dat* clicked his tongue. "It's not easy when a *maedel* turns you down. I've been there more than once, actually. Your *mamm* wasn't my first girlfriend, but she was worth all the emotional pain I faced before I met her. You'll meet someone else, and you'll realize what true love is supposed to feel like. I know it hurts right now, but it will get better. You just have to be patient."

"No." Jason's tone was sharper than he'd planned, and *Dat's* eyes widened. "I know she's the one. I can feel it in my soul, and I'm certain she feels it too."

Dat shook his head. "If she felt the same way, then she wouldn't have said no. You can't force someone to love you."

"I know that." Jason gingerly pulled on his shoe, wincing at the searing pain that shot through his toes. "She didn't seem like herself tonight. She wasn't the funny, genuine *maedel* I've seen over the past couple of weeks. She was upset. She seemed as if she didn't want to say no, but she had to. She told me she wasn't ready to be my girlfriend, but her eyes seemed as if she wanted to tell me yes."

"Why would she say no if she really meant yes? That doesn't make any sense."

Thunder rumbled outside while the rain continued to drum on the barn roof.

"It's complicated," he said. He wasn't sure he wanted to tell his father the whole story.

"Jay, you've lost me. I don't understand how it's complicated. She either wants to date you or she doesn't."

Jason cupped his hand to the back of his neck. "She's Seth's fiancée."

Dat paused, processing this information. "Are you talking about Seth Lapp?"

"*Ya.*"

"Jason, you realize Seth has been gone only a few months."

"I'm quite aware of that," Jason muttered.

"Then you should be sensitive to the fact that she may not

be ready to see anyone else yet." *Dat* paused. "Were you *freinden* with her before his accident?"

"No," Jason said softly. "I met her after the accident. I went to her bake stand to get her raspberry pies."

"Oh." *Dat* fingered his long beard. "So *she* makes those *appeditlich* pies."

Jason nodded and frowned when he recalled the two pies he'd just brought home for his mother. Were they the last pies he'd ever receive from her? Would she even talk to him if he went back to her bake stand?

"Did you know she was Seth's fiancée when you went to her bake stand?"

"*Ya.*" Jason couldn't lie to his father. "Well, I didn't know she was the *maedel* who made those pies until after I got to the stand. I realized who she was when I saw the sign and then heard her *schweschder* call her Veronica." He rested his hand on his aching foot. "I know she just lost Seth. I miss him, too, and I'm sensitive to her grief. At the same time, she and I clicked. She makes me laugh, and I make her laugh. She's *schee* and funny and *schmaert*. I know she feels the same deep connection I do, and I can't let her go. I just can't. I feel like I have a hole in my heart now."

Dat shook his head. "I'm sorry she hurt you. If you truly believe you share a strong connection with her, then you should keep trying to convince her you belong together."

"How?" Jason's voice reverberated with desperation.

"Find a way to show her how much you care for her. Visit her as often as you can. Make her something or give her something to show her how you feel. She's hurting right now, so tell her you're willing to wait as long as she needs you to before she's ready to date again."

"*Ya,* that makes sense." Jason felt a spark of hope ignite in his soul. His frown deepened when he realized it would never be that easy. "There's another issue, though. I haven't been completely honest with her."

"What do you mean?"

"I've never told her I saw her at the visitation at Seth's mother's house," Jason began. "She thinks we met for the first time when I came to her bake stand. I hadn't actually met her at the visitation, but I remember her clearly. She has no idea I knew Seth. I know a lot about her because of Seth, since he talked about her constantly."

Dat grimaced. "She has no idea you knew Seth?"

Jason shook his head. "It was *Mamm's* idea for us to go to the Fisher bake stand for those first pies, and I originally planned to express my condolences if she turned out to be the right Fisher. But when I met her, I couldn't even bring myself to tell her who I was, let alone that I was Seth's *freind.*"

"Why?"

"I was attracted to her right away, and I was afraid it would be so emotional for her that she wouldn't want to get to know me." Jason glared at the offending wall where he'd injured his foot. "I thought I could tell her eventually, but I couldn't bring myself to do it. I was so afraid of losing her by telling her the truth, but in the end, I lost her anyway."

Dat fingered his beard again, more thoughtfully this time. "If you truly care for her, then you need to fight for her and also be honest with her. Be the *freind* she needs right now and help her through her grief. Don't push her. Just be there for her. But also tell her the truth. She needs to know you were *freinden* with Seth. She deserves to know you were there when he died."

Jason nodded as the glimmer of hope brightened a tiny bit. "I can be her *freind.*" *But I don't know how to tell her the truth.*

"If you want her to trust you, she has to know the truth."

"*Ya*, I know." Jason shook his head as dread consumed him. "I've made a bigger mess than I ever meant to."

"It will be all right." *Dat* patted Jason's shoulder. "Have faith, and be the *freind* she needs."

"I will. *Danki, Dat*."

Jason stood and walked carefully on his throbbing foot as he followed *Dat* through the barn. He retrieved the pies from the buggy before walking with his father toward the house. Jason limped through the mud as the rain soaked through his shirt and trousers. His toes ached, but it was the pain of losing Veronica's friendship that stole his breath.

When they reached the kitchen, Jason placed the pies on the counter for his mother before hobbling up the stairs to his room. He considered telling his mother about his failed visit with Veronica, but he was too emotionally drained to rehash it once again. He just wanted to be alone.

After taking a quick shower and changing into his shorts and undershirt, Jason crawled into bed. His conversations with Veronica and his father replayed in his thoughts. He couldn't shake the notion that Veronica had wanted to tell him yes. He was certain Veronica did care for him. His father's advice to be her friend was the best plan for him to follow. He recalled Seth telling him some of the things Veronica loved. He would shower her with gifts, and he'd be her friend and support her while she grieved. And, most importantly, he would find the courage to tell her the truth.

Jason breathed in a deep, ragged breath and prayed he could convince Veronica that he cared enough to wait as long as it took for her to accept him into her precious heart.

CHAPTER 11

Jason guided his horse up the Fishers' driveway the following Saturday afternoon and halted it by the bake stand.

Though the Closed sign was not up, no one was in the bake stand, and he stared at the gift bag beside him as he tried to decide what to do next. He had set out early that morning and visited the Bird-in-Hand Farmers Market to buy a vanilla-scented candle and a pink umbrella. Next, he visited the Good Books bookstore in Intercourse and purchased two Christian novels he hoped Veronica hadn't read. Last, he stopped by the Bird-in-Hand Bake Shop for two homemade pretzels.

Jason had spent most of last night working on the letter he included with the gifts. He'd written and rewritten it four times before settling on the version he'd signed and slipped into an envelope before dropping it into the bag. Then he lay awake worrying how Veronica would react when he arrived this afternoon. Would she reject him? Would she speak to him but then coldly rebuff his gifts? Or, worst of all, would she refuse to see him at all?

He got out of the buggy, saw the sign saying customers should knock on the door, and walked slowly toward the front porch. He gripped the handle of the gift bag. When he reached the door, he took a deep breath and knocked.

VERONICA'S HEART RACED IN HER CHEST WHEN SHE HEARD the *clip-clop* of a horse coming up the driveway. She felt sure even without looking that the buggy belonged to Jason, so she had sprinted inside the house before he could see her. Peeking out the kitchen window, she spotted him climbing from the buggy and holding a large pink gift bag. She gnawed her lower lip, silently debating if she should speak to him. She longed to apologize to him for rejecting him, but she couldn't risk losing her heart to him.

Jason walked toward the door, and her courage faltered. She rushed through the family room toward her parents' bedroom at the back of the house. She found her mother folding her father's shirts.

"*Mamm*," Veronica said breathlessly. "I need you to go talk to Jason for me. He's at the door. Tell him I'm not feeling well and I've gone to bed for the day."

Mamm frowned. "You should speak to him yourself. Just tell him you need some space."

A loud knock sounded from the front of the house, and Veronica's pulse leaped like a horse running through her father's pasture at a full gallop.

"Please, *Mamm*." Veronica folded her hands as if she were praying. "I don't have the strength."

"He doesn't want to see me," *Mamm* said. "Why don't you talk to him?"

"*Mamm*, I'm begging you to handle this for me." She pointed toward the shirts. "I'll finish folding these for you."

Another knock sounded.

"Fine." *Mamm* held up her hands in surrender. "I'll talk to him, but I'm not going to outright lie for you, and he's going to want an explanation sooner or later."

"*Danki.*" Veronica squeezed her mother's hand. "I will talk to him eventually. I just need some time to sort through my feelings."

Mamm hurried off, and Veronica sank onto the corner of the bed. She hoped her mother could say something to Jason to convince him to give up on her. She needed to stay away from him. She knew if she looked into his honey-colored eyes again too soon, her determination might crack, and she just might tell him yes.

JASON KNOCKED A THIRD TIME AND THEN TURNED TOWARD the harness shop located across the pasture. He considered walking over there to see if perhaps the family was in the store helping her father with his work. His intuition told him, however, that Veronica most likely was in the house. She had to be nearby since her bake stand was clearly not closed, and if she wasn't outside, then she was probably hiding from him. The notion sent disappointment coursing through him.

The door opened, revealing Veronica's mother. He recognized her from that day at Seth's visitation and when he saw her again with Emily at his district's church service. She smiled at him as the warm and sugary smell of raspberry pie mixed with freshly baked bread wafted from inside the house. Someone had been busy baking this morning, and he suspected it had been Veronica.

"*Gude mariye,*" she said. "I'm Mattie. How are you?" Her smile was wide, almost a little too cheerful.

"I'm fine, *danki*. And you?" Jason shifted his weight on his feet. He doubted he needed to introduce himself.

"Fine, fine." Mattie gestured toward the bake stand. "Are you here for one of Veronica's pies? Veronica isn't up to managing sales today, so I'm helping her with her bake stand."

His stomach twisted. This was just what he'd been fearing—the dismissal. If Veronica truly was not up to working in her bake stand, then who had been baking earlier? "I'm sorry to hear she's not, uh, feeling well. I was hoping to talk to her. I have something for her." He held up the bag.

"Oh, isn't that nice." Mattie reached for the bag. "I'll be sure to give this to her."

Jason frowned. "Is she okay?"

"Oh, *ya*." Mattie waved off the question. "She just isn't feeling her best today. She's resting, but I promise she will receive this."

"*Danki*." Jason handed Mattie the bag, but frustration washed through him. He wanted to see Veronica's expression when she pulled out the gifts. He had to trust that his father's advice would work and Veronica would see the gifts, read the letter, and realize that he wanted to be her friend and her supporter. He longed for her to realize their relationship should have a chance. "How many pies would you like?" Mattie asked. His heart sank as he realized she was not even going to invite him in.

"One is fine."

Mattie disappeared inside. He craned his neck and peered through a window, wondering if he would spot Veronica standing just out of sight, blatantly avoiding him. When he didn't see anyone lurking there, he began to wonder if Veronica truly was ill, and his frustration was replaced with worry.

"Here it is," Mattie said as she returned to the porch.

Jason pulled out his wallet and paid her, and she handed him the pie.

"*Danki* for your business," Mattie said, still sounding a little too upbeat. "I'll let Veronica know you were here."

Jason paused and contemplated her expression. He wanted to know the truth, and he couldn't stop the question as it leaped from his lips. "Mattie, is Veronica avoiding me?"

Mattie sighed, and her smile faded. "I'll walk you to your buggy."

She was going to tell him the truth. The tension in his shoulders released slightly as they walked together toward his horse.

"To answer your question," she began while they stood behind his buggy, away from the kitchen windows, "*ya*, she is avoiding you."

Jason's shoulders slumped, and he deflated like a balloon.

"Now, wait," Mattie said. "I need you to be strong. I want you to promise me you won't give up on her."

"What do you mean?" Jason asked, confused. "Why are you encouraging me to pursue Veronica when she refuses to see me?"

Mattie looked toward the house as if checking to see if someone was spying on them. "Veronica is confused right now. She feels as if she'll hurt Seth if she sees you. She's still grieving, and she's not sure what she wants." Her lips formed a real, genuine smile. "I know she has feelings for you, Jason."

"She does?" He was certain his grin was goofy.

"*Ya*, she does. She's just afraid of what she's feeling, but I need you to give her a chance. If you're patient, then I know things will turn out the way you want them to."

A renewed hope bloomed inside of him. "I will wait as long as she needs me to."

Mattie's eyes misted over as if she might cry. "I'm *froh* to hear you say that. Just be patient with her and give her some time. You might even want to give her a little space and let her come to you."

Jason swallowed. He wasn't sure he could stay away, but he would do whatever Mattie thought was best. "All right."

"*Wunderbaar.*" Mattie nodded. "I'll give her your gift bag. I have a feeling you'll be hearing from her soon."

"*Danki,*" he said as he climbed into the buggy. As he guided the horse toward the road, he sent a silent prayer up to God, asking him to grant him patience and to help Veronica through her grief.

VERONICA RUSHED INTO THE KITCHEN AS SOON AS SHE heard the door shut. She peered out the kitchen window above the sink just as Jason's buggy moved down the driveway toward the road. Regret and relief warred inside of her. She longed to call him back and push him away at the same time. What was wrong with her?

Mamm stepped in, holding the pink gift bag Jason had been carrying.

"What happened?" Veronica asked as she crossed the kitchen and met her mother at the table.

"Jason wanted to talk to you, and he wanted you to have this." *Mamm* held out the bag. "I promised to give it to you."

Veronica pondered his bringing her the bag. "Why would he bring me a gift after I pushed him away?" she whispered.

"Open it." *Mamm* nudged the bag toward her. "He was adamant that I give it to you."

Veronica's hands trembled as she took the bag and placed it on the table. She opened it and pulled out a bright-pink, collapsible umbrella and turned it over in her hand. Was this a reference to his weather reports? She stuck her hand back into the bag and retrieved two large baked pretzels. She breathed in the warm smell, and her stomach gurgled.

"Your favorite," *Mamm* said.

Veronica looked at the pretzels and then set them on the table. "How did he know?" Then she pulled out a jar candle and turned it upside down to read the fragrance—vanilla. Last, she took out the novels, which were written by two of her favorite authors. She pored over the gifts and then looked at her mother.

"How could he possibly know I liked all these things?" Veronica lifted the top off the candle and breathed in the sweet scent of vanilla, and tears pricked her eyes. Why would a man whom she'd rejected bring her such thoughtful gifts?

Mamm peered into the bag and pulled out an envelope. "You missed this."

Veronica took the envelope, finding her name written on the front in neat, slanted cursive. She looked at the handwriting and imagined him writing this for her. Why would he take the time to write her a letter after she'd told him to pursue Mary instead of her?

"Read it," *Mamm* gently prodded.

Veronica opened the envelope and unfolded a letter written in the same neat cursive on plain white paper.

To My Favorite Expert Stone Skipper,

I've written and rewritten this letter more than three times while trying to figure out exactly what I wanted to say. After much thought, I realized that I need to apologize to you.

I'm sorry for pressuring you when you had clearly told me you weren't ready to date yet. You had shared at the youth gathering that you missed Seth so much that your heart ached. I'm deeply sorry for adding to your pain. It's my fault for misreading our special friendship as something more. I take full responsibility and hope you will forgive me.

Please accept these gifts from me as tokens of our friendship. I promise I won't pressure you about dating me. All I
want from you is friendship. I hope you can find it in your
heart to forgive me because I truly will miss our friendship
if you can't.

Sincerely,

Your Weatherman

P.S. I heard it might rain on Tuesday, so please be sure to
carry the umbrella.

Veronica read the letter until she nearly had it committed to
memory. Her vision blurred as tears flooded her eyes and then
trickled down her hot cheeks. Why would he want to be her
friend when she'd hurt him? If she let him be her friend, would
he slowly make his way into her heart and try to squeeze out all
the love she'd saved for Seth's memory? How could she possibly
even consider being Jason's friend when she could see herself
falling for his warm, caramel-colored eyes, his radiant, crooked
smile, and his easy sense of humor? Jason could quickly steal her
affection, and she wasn't ready for that.

"Veronica?" *Mamm's* voice was soft and comforting as she
placed her hand on Veronica's shoulder. "Are you all right?"

Veronica sniffed and brushed away the tears. "What did he
say to you?" she asked, ignoring *Mamm's* concerned expression.

"He wanted to see you, and I told him you weren't feeling
your best. He asked me to take the bag, and I sold him a pie."
Mamm paused as if debating if she should share something or not.
"He asked if you were avoiding him, and I told him the truth."

Veronica gasped. "What did you tell him?"

"I told him you are struggling with your grief, and I asked

him not to give up on you. I told him I am sure you have feelings for him." She said the words matter-of-factly, as if she were ordering at the deli counter in the Bird-in-Hand Farmers Market.

"Why would you say that?" Veronica's voice rose as anger radiated through her. "Why would you tell him not to give up on me when you know I can't possibly allow myself to fall in love with him?" Another tear escaped her eye, and she brushed it away with a shaky hand.

Mamm's expression remained calm. "*Mei liewe,* you need to allow yourself time to grieve, and then you need to find your way back to this life." She pointed toward the letter. "May I ask what the letter says?"

"You wouldn't understand it, but here." Veronica handed her the letter and then focused her attention on her apron while *Mamm* read it. Thoughts swirled in her mind and a headache brewed in her temples. Why had *Mamm* told him to wait for her? Why was Veronica so confused? When would she feel like herself again?

"'Expert Stone Skipper and Weatherman'?" *Mamm* shook her head as she set the letter down on the table.

"I told you that you wouldn't understand it." Veronica grabbed the letter.

"Veronica," *Mamm* said with a smile. "Don't you see that he loves you?"

"Don't say that!" Veronica shook her head. "He can't love me. I'm not ready for this! And maybe I'll never be ready for this again. Maybe Seth was the only one for me."

"That's not true." *Mamm* reached for Veronica's arm, and she stepped out of her reach.

"*Ya,* it is. And you just made it worse." She trembled as the reality of her strong feelings for Jason swept over her.

"How did I make it worse?" *Mamm* asked. "I only told him

to wait for you. I told him to give you time and not to give up on you."

"But that's not what I want." Veronica pointed to herself. "I want to be left alone!" Her tears were pouring out of her eyes now. "I'm going for a walk."

Veronica jammed the letter in her apron pocket and stalked out the door and down her driveway. She needed to talk to someone. She needed Margaret. Only Margaret could help her sort through all these confusing emotions. She hurried down the street to Seth's mother's house and knocked on the door. She blew out a sigh of relief when his mother answered the door.

"Veronica." Margaret's eyes widened with worry. "Are you all right?"

"Do you have a minute to talk?"

"*Ya.*" Margaret opened the door wide and motioned for Veronica to come in. "Let's have a cup of tea together."

"*Danki.*" Veronica rubbed away the last of her stray tears and stepped into the house she used to consider her second home. "Where is Ellie?" she asked as she took two teacups from the cabinet.

"Ellie is working today." Margaret put the kettle on the stove.

"Ellie's working now? I didn't know that."

"She insisted on getting a job." Margaret frowned. "Things are tight since we lost Seth. He helped us so much after Abner died." She shook her head. "Now we're having a difficult time keeping the farm going with Abner and Seth both gone. I don't know what we're going to do."

"I'm sorry." Veronica's stomach tightened. Seth lost his father when he was twelve, about the same time his grandmother made the quilt for him. Her heart broke for Margaret. She'd lost her husband and then her only son. "How are you doing?"

"I have *gut* days and bad days." Margaret's green eyes clouded. "Some days I expect him to run into the kitchen and kiss my cheek on his way out to the stable to take care of the animals after work. And then I remember he can't do that anymore."

"I know," Veronica whispered.

Margaret brought a plate of cookies and two tea bags to the table. When the kettle whistled, Veronica filled the cups and then sat down across from Margaret.

"So," Margaret began, "what did you want to talk about?"

Veronica's bottom lip quivered, and she willed herself not to cry again. She'd cried too many tears for one day. "There's a young man who likes me."

"Oh?" Margaret lifted her teacup. "Do you like him?"

Veronica nodded. "*Ya*, I do, and I feel . . . guilty."

"Why do you feel guilty?" Margaret looked incredulous as she lifted a snickerdoodle from the plate.

"It doesn't feel right to have feelings for someone else." Veronica was thankful that she had willed herself not to cry. "I don't want to betray Seth's memory by being with someone else. Seth was my first and only love. How can I possibly think of someone else?"

To Veronica's surprise, Margaret smiled. "*Ach*, Veronica. You're young. You have your whole life to live." She reached over the table and touched Veronica's hand. "Seth loved you. He couldn't wait to marry you."

Veronica sniffed and cleared her throat. *Don't cry! Don't cry!*

"You can rest assured that Seth would want you to be happy. He wouldn't want you to stop living now. It's only natural to want to marry and have *kinner*. Jesus tells us we should go forth and bear fruit, and Seth would want you to move on and be *froh*."

"You think so?" Veronica asked, gripping the teacup in her hands.

"I'm absolutely certain of it. How would you feel if you knew you were going to be the one who wasn't with us anymore?"

Veronica considered this. "I would want Seth to fall in love, get married, and have a family."

"There's your answer." Margaret tapped her teacup for emphasis. "You're still here. You need to live your life, and you can do that and still keep those precious memories of Seth in your heart."

"*Danki.*" Veronica let that sink in, then nodded. This was what her mother and sisters had been trying to tell her, but somehow it mattered most coming from someone who loved Seth as much as she did.

"I will." Hope took hold of her. With Margaret's blessing, she knew she didn't need to be alone.

CHAPTER 12

MARGARET'S WORDS TWIRLED THROUGH VERONICA'S MIND as she walked home, the afternoon sun shining in the bright blue sky and birds singing in nearby trees. Veronica and Margaret had turned the conversation to mundane things while they finished their tea and cookies, then Veronica thanked Margaret again before making her way back home.

She felt a mixture of relief and guilt when her driveway and the sign advertising her bake stand came into sight. She was so relieved Margaret had given her blessing to date Jason, but Veronica was drowning in guilt for how she'd spoken to her mother. She needed to get home and make things right.

While walking up the rock driveway, Veronica pulled the letter from her pocket. She had craved Margaret's blessing, and now that she had it, she needed to find a way to release her overwhelming grief.

She stopped by the bake stand and reviewed the letter, taking in the words with fresh eyes. Her mother was right; Jason did care for her. But one question still puzzled her—how did Jason know baked pretzels, vanilla-scented candles, and novels were among her favorite treats? Could he read minds? No, that certainly wasn't possible, but how else could he have known? Had her mother or sisters given Jason ideas for what gifts to buy her? She folded the letter and pushed it back into her pocket.

Veronica went around the house, climbed the back porch steps, and pushed open the back door. She found her mother standing at the kitchen counter perusing a cookbook.

"Veronica?" *Mamm* looked over her shoulder and relief softened her expression. "I've been worried about you."

Veronica crossed the kitchen and enveloped her in a hug. "I'm so sorry, *Mamm*." Her voice reverberated with regret. "I'm sorry for yelling at you. You were right all along, and I should've listened. Please forgive me. I hope the bake stand wasn't too busy while I was gone."

"*Ach*, it's okay. Your customers were fine, and I understand how you feel. You feel as if you're drowning, but it will get better." *Mamm* smiled at her. "Where were you?"

"I went to see Margaret." Veronica sniffed and then shared the conversation she'd had with Seth's mother. "I suppose I felt like I needed her blessing. If she tells me it's okay to move on, then it's almost as if Seth is giving me his blessing as well." She shrugged. "I know that sounds *gegisch*."

"No, not at all. You have to follow your heart, but I also don't want to see life pass you by. I'm sure Jason's feelings for you are genuine. You pushed him away, but he came back. He's not giving up on you, and he even said he'll wait for you."

Veronica considered the letter. "I'm really surprised he wants to wait for me. I even told him to pursue another *maedel* who obviously has feelings for him."

"If he were interested in her, then he wouldn't come to see you, would he?"

"No." Veronica shrugged. "I'm just shocked." She pointed toward the gift bag, which still sat on the table, surrounded by the items he'd packed in it. "How did he know what I liked? How did he know I love pretzels, vanilla candles, and books?"

Mamm's smile was warm. "Maybe he knows you better than you think he does."

"But that doesn't make sense. I've never told him I like those things."

"Could it be instinct?" *Mamm* picked up one of the books and scanned the back. "Does he have a *schweschder*? Maybe she gave him some advice and these are things she likes."

"No, he only has a younger *bruder*. But I suppose his *mamm* could have helped him. She seemed very nice when I met her." Veronica sank into a chair at the table, unwrapped one of the pretzels, and broke off a piece. Even though it was no longer warm, it melted in her mouth. She closed her eyes, savoring the taste. She broke off another piece and handed it to her mother. "It's *appeditlich*."

Mamm sat down across from her, ate the piece of pretzel, then used one of the napkins in the holder. "May I ask you something?"

"Of course." Veronica ate another piece and handed one to her mother.

"Why did he call himself your weatherman and refer to you as the expert stone skipper?" *Mamm* popped the pretzel into her mouth.

Veronica cleaned her fingers on a napkin and told her mother about Jason's weekly bake stand weather reports and how she taught him to skip stones at the youth gathering. As *Mamm* listened, her smile widened.

"Why are you smiling like that?" Veronica asked as she broke the last piece of pretzel in half.

"It sounds like you two have a very special friendship."

Veronica nodded as worry seeped into her thoughts.

"Is something wrong?"

"I guess I'm scared."

"Don't be. Just take your time and get to know him."

Veronica considered this. "I don't even remember how to date. It seems like it was a long time ago when I first started dating Seth—four years. How do you start over again?"

"That's a *gut* question." She rubbed her chin. "I suppose it's like making new *freinden*, right? You slowly get to know each other. Just be his *freind*."

"Right." Veronica sighed. "It's all so overwhelming."

"Don't let it be. Just be yourself."

Veronica tried to imagine what it would be like if she dated Jason. Would she think about Seth every time they held hands? Would she compare him to Seth every time he spoke? She had to let her worries go and have faith.

RACHEL LURKED IN THE DOORWAY BY THE STAIRS. SHE didn't mean to eavesdrop, but she didn't think anyone was in the kitchen with *Mamm* until she heard the voices. When she heard Veronica mention Jason, she stopped and listened. She should have gone back upstairs, but she was intrigued by what she was hearing. She smiled, hopeful that her sister was finally going to find happiness again.

Rachel had to find a way to encourage Veronica to trust her instincts and let herself find love again. It would be the best way for her older sister to heal. Rachel and Emily had been so worried about Veronica. God had definitely answered their prayers. She couldn't wait to tell Emily!

LATER THAT EVENING, RACHEL STOPPED BY VERONICA'S room on her way to her own bedroom. She found Veronica sitting on her bed reading a book while a flame danced from a sweet-smelling candle on her nightstand. She was dressed in her white nightgown with her long, blonde hair falling in waves to her waist. Her expression was serene as she focused on the book and turned a page.

For the first time in months, Veronica actually looked relaxed. Hopefully Jason would be the key to Veronica's happiness. Her sister had suffered so much during the past three months, and Rachel was thankful that her older sister was finally happy again.

"Is that a new book?" Rachel stepped into the room.

Veronica looked up at her and smiled. *"Ya."* She held it up so Rachel could read the cover. "It's one I saw in the bookstore last week, and I was waiting to buy it."

"It looks *gut.*" Rachel crossed the room to the end of the bed. *"Mamm* said you were gone for a while earlier today. Did you go to the library?"

"No, I wasn't at the library." Veronica looked at the cover. "The book was a gift—an unexpected gift, actually."

"Oh." Rachel lingered, hoping her sister would share more. From what she'd heard her mother and Veronica discussing earlier, it sounded like Jason had brought her gifts. Was the book one of them? "Where did you get it?"

"It's from Jason." Veronica's cheeks blushed bright pink.

"Jason brought you gifts?" Rachel sat down on the edge of the bed. "I didn't know he'd come to see you today."

"He stopped by, but I refused to see him." Veronica grimaced. "I didn't want to face him after I'd turned down his offer to date me."

"You turned him down?" Rachel gasped.

"Ya." Veronica sighed and placed the book beside her on the bed. "When he visited me last Sunday while you and Emily were at the youth gathering, he was about to ask me if I would be his girlfriend, and I told him no before he could even do it."

Rachel shook her head. "I had no idea. Why didn't you tell me?"

"I'm sorry. I should've told you and Emily." Veronica shrugged. "I guess I was too upset. I told *Mamm*."

"It's okay." Rachel understood. She didn't tell her sisters everything either. Lately she'd found herself wondering if something was going wrong between her and David since he'd been so cool toward her, but she hadn't admitted it aloud to her sisters or anyone else. "So Jason came by to see you today, and you didn't want to talk to him?"

"Right. He talked to *Mamm* and left me a bag of gifts."

"What did he give you?" Rachel asked. Her eyes widened with surprise as Veronica showed her the gifts and then told her about visiting Margaret.

"So you feel better after talking to Margaret?" Rachel asked.

"*Ya*, I do." Veronica's eyes clouded as if she might cry. "I needed to hear her say she would be comfortable seeing me date another man. I didn't want to hurt her or Ellie."

"I understand." Rachel fingered the bedspread. "So you're going to see Jason?"

"I guess so." Veronica gnawed her lower lip. "I'm so *naerfich*."

"Oh, don't be. Everything will be fine. I'm *froh* for you." Rachel beamed. "Emily told me it was obvious Jason liked you when you ran into him at the market. I think you're right to give him a chance. He seems very genuine, like he really cares for you." She turned toward the candle and watched the flame dance. "That smells *appeditlich*, and vanilla is your favorite."

"I know." Veronica looked curious. "I can't figure out how he knows me so well. He also gave me two pretzels. He's very intuitive."

"That's rare," Rachel said. "It seems like David doesn't understand me at all." The words slipped from her lips before she could stop them. Maybe she'd subconsciously wanted to share her worries with her older sister.

"What do you mean?" Veronica asked, her tone full of concern.

"I don't know." Rachel sighed. "I can't really put it into words. We just don't seem to communicate well anymore. He acts almost aloof lately. When I ask him if everything is okay, he just shrugs. I feel like I'm missing something."

"Oh." Veronica frowned. "I'm sorry. Don't give up on him. You both have had some really *gut* times. Just try to work things out. Keep talking to him."

"I promise I will. You know I don't give up on things easily." Rachel smiled again. "What are your plans with Jason? Did he say he'd come back, or are you going to call him or go see him?"

"No, he didn't say he was going to come back. He just asked *Mamm* to give me the gift bag, so I don't know what to do. I was just wondering about that earlier." Veronica shook her head. "He told me he works construction, but I don't know exactly where. I don't even know where he lives, though I know now which church district is his." She turned her attention to the book again. "I need to thank him. He's very generous, and I don't deserve these things after the way I treated him."

"*Ya*, you do," Rachel said gently. "He knows you've had a difficult time, and I'm sure he understands that you're still grieving. He cares for you, so he wants to show you." She touched Veronica's arm. "I'm just so thankful that you and Jason found each other. You've been through a lot, and you deserve to be *froh* again."

"*Danki.*" Veronica sighed and stared at the quilt folded at the bottom of the bed. "I didn't think I could find happiness ever again, but with Jason, I just might." She looked hopeful instead of sad.

"You will. I promise you." Rachel hugged Veronica. "I'm going to go to bed. *Gut nacht.*"

"*Gut nacht.*" Veronica smiled.

Rachel hurried down the hallway and stopped at Emily's bedroom door. She couldn't wait to tell Emily the exciting news about Veronica and Jason. She knocked quietly and then entered when Emily called. She stepped inside and softly closed the door behind her. She found Emily wearing a pink nightgown and propped up in bed, writing in her journal.

"Hi," Emily said. "*Wie geht's?* You look awfully excited. What's going on?"

"Did you know Jason came by to see Veronica today?" Rachel whispered as she sat down in a chair next to Emily's bed.

"No." Emily's blue eyes widened with surprise. "When was he here?"

"He came by this afternoon. I was cleaning upstairs, so I missed it. You must've been helping *Dat* in the store." Rachel recounted what Veronica had shared. "Margaret convinced Veronica it was okay to date Jason, so Veronica is going to give him a chance."

"Oh!" Emily gasped. "That is *wunderbaar* news!"

"Shh." Rachel warned. "She might hear you and come down to see what we're talking about."

"I'm sorry." Emily grinned. "I'm just so *froh* and thankful he hasn't given up."

"I know." Rachel sighed. "We have to help her. She doesn't know where he works or how to get in touch with him. We have to get them together."

Emily twirled her finger through her waist-length, wavy blonde hair while she thought a minute. Suddenly her eyes widened, and she snapped her fingers.

"I've got it!" Emily announced. "The Bird-in-Hand mud sale

is Friday. We'll make sure she goes. I'm positive we'll run into Jason there. If we don't, then we can ask around to find out if anyone knows where he lives."

Rachel instantly considered that event for their purpose. At the Bird-in-Hand mud sales, community members came together to sell items as a way to support the local volunteer fire department. Members of the community sold a variety of items, including farming equipment, furniture, quilts, and even livestock. The event was called a "mud sale" since many of the items are sold outside during potentially muddy spring conditions.

Yes, it was just the kind of place where she and Emily could accomplish their goal. And they already had a booth to sell quilts.

Rachel gasped as excitement overtook her. "That's a *gut* idea. We can convince her to sell her pies, relishes, and jams there. She'll want to do that. And, just as you said, if Jason isn't there, we'll find someone who knows him. I know it will work."

"Great." Emily gently squeezed Rachel's arm. "This is going to be *wunderbaar*. Veronica will be *froh* again."

"*Ya*." Rachel sighed. "I can't wait."

JASON SAT ON THE PORCH LATER THAT EVENING AND heaved a deep sigh. He knew he wouldn't sleep tonight. Instead of tossing and turning in bed, he'd headed out to the porch to get some fresh air and think. Had Veronica opened the gift bag, or was she so upset with him that she'd thrown it out? What had she thought of the letter? He slumped back on the bench and looked out across the pasture toward the pond. Of course, staring at the pond reminded him of the evening he'd spent sitting with her at the youth gathering. He longed to walk out to the pond and try skipping stones the way she'd taught him, but he couldn't imagine skipping stones without her.

The front door opened with a squeak, and *Dat* stepped out from the house.

"There you are," he said. "Your *mamm* sent me to find you. She was worried when you weren't in your room."

"I came out here to think."

"Oh." *Dat* nodded. "May I join you?"

"*Ya*, of course." Jason slid to the other side of the bench, and *Dat* sat beside him.

"Is everything all right?" *Dat* asked.

"*Ya*." Jason ran his fingers down the arm of the bench. "I took your advice about Veronica. I went to see her today."

"How did it go?" *Dat* looked hopeful.

"Well, she wouldn't see me, but I left her a gift bag with a few of her favorite things and a letter." Jason sighed. "I can't stop wondering if I made a mistake. What if she threw the gifts away and burned the letter?"

Dat shook his head. "I have a feeling she didn't."

"But what if she did? What will I do then?" His voice quavered, and he longed to have better control of his feelings. As his mother said, he often wore his heart on his sleeve.

Dat gave him a rueful smile. "If she threw away your gifts and your letter, then she isn't the *maedel* for you."

Of course *Dat* was right, but Jason didn't want to hear it. He wanted to hear that Veronica would be thrilled with the letter and gifts and would tell him she wanted to be his friend, if not more.

"Jason," *Dat* began, "you will find the right *maedel* someday. Just be patient. I know Arie hurt you, and now Veronica, but you'll find someone else."

"Right." Jason's voice was low as he looked up at the stars in the clear night sky.

"What was in the gift bag?"

"I wrote her a letter and gave her a few things Seth mentioned she liked. I picked up a couple of pretzels, a vanilla-scented candle, and a couple of books." He paused, debating if he should explain the weatherman joke and tell him about the umbrella. Finally, he said, "I also gave her an umbrella because she calls me her weatherman." He explained how Veronica had asked him for a pretend weather forecast every time she saw him. When his father remained silent, he turned toward him. "Do you think it was a bad idea?"

Dat rested his hands on his suspenders. "No. Actually, I think it was a great idea."

The tension coiling in Jason's stomach lessened ever so slightly. "You do?"

"*Ya.*" *Dat* smiled. "And if she's not impressed with the gifts and the letter, then, again, I don't think she's the *maedel* for you."

But I know she is. Jason nodded. "Should I go see her or wait for her to come to me? Her mother talked to me. She's supportive, but she thinks I should let Veronica come to me."

"I agree. Just give her a little while and see if she contacts you before you do anything else." *Dat* tapped the bench. "I'm going to go to bed. Don't stay out here too long."

"*Gut nacht, Dat.*"

"*Gut nacht.*" *Dat* disappeared into the house, and the door clicked shut behind him.

Jason lifted his eyes to the sky and blew out a deep breath. He hoped Veronica enjoyed the gifts. And even more, he hoped he wouldn't have to wait too long to find out.

CHAPTER 13

JASON FOLLOWED STEPHEN, LEAH, AND MARY THROUGH THE Bird-in-Hand mud sale Friday afternoon. While an auctioneer yelled out prices for livestock, they made their way past tables where vendors were selling baked goods. He scanned the tables, absently wondering if Veronica was there.

When his thoughts turned to Veronica, he frowned. All week his *dat's* words repeated through Jason's thoughts—*And if she's not impressed with the gifts and the letter, then I don't think she's the* maedel *for you.* He hadn't heard from her, and he wondered if that meant she wasn't interested.

"Jason?"

Mary looked over her shoulder at him with a concerned expression. "Are you all right? You've been so quiet today."

"I'm fine, *danki.*" Jason forced a smile. "I'm just tired."

Stephen gave him a look of disbelief. Jason hadn't told Stephen that Veronica had turned him down; nor had he shared his last visit to her house with the gift bag. He didn't want to hear his brother say, "I told you so." Instead, Jason had kept his woes to himself at work and pushed through the week.

"Did you want to buy anything in particular?" Mary said.

AMY CLIPSTON

Jason rubbed his chin. "I suppose I could pick up a few cows," he said, joking.

"We're carpenters, not dairy farmers." Stephen raised an eyebrow. "Tell me you're not serious."

"Aren't I?" Jason asked, and Mary laughed. She still talked all the time, but at least she wasn't acting as much like she had a crush on him.

"Oh, Leah," Mary gushed. "Look at that gorgeous quilt." She grabbed her sister's hand and pulled her toward a table covered with homemade quilts. They stood close to each other, speaking softly about the workmanship.

"What's wrong, Jay?" Stephen asked while the women were preoccupied. "You've been quiet all week."

"Nothing's wrong." Jason stuck his hands in the pockets of his trousers and surveyed the sea of people purchasing a variety of items at the mud sale.

"Jason!"

He spun around and spotted Emily Fisher trotting toward him, grinning and waving. He gasped with surprise. *If Emily is here, then Veronica most likely is too!*

But she doesn't want to see me.

"Jason." Emily worked to catch her breath. "Could I talk to you for a moment?" She smiled at Stephen. "Hi."

"Hi," Stephen said, clearly recognizing Emily from that first day at the bake stand. "I'll give you two a moment to talk." He walked over to Leah and Mary. "What are you two looking at?"

"Will you check out this quilt?" Leah asked Stephen. "Tell me if you like this pattern, and I can try to make one for you."

Emily motioned Jason to move away from the crowd of people. "Veronica is here," she began as they walked side by side toward a less populated area. "Would you please come and talk to her?"

Jason suppressed the excitement building inside of him. "She doesn't want to see me. When I went to your house last Saturday, she refused to come to the door."

"Please, Jason. Give her another chance," Emily pleaded. "She really enjoyed the gifts."

"If she liked them so much, then why didn't she contact me to tell me?" He didn't mean for the question to come out so forcefully.

Emily gave him a wry smile. "She doesn't know how to get in touch with you. She doesn't have your phone number or address. She doesn't even know where you work."

She's right about the address and phone number. I never gave those to her! But it's actually a good thing Veronica doesn't know where I work.

"Oh, right." Jason considered the possible consequences if he talked to Veronica as Emily requested. If she rejected him, at least he'd know he'd tried one last time before having to accept that his father was right that she might not be the girl for him. "Where is she?"

Emily grinned and made a little squealing noise in her throat. "She is going to be so excited that you're here. Rachel and I convinced her to sell her pies, relishes, and jams here so she'd come to the sale today. My *mamm*, Rachel, and I already had the booth to sell quilts, and we told her she could have half of it. We were hoping you'd be here so you two could talk."

"Wait a minute." Jason held up his hand to slow her down. "You and Rachel asked Veronica to come and sell her homemade goods so you could find me and get her to talk to me?" When she nodded he evaluated her possible motives with puzzlement. "Why are you so determined to get Veronica and me together?"

Emily gave him an incredulous expression. "You've given her hope and made her *froh* for the first time since she lost Seth. Rachel and I are rooting for you."

Jason blinked. "Really?"

"*Ya.*" Emily folded her hands. "So will you come with me and talk to her?"

"*Ya.*" Jason nodded as a renewed optimism rang through him. "I will." He looked over his shoulder to where his brother stood with Leah and Mary. "Let me just tell them where I'm going."

VERONICA HANDED A WOMAN TWO OF HER PIES, TOOK THE money, and thanked her. She glanced around the vending area and silently marveled at the crowd of people. She'd sold more than a dozen pies in only a few hours. She was thankful that she'd filled four coolers before they came out to the mud sale. She'd considered staying home today, but her sisters had insisted she come with them. It had been a profitable morning considering all the food she'd sold, but it was crowded and humid at the mud sale grounds.

After two women each bought a jar of relish and a jar of jam, Veronica turned toward Rachel, who was standing behind the booth with David and her best friend, Sharon. "Where did Emily go?"

Rachel shrugged. "I'm not sure. She was here a few minutes ago."

Mamm stepped over from her end of the booth where she had quilts on display. "She went to find the restrooms."

"Oh." Veronica couldn't shake the feeling that Emily was acting a little preoccupied earlier. She'd been surveying the crowd as if she were looking for someone.

"There she is!" Rachel called, a smile turning up the corners of her mouth as she pointed toward a group of people walking toward the booths.

Veronica followed Rachel's gaze and gasped when she

spotted Emily walking with Jason beside her. She turned back toward Rachel, who was flashing a knowing expression, and all the events clicked together in Veronica's mind. *This whole sale idea was a plot to get Jason and me together again!*

Rachel stepped over to Veronica and lowered her voice. "Don't look so terrified. He likes you, and you like him. Go tell him how you feel."

"You and Emily planned this," Veronica accused.

Rachel nodded. "*Ya*, we did, because we care about you, Veronica. We want to see you *froh* again."

"Excuse me," Jason said with a weak smile as he approached the booth. "I heard you sell raspberry pies here. Could I possibly purchase one?"

Emily bit her lip to suppress a smile as she looked at Veronica and then back at Jason.

"*Ya*, you may buy one," Veronica began, "but you have to go for a walk with me first."

Jason rubbed his chin as he feigned indifference. "I don't know if I have time to go for a walk."

"What if I promise you a stone-skipping lesson?" Veronica held her breath, hoping he'd give her a chance to explain herself. She'd thought about him all week, and she'd watched out the window every evening, hoping he'd visit her again. She was so grateful that her sisters had orchestrated this meeting, and she made a note to thank and hug each of them later.

"Sold!" Jason grinned, and her knees wobbled. She'd forgotten how gorgeous his smile was. Oh, how she'd missed it all week!

Veronica turned toward her mother. "Would you watch my booth for me?"

"I'll take care of it." Emily moved behind the table. "Go take your time."

"*Danki*," Veronica whispered to her. She handed her the money box and then slipped out from behind the table. "Let's go find a quiet place to talk."

They walked side by side while weaving through the knot of people clogging the field until they reached a snack bar.

Jason drew his wallet from his back pocket. "Would you like a soda and a pretzel?"

"*Ach*, I left my money back at the table." She looked over her shoulder toward the vending area.

"Veronica," he said. "I have money."

"You've already given me too much. I couldn't possibly expect you to—"

"So that's one pretzel and one soda," he said.

Before she could protest, he purchased two pretzels and two Cokes and handed her one of each.

"*Danki*," she said.

"*Gern gschehne*." He pointed toward an area with tables and chairs. "Want to go sit down?"

"*Ya*, that would be nice."

The noise of the crowd and the auctioneer's voice faded as they ambled toward the back of the eating area.

"How was your week?" he asked as he motioned toward a chair.

"*Gut*," she said. "How was yours?" She sat down, and he sat across from her.

He lifted and dropped one shoulder in a halfhearted shrug. "Uneventful."

"I used my umbrella on Tuesday." She met his eyes, and he raised his eyebrow. "Your weather forecast was very accurate."

He gave her a lopsided grin, and her heartbeat raced. "I just happened to guess right." He took a sip from the can of Coke and then broke off a piece of pretzel.

"You could get a part-time job doing the weather report for the radio station."

"Do you think it pays well?" he asked.

She laughed and then took a bit of the warm pretzel, which melted in her mouth. "I loved all of the gifts. They were perfect. *Danki.*"

He nodded. "I'm glad you liked them."

"I've already finished the books. How did you know they are my favorite authors?"

He shrugged again. "Good guess."

"The candle is perfect. I like to light it at night while I read."

He seemed to search her eyes for something. He was waiting for her to talk about her feelings. She took a depth breath and mustered all the emotional strength she could find.

"I'm sorry for pushing you away," Veronica began with both her hands and her body quaking with a mixture of anxiety and raw emotion. "I was afraid." She kept her eyes trained on the pretzel. "I thought if I let anyone into my heart again, I would somehow betray Seth. And I think, deep down, I'm also afraid of losing someone again. Seth meant everything to me. We had all these plans. We were going to be married on November twenty-seventh, and we were going to build a *haus* on his parents' property. We even had talked about what we would name our six *kinner.*"

She gave a little laugh and looked up, surprised to see that he looked stricken. "I was a coward on Saturday, and I'm sorry. When I saw you in the driveway, I asked my *mamm* to talk to you. I couldn't face you because I knew I'd hurt you. I hope you'll forgive me."

"Of course I forgive you." Jason started to reach for her hand and then pulled his arm back. "I could never be angry with you."

"*Danki*, but I don't deserve that. I was wrong to hide in the *haus*." She pulled a napkin from the metal dispenser in the center of the small, round table and fingered it as she spoke. "After you left, I opened your gifts, and I was really overwhelmed by your generosity. My *mamm* told me she asked you to give me a second chance, and I was furious."

Jason's eyes continued to explore hers. "Why were you furious?"

"I was confused and hurt. I didn't know what to do or how to feel. I went to see Seth's mother, and I told her I was interested in someone. She gave me her blessing."

"She gave you her blessing?" he asked.

"Margaret told me I should live my life. She said Seth would want me to move on." Veronica paused and sucked in a trembling breath. "If you are still interested in me, then I would like to get to know you better."

Jason's face lit up. "Are you sure?"

"*Ya.*" Veronica smiled, and her cheeks heated. "I need your weather reports to get through the week." She laughed and then broke off another piece of pretzel.

JASON THOUGHT HE MIGHT BURST WITH EXCITEMENT. Veronica wanted to get to know him! His father's advice had worked, and she had changed her mind. He was so thrilled he thought he could dance and sing right there in the middle of the refreshment area. She looked breathtakingly beautiful today with her blue dress complementing her eyes. The bright sunlight gave the blonde tendrils escaping her prayer covering a golden hue. Her smile was bright and warm. He was falling for her—fast.

I need to tell her the truth about Seth now!

The thought took him by surprise. It was time for him to be honest with her before the truth tore them apart.

"I know how you feel," he said as he broke off another piece of pretzel. "I lost a close friend recently."

"Really?" she asked. "I'm sorry to hear that."

"*Danki*." He cleaned his hands on a paper napkin. "It's difficult when you expect to see them every day and you don't."

Veronica sighed and nodded. "*Ya*, it is. Some days are more painful than others."

"That's true." Jason sipped his drink and then looked down at the half-eaten pretzel. He had to tell her before he lost his nerve. But how should he start? Should he apologize? Should he tell her he saw her at the visitation at Seth's mother's house? Should he just flat out say he had worked with Seth?

"I need to apologize for something," Veronica suddenly blurted out, her beautiful face flushed with embarrassment. "I said something terrible to you, and I didn't mean it. I just want to clear it up with you now."

"Oh?" He shook his head. "You don't need to apologize for anything."

"*Ya*, I do." She nodded with emphasis, her eyes serious. "Two weeks ago when you came to see me, I told you that you should date Mary." She leveled her gaze with his. "I didn't mean it."

Jason bit the inside of his lip to stop himself from laughing at her serious expression. "You don't need to be concerned about that."

"Okay." She took another bite of pretzel, but she didn't seem convinced.

"Did you really think you were going to lose me to her?" He was stunned.

She nodded and sipped her soda. "She really likes you. When I saw her at church, I could tell she wasn't *froh* to see me. I think she sees me as a threat."

That's because you are. "Don't worry about Mary."

"Okay." This time Veronica looked relieved. "I was hoping I hadn't pushed you toward her."

"No." Jason shook his head. He was amused and somehow comforted by the worry in her eyes. Was she as afraid of losing him as he was of losing her?

She finished the pretzel and then looked at him. "How did you know I love pretzels and vanilla-scented candles?"

The question was simple, but a wave of worry flowed through him. Jason's shoulders stiffened with apprehension. He'd been caught red-handed.

"Didn't you tell me you liked them while we were sitting at the pond?" His lie was feeble, and he was sure she'd see right through it.

Veronica shook her head. "No, I don't think so." She smiled. "You have *wunderbaar* intuition."

"*Danki.*" He inwardly sighed with relief. He'd dodged that one with ease.

"Now I need to know your favorite things. What foods do you like?"

"Raspberry pies." He grinned, and she tossed her crumpled napkin at him.

"That doesn't count," she said with a laugh. "You have to like something else."

"Let me think." Jason smiled. "I like *maed* with blonde hair and blue eyes. They have to like to bake and skip stones."

Veronica rolled her eyes. "Tell me something I don't already know."

He laughed, and she soon joined in. He enjoyed the sweet melody of her laughter.

"This is fun," she said before finishing the last piece of her pretzel.

"*Ya*, it is." He held up his can of Coke as if to toast her.

"You're not going to get away with avoiding my question." She wagged a finger at him and looked adorable. "What are your favorite things?"

Jason touched his chin while considering the question. "I've never really thought about it. I suppose I like peanut butter cookies and chocolate cake."

Veronica sat slightly taller. "I can make those."

"I also like picnics and quiet walks by a pond." He paused for a moment, as if gathering his nerve. "I just like being with you."

Her cheeks flushed, and she glanced down at her Coke.

"Veronica," he said, and she looked up at him. "May I see you again?"

"I'd be disappointed if you didn't." Her expression was serious.

"*Gut.*" His heart soared. This was what he'd dreamed of since the first time he'd met her at the bake stand. Now he had to find a way to tell her the truth about Seth.

VERONICA FELT AS IF SHE WERE WALKING ON AIR AS SHE AND Jason made their way back to the vendor area. Her lips formed a permanent smile, and her stomach fluttered with excitement. She had worried for so long about feeling guilty, but all she felt now was happiness—pure, uplifting happiness.

They weaved through the crowd to the table where Emily was telling a customer about the assorted jams while her mother talked to someone about a colorful log cabin pattern quilt. Rachel sat on a chair and frowned while flipping through a quilting magazine.

Veronica stood by the table and turned to Jason. "*Danki* for the snack. I had a nice time."

"*Gern gschehne,*" Jason said. "I had a nice time too." He

motioned toward the table. "How long do you think you're going to be here today?"

"I'm not sure." Veronica looked over at her mother, who smiled. "Do you have plans?" she asked Jason.

"I'm here with my *bruder*, Leah, and Mary," he said. "I told them I'd be back in a few minutes, but I think that was over an hour ago."

Veronica laughed. "I wonder if they're looking for you. You probably should go find them."

"Okay." He seemed to hesitate, as if he didn't want to leave. She didn't want him to go either.

"I think you should come over tomorrow to get a pie," she suggested quickly. "I imagine you're out of raspberry pie, and you know my stand is open on Saturdays." She clicked off a mental list of ingredients for chocolate cake and peanut butter cookies. She could whip them up quickly tonight and have them ready for him tomorrow. Excitement rushed through her. She couldn't wait to bake for him.

"That's a *gut* idea." He touched her hand, and the warmth of his touch sent her heartbeat thumping wildly in her chest. "I'll see you tomorrow."

"*Gut*," she said. "I expect a new weather report. My umbrella is ready just in case."

"I'll have one." He waved at her mother and sisters and then smiled at her. "See you tomorrow."

"I look forward to it." She stood by the table and watched him saunter away, taking in his confident stride and tall frame.

"Looks like you had a great time." Emily's comment snapped Veronica back to reality.

Veronica ran her hands down her apron. "*Ya*, I did. *Danki* for running the table for me. Did you make a lot of sales?"

Emily jammed a hand on one of her small hips. "I don't want to talk about how many jars of jam I sold. I want to hear about you and Jason."

Rachel sidled up to them. "So do I. You two looked really *froh*."

Mamm joined them. "I have to agree with your sisters. You and Jason seemed awfully cheerful."

Veronica smiled. "We went to the concession area and had a pretzel and a drink. We talked, and it was really nice. He's coming to see me tomorrow."

Her sisters clapped their hands and hugged her. Apparently that was all they needed to hear.

"I'm so *froh* for you," Emily gushed while squeezing Veronica's hand.

"I knew it would work out," Rachel chimed in with a slight smile.

Mamm touched Veronica's shoulder. "I'm glad you gave him a chance."

An *Englisher* woman appeared at *Mamm's* end of the table and asked about one of her wedding ring quilts, and *Mamm* turned to help her.

Emily continued to grin. "I'm glad you're not angry with me for finding him and bringing him over to see you. I was afraid you'd ask him to leave and then yell at me."

"I would never do that," Veronica said, shaking her head. "I'm thankful you knew what I needed before I did."

Emily began to arrange the remaining jars of relish and jams on the table, and Rachel retreated to the chair at the back of the booth area. She picked up the quilting magazine and stared at the cover as a scowl deepened on her pretty face.

Veronica couldn't let her sister suffer in silence. She moved a chair beside her and sat. "Is something wrong, Rach?"

Rachel shrugged and shook her head. "No, not really."

Veronica took in her sister's brown eyes. "You're not telling me the truth."

Rachel sighed. "I have this feeling I can't seem to shake off." She glanced down at the cover of the magazine as if it held all the answers she craved. "David doesn't seem interested in me anymore. He talks to Sharon more than he talks to me, and when Sharon suggested they go to the auction, they left without me."

Veronica frowned. How could she be so happy when her sister was so sad? "I'm sorry. Maybe they thought you had to stay and help *Mamm* and Emily since I was gone."

"No, I'm sure it wasn't that." Rachel shook her head. "This isn't your fault. This is something that has been bothering me for a while."

"I think you need to talk to David alone and tell him how you feel," Veronica said. "Be honest with him and explain how he hurt your feelings today."

"Okay." Rachel nodded. "I'll do that tonight."

Veronica stood. "Would you like to help us with the booth? Or do you want to go find David and Sharon?"

Rachel shook her head. "I'd rather help you and Emily."

Veronica stood between her sisters as a few *Englishers* approached the booth and asked about the jams and relishes. She was grateful for her family, and she looked forward to the possibility of getting to know Jason better, thanks to her thoughtful sisters.

CHAPTER 14

Veronica's heart fluttered when she spotted Jason's buggy moving down the road toward the bake stand Saturday afternoon. She'd waited for him all morning, eager to give him the peanut butter cookies and chocolate cake she'd baked for him the night before. When he didn't arrive by noon, her excitement waned and doubt crept into her soul. Had she imagined the connection they'd shared yesterday in the concession area at the mud sale? Did he say he'd *try* to stop by the bake stand instead of promising he'd be there?

The sight of his buggy caused her worries to evaporate. He'd kept his promise.

Jason halted the horse in front of the stand and climbed from the buggy. *"Wie geht's?"* He got out of the buggy and walked to the stand. "I heard you sell the best raspberry pies in Bird-in-Hand. Is that true?" His eyes sparkled with humor.

"No, that's not true." Veronica grinned, playing along with this game. "I do have something that might interest you instead." She reached into a cooler beside her and extracted the tin of peanut butter cookies and the plastic cake saver that held his chocolate cake. She set them on the counter in front of her. "A little bird told me you like peanut butter cookies and chocolate cake."

Jason looked at the tin and the cake saver with surprise. "You made these for me?"

She nodded.

He opened the tin and found the cookies. "When did you make them?"

"Last night." She shrugged as if it hadn't taken her a few hours. "I wanted to have them ready for you when you came by." *And I worried all morning that you weren't going to come.*

"*Danki.*" He plucked a cookie from the tin and took a bite. "Oh, this is the best peanut butter cookie I've ever had. But don't tell my *mamm* that."

"I'm so glad you like it." Veronica tapped the cake saver. "I hope you enjoy the chocolate cake too. You may want to skip the raspberry pie this week and only take home the cake."

Jason shook his head. "No, the raspberry pies are for my parents and my *bruder*. The chocolate cake is all mine." He lifted the top of the cake saver, and the aroma of chocolate wafted up. "I can't wait to have a piece."

She smiled. "I hope you like it too."

He offered her a cookie, and she took it. "I wanted to be here earlier, but I had to help my *dat* with a project at the *haus*. We're replacing some old boards on the barn. We're doing a little bit each Saturday. It's going to be a brand-new barn soon."

"Oh." She bit into the cookie. "These are pretty *gut*."

"Pretty *gut*?" he asked. "They're more like perfect." He bit into another one. "How are sales today?"

"They've been okay." She shrugged. "A group of tourists stopped by earlier and bought nearly all my pickles and relish. They bought one of my pies. I only have a few left since I sold so many yesterday. I baked only a few more last night—"

"Because you were busy making my goodies." He finished her sentence, and she nodded.

"*Ya*, that's true." Veronica leaned on the counter. "What is the weather report this week?"

"Hmm." Jason leaned across from her, his hands only a millimeter from hers. He looked up at the cloudless sky and then at her. "No rain this week. In fact, every day the sky will be blue, almost as *schee* as your pale-blue eyes." His expression and eyes were intense, sending a shiver of excitement dancing down her spine.

"I suppose I won't need my umbrella then?" she asked.

"Nope." He shook his head. "You won't."

"That's *gut* to know." She couldn't stand the thought of his leaving, and an idea occurred to her. "What are your plans for later today?"

Jason took another cookie. "I don't think I have any. Why?"

"I'm going to close up the bake stand in about an hour. Would you like to stay for supper?" She held her breath, hoping he'd say yes.

"I'd love to." He looked surprised by the offer. "*Danki*."

"Great." She grabbed a sign from under the counter. "I'll pick up here, put out my sign, and then we can go inside to visit with my family."

Jason nodded. "That sounds *gut*. I'll park my horse and buggy by the barn if that's okay."

"*Ya*. I'll meet you at the *haus*." While Jason guided the horse toward the barn, Veronica stowed her pies in the cooler and then set out the sign that said, "Please knock on door for service." She carried his tin of cookies and the cake saver toward the back door.

Veronica spotted Jason standing by the barn while gazing toward her father's harness shop. She walked over toward him. "Do you want to see my *dat's* store?"

Jason smiled. "I'd love to."

"Let me put the cake and cookies inside, and then I'll take

you over there. My *dat* would enjoy talking with you." She nodded toward the house. "Walk with me."

He took the cake saver from her hands. "You didn't have to carry all of this."

"I thought you wanted me to." She teased. "After all, you left it on the counter for me."

Jason's cheeks turned slightly pink. He was blushing! "I didn't mean to. I guess I was so surprised that you'd invited me for supper that I wanted to move my horse and buggy before you changed your mind."

She stopped walking and looked at him. "Why would I change my mind?"

He shrugged. "It was a joke."

"Jason, I really want you to stay and meet my *dat*."

He smiled, and she could hardly contain her joy. "*Danki*. I'm honored."

They climbed the back porch steps and entered the house through the mudroom. Veronica stepped into the kitchen and found *Mamm* sitting at the table making a shopping list.

"*Mamm*," Veronica said. "Jason came to visit, and I invited him to stay for supper."

Mamm looked up and smiled. "Jason. It's so *gut* to see you. I'm glad you can stay." She gave Veronica an approving look, and the tips of Veronica's ears heated.

"I'm going to take Jason out to see *Dat*'s store, and then I'll be back to start cooking." Veronica placed the cookie tin and cake saver on the counter and started for the door.

JASON FELT OVERWHELMED AS HE WATCHED VERONICA place the cake saver and tin of cookies on the kitchen counter. When he arrived at her stand today, he'd never expected her to hand him baked goods she'd made especially for him. And never in his wildest dreams had he imagined she would invite him to stay for supper and meet her *dat*. He had hoped to spend an hour or so visiting with her, but now he felt as if she were making him a part of the family.

"Let's go see my *dat*," Veronica said as she crossed the kitchen toward the mudroom. "He enjoys people visiting his store."

Jason followed her through the mudroom and out to the porch.

"My *dat* and our neighbor, Hank Ebersol, built the shop when they were in their twenties," Veronica explained while they walked. "They run it together. Emily helps out with the books every week, and sometimes she'll run the front counter and answer the phone. Mostly it's just *Dat* and Hank, though."

Jason nodded and noticed a large sign boasting the Bird-in-Hand Harness Shop. His stomach knotted as they approached the store. What if her father didn't approve of him? After all, he hadn't asked her *dat*'s permission to see Veronica. Would her father ask Jason why he hadn't visited the store and introduced himself before coming to visit her?

The worry settled into his stomach as they walked up to the one-story, white clapboard building. A hitching post by the front door welcomed horses and buggies, and three empty parking spaces greeted motor vehicles.

Jason pulled the door open, and Veronica stepped inside as a bell over the door announced their entrance. As Jason followed her inside, the aroma of leather engulfed his senses. The one-room store was clogged with displays featuring harnesses, leashes for pets, pet collars, saddles, saddle blankets, doorknob hangers with bells, rope, pouches, bags, and various other horse accessories. The sales counter sat in the center of the crowded showroom with a small round display that included leather key chains in shapes varying from cats to horses.

Beyond the showroom was an open area where two middle-aged men worked.

"Hi, *Dat*," Veronica said. "Hi, Hank. Jason is here to visit."

"Jason." A tall man with graying light-brown hair and a matching beard stood from the workbench and approached. "*Wie geht's?*" He shook Jason's hand with a confident, strong grip.

"I'm doing well." Jason gestured around the store. "You have a *schee* store here. You do fantastic work."

"Oh, no." Her *dat* pointed toward the other man sitting at the workbench. "Hank does the *gut* work. I do the mediocre stuff."

"Don't listen to Leroy," Hank chimed in. "He's not as *gut* as I am, but I wouldn't call him mediocre."

Leroy gave a loud, boisterous laugh, and Veronica shook her head.

"I'll leave you *buwe* to argue about who does the best work." Veronica smiled at Jason, and his heart skipped a beat. "I need to get started on supper. Come in around five thirty." She waved and then strode out of the shop, the door clicking shut behind her.

"What kind of work do you do?" Leroy asked Jason.

"I'm in construction," Jason said, leaning against the cashier counter. He glanced around the shop, silently admiring the craftsmanship.

"What kind of construction do you do?" Leroy asked.

Jason paused and gathered his thoughts. He wanted to tell Leroy the truth about where he worked, but he had to tell Veronica first. "I build sheds." He said the words and then waited for Leroy to make the connection.

"You build sheds?" Leroy's eyes widened in surprise. "Veronica's fiancé was in the shed business. He was killed in an accident."

I know. "I had heard that." Jason dodged the connection. "It was *bedauerlich*."

"*Ya*," Leroy said, frowning. "It was horrible. It happened while he was working. He fell from the rafters and the impact broke his neck. He died instantly. There was nothing the EMTs could do for him."

"What a shock." Hank sighed and then returned to the leather strap he was creating.

"That's terrible." Jason had to steer the conversation elsewhere. He pointed toward a saddle. "Do you make the saddles here?"

"No, no." Leroy shook his head. "We order the saddles from wholesalers. We only do leatherwork here. Let me show you." He waved Jason toward the work area and pointed out the tools.

Jason sat on a stool and enjoyed listening to Leroy talk about his work. Leroy was a friendly, confident man, and he reminded Jason of his own father. Jason imagined himself becoming close friends with Leroy. He hoped he would have the opportunity to get to know him better as his friendship with Veronica grew.

At five thirty, Leroy and Hank closed up the shop. After saying good night to Hank, Jason and Leroy walked to the house. When they stepped inside they found Veronica, her sisters, and their mother flitting around the kitchen. Delicious aromas overtook Jason's senses as he surveyed the long table, which was already set for six.

Leroy washed his hands at a small sink outside of the mudroom, and Jason followed suit. Leroy sat at the head of the table and then pointed to a chair to his right.

"Have a seat," Leroy said.

"*Danki*," Jason said.

Veronica met his curious expression as she brought a tray of breaded pork chops to the table. "Do you like iced tea?"

"*Ya*, I do." Jason nodded. "*Danki*."

"Here you go," Emily said, handing him a glass of tea, then

placing a glass of tea at each table setting while Rachel delivered two baskets of sliced bread and two plates of butter.

"Did you have fun in the shop?" Mattie asked Jason.

"*Ya*," Jason said. "Leroy let me help him make a harness." He fingered the cool glass of tea. "I really just watched while he finished it."

"No, you helped." Leroy grinned. "You handed me tools." He laughed and Jason nodded.

"That's true," Jason said.

Veronica and her sisters laughed while delivering the rest of the meal to the table, including green beans and mashed potatoes.

"I think we're ready now," Mattie said as she stood at the opposite end of the table.

Veronica sat down across from Jason, and Emily sat beside him. Rachel sank into the chair beside Veronica. After a silent prayer, they filled their plates, utensils scraping and the murmur of conversation filling the large kitchen. As Leroy asked Jason more about what he thought of the harness shop, the women discussed what menu to provide for the group of *Englishers* who'd made a reservation for supper in a couple of weeks.

Soon their plates were empty, and Veronica brought out coffee along with a lemon meringue pie for dessert. After eating two pieces of pie and drinking two cups of coffee, Jason was so full he thought his stomach might burst.

Leroy went outside to take care of the animals, and Jason collected the dirty dishes and carried them to the sink, where Mattie was washing and Rachel was drying.

"Should I go help your *dat* with the animals?" he asked Veronica, who was carrying cups to the counter.

"No," Emily said. "You and Veronica can go outside and visit." She gave Veronica a pointed expression. "Rachel, *Mamm*, and I will clean up."

Veronica and Emily exchanged unspoken words in conversation with their expressions, and Jason watched them in awe. He was always amazed at how sisters could talk to each other with their eyes without men having the faintest notion what they were saying. He'd seen it lately with Leah and Mary.

"That's a great idea," Rachel said. "Take some of *Dat's* root beer with you."

"*Ya,*" Mattie chimed in. She peered into the propane refrigerator and then handed Jason two bottles. "Go sit on the porch or go for a walk. We'll clean this up."

"Supper was *appeditlich,*" he told Mattie. "I really enjoyed it. *Danki* for having me."

"*Gern gschehne.*" Mattie's smile was warm. "Veronica did most of the cooking. I was only the assistant." She motioned for Veronica to leave. "Go enjoy your company. We'll take care of this."

Veronica touched Jason's arm, and warmth rushed through him. "Let's go out to the porch."

Jason followed her through the family room and past a spiral staircase to the front door. She opened the door to the wraparound porch that spanned the front of the house. The evening air was warm, but it was not quite as humid as it had been earlier.

Veronica sat down in the wooden swing and patted the spot next to her. He remembered when they had sat out here and she had rejected him. Now the sparkle in her eyes had turned from hesitant to certain in a matter of only a couple of weeks. He was thankful for his father's sound advice.

Jason sat beside her and handed her a cold bottle of root beer. "Your *dat* does leatherwork and makes root beer. The talent in your family is overwhelming."

"Also, he and Hank built my bake stand in only two weeks." She lifted her bottle. "You should be really impressed now." She giggled and then took a sip.

Jason shook his head. He could listen to her laugh all day long. He was definitely smitten with her. He sipped his own root beer and enjoyed the cool carbonation as it slid down his throat. "I've had a *wunderbaar* day."

"I have too." Veronica smiled at him. "I know my family has enjoyed getting to know you today, and I have too."

Jason covered her hand with his, and her smile deepened. His head was dizzy with delight. Did she feel the same, overwhelming bliss he felt? Was she also falling fast for him?

"Would it be all right if I came to visit you more often?" Jason asked. He held his breath as he waited a moment for her response.

"*Ya*, but I'm afraid I may run out of raspberries soon since the season is ending," Veronica said coyly. "I'll have to supplement with the peanut butter cookies and chocolate cake."

"I suppose that will have to do." He feigned an annoyed sigh. "I expect to be the first on your list for raspberry pies next year when they come back into season."

Veronica eyed him for a minute and then nodded. "I would love to make the first pie next season for you if you'll promise to visit my bake stand."

Jason reached over and pushed the ribbon from her prayer covering behind her ear, his finger brushing her warm cheek. She seemed surprised by his touch but didn't move away from him.

"I will be the first person at your bake stand next season," he promised. "Or maybe I'll be here to help you open it on the first day."

"I'd like that." She took another sip and gave the swing a gentle push with her foot. "I love to sit out here and look at the stars after dark. It reminds me of how beautiful God's creation is."

"*Ya*, I agree." The swing moved back and forth, and Jason breathed a soft sigh. He hadn't been this happy in a long time.

They sat on the porch and talked for nearly an hour. Soon the sky was growing dark, and Jason had to face the five-mile trek home to Gordonville. After saying good night to Veronica's family and grabbing the tin of cookies and cake saver, Jason walked out to his buggy with Veronica at his side.

"*Danki* again for a *wunderbaar* afternoon and evening," he said after stowing the cookies and cake on the passenger side of the buggy. "I'll see you soon."

She nodded. "I look forward to it."

Jason hesitated. He longed to kiss her, but he knew it was too soon. He didn't want to pressure her and unintentionally push her away again.

Instead, Jason climbed into the buggy and waved as he guided the horse toward the road. He spent the whole ride home replaying the afternoon and evening in his mind. He recalled her smile during dinner, the feel of her hand as they sat on the swing, the smell of her lavender shampoo when he pushed the ribbon away from her face.

He was still grinning more than an hour later when he guided the horse up his driveway. He unhitched the horse and led him into the barn and to his stall. He was rubbing the horse's ears and talking softly to him when his father appeared behind him.

"How was your day?" *Dat* asked. "I guess it went well at Veronica's since you didn't make it home in time for supper."

Jason nodded. "It was a fantastic afternoon and evening." He told his father about visiting Leroy's shop, eating supper with the family, and drinking root beer on Veronica's porch. "It couldn't have been any more perfect."

Dat leaned on the stall door. "I'm *froh* for you."

Jason stepped out of the stall and brought Maximus fresh water before looking at his father again. "*Dat*, how did you know you were in love?"

Dat considered the question. "I suppose I just knew. With

your *mamm*, there was never any doubt in my mind. I was positive she was the *maedel* for me the first time I met her and we went for a walk together. It was just something I knew deep in my heart."

Jason smiled. "I think I understand. I feel such a deep connection with Veronica. It's deeper than anything I ever felt with Arie."

Dat placed his hand on Jason's shoulder. "I'm *froh* to hear you say that. I know Arie hurt you deeply, and I've been hoping you'd find someone else who made you happy."

"There's just one problem." Jason grimaced. "I still haven't told Veronica I knew Seth." He leaned back against the stall door, and Maximus rested his snout on Jason's shoulder. "I even had the opportunity to tell her *dat*, and I chickened out." Jason recounted the conversation he'd had with Leroy in the harness shop. "I just can't bring myself to tell her the truth about how I found her. I don't know how to do it. I don't know what to say. Every time I convince myself it's the perfect time, I freeze up."

Dat shook his head with a concerned expression. "You have to tell her. Just start by telling her where you work, and the rest will come to you."

"But I can't bear the thought of losing her." Jason lifted his hat and raked his hands through his hair. "I can't bear it."

Dat's brown eyes were sympathetic. "Do you think she feels the same way for you as you feel for her?"

Jason nodded. "I do."

"If that's true, then she will forgive you. She'll understand why you wanted to wait until the right time. Just tell her you care for her and you don't want to lose her."

Dat made it sound so easy, but every time Jason had attempted to tell her the truth, the words had evaporated, leaving him speechless and nervous. "I'll try," he promised.

"Let's go inside," *Dat* said. "It's late. We have church tomorrow."

As Jason walked with his father toward the house, he silently vowed to tell Veronica the truth as soon as he could. Somehow he'd convince her he wanted to tell her sooner about his friendship with Seth, and somehow she'd have to understand and forgive him.

CHAPTER 15

"Jason is so sweet," Veronica told Mamm as they planted pansies together Thursday afternoon. "He's so funny. He gives me a weather prediction every time I see him."

"Oh *ya?*" Mamm smiled while wiping her brow. "What did he say for this week?"

"No rain." Veronica laughed. "And he was right. I don't know how he predicts it so well."

Mamm shook her head. "It's a gift, I suppose." She picked up the watering can and began to water the flowers. "You really like him, don't you?"

"*Ya*, I do." Veronica considered her feelings as she continued to pat the new soil with her trowel. "I was so worried that I would feel guilty, but I don't. I'll never forget Seth, and he'll always have a special place in my heart. My feelings for Jason are different since he's a different person. Does that make sense?"

Mamm nodded while keeping her eyes trained on the colorful pansies. "*Ya*, I understand."

"My nightmares have stopped," Veronica said.

Mamm looked over at her. "What nightmares?"

"I used to dream I was with Seth when he had the accident. Sometimes I was trying to save him but he died in my arms.

Other times I was too far away to get to him as he fell." Veronica dug another hole and stuck a purple pansy in it. "Now I dream about happy times with Seth, or I dream about spending time with Jason."

"That's *gut*." *Mamm* smiled again. "I've been worried about you. I'm thankful that you're working through your grief and feeling better."

"*Danki, Mamm*. I'm feeling much better." Veronica surveyed the garden, which they had been working on all week long. "We're almost ready for church on Sunday."

Mamm sighed. "We have so much to do. I'm glad Emily is taking a break from *Dat's* books and helping me by cleaning the floors today."

"Don't worry, *Mamm*," Veronica said. "We'll get it all done. The *haus* will be ready in time."

A buggy moved up the driveway, and Veronica stood up straight. "Were you expecting company today?"

"No." *Mamm* shook her head. "Who is it?"

"I'll find out." Veronica wiped her hands down her apron and walked toward the driveway. She gasped when Jason climbed out of the buggy. She was a mess! Her dress and apron were caked in dirt, and she needed to wash her hands.

"Jason. What are you doing here?" She continued to rub her hands down her apron as he approached her. She longed to run into the house and change as he stood in front of her, looking perfect with his clean trousers and crisp, green shirt.

"It's nice to see you too." He gave her a playful grin, and her knees nearly buckled. "I was wondering if you wanted to go for a picnic with me. I thought you might like to take a break from your work today."

Veronica gaped at him with surprise. "You want to go for a picnic now?"

He grimaced. "I guess it's not a *gut* time? I suppose I should've called first, but I managed to get out of work early and wanted to come and see you as soon as I could."

She bit her lip and turned toward her mother, who was watering the last of the flowers they'd planted.

"I understand. It's not a *gut* time." He jammed a thumb toward the buggy. "I'll go and come back another time."

"No," she said quickly. She couldn't allow him to leave. It had been five long days since she'd seen him. "Just wait a minute, okay?"

"Take your time." He leaned back against his buggy.

Veronica rushed into the garden. "*Mamm*, Jason wants to take me on a picnic. Is it all right if I go for a while? I promise I'll get back here as soon as I can, and I'll finish the garden. I'll mow and then finish up the weeding."

"Go have fun." *Mamm* brushed her hands on her apron. "I'll finish up here, and we'll see what else needs to be done when you get back."

"Are you sure?" Veronica hesitated. "I hate leaving the work for you."

"Emily can help me as soon as she finishes the mopping." *Mamm* waved at Jason, who returned the gesture from the back of the buggy. "A handsome man is waiting to take you on a picnic. Go change your dress before he leaves without you."

"*Danki, Mamm*." Veronica squeezed her mother's hand and then hurried toward the porch. "I'll be right out!" she called to Jason.

"Grab one of your pies!" he hollered back with a grin.

She rushed up the stairs to her room. After washing up and changing into a purple dress and black apron, she checked her hair and head covering in the mirror. Once she felt she was presentable, she hurried back down the stairs. Emily was on her knees scrubbing the kitchen floor. Veronica gingerly stepped around her and grabbed a pie from the refrigerator.

"Where are you going?" Emily asked, sitting back on her heels and wiping her sweaty brow.

"Jason is here. He's taking me on a picnic. I'll be back as soon as I can to help finish up today."

Emily smiled. "Have fun."

"I will," Veronica promised.

She rushed out the back door, surprised to find her mother talking to Jason as he stood leaning against the buggy. He was so handsome as he crossed his arms over his wide chest and smiled. He met Veronica's stare and waved.

"I'm ready," Veronica said.

"Great," Jason said. "I promise I'll have her back soon."

"Take your time," *Mamm* said. "We've been working hard all week. She deserves a little break."

"*Danki, Mamm.*" Veronica climbed into the passenger side of the bench seat and blew out a sigh as Jason climbed into the driver's side. "How did you know I needed a break today?"

"It was just a feeling I had." He guided the horse down the driveway, waving at her mother as they made their way to the road.

"I'm amazed by how well you know me." She looked at him, and he kept his attention focused on the road. "It's like you've known me for years instead of just a few weeks."

Something in his smile changed, but she couldn't put her finger on why.

"I guess sometimes you just have a special connection with people." He gave her a sideways glance, but the look in his eyes seemed hesitant.

"*Ya*, I suppose you're right." She looked over a shoulder and found a picnic basket. "You packed lunch?"

"How am I supposed to take you on a picnic without food?" His grin teased her. "I came prepared for this special date."

Veronica contemplated his thoughtfulness. How had this perfect man found her when she'd needed someone like him to heal her broken heart? He felt like an answer to a prayer. Did God send him to her?

Jason's smile disappeared. *"Was iss letz?"*

"Nothing is wrong." She tilted her head and smiled. "I was just wondering how you found me."

THE QUESTION CAUGHT JASON OFF GUARD. DID SHE SUS-pect something? Did she know he wasn't being honest with her? The fear slithered through his stomach, coiled up, and then settled there like a heavy brick. He had to tell her the truth. He braced himself while remembering his father's advice to first tell her where he worked and then let the rest of the information come out slowly while reminding her how much he cared for her. He could do this.

He *had* to do this and finally confess once and for all.

Jason opened his mouth to speak, and she cut him off with a question.

"Where are we going?" Veronica asked. She was holding the pie on her lap. Its sweet smell filled the buggy and caused his stomach to growl.

Jason was speechless for a moment. He had prepared himself to tell her the truth about his relationship with Seth, but then she completely derailed him with a mundane question. She'd asked a question that rocked him to the core and then dropped it as if it were nothing. Veronica was truly unpredictable.

"Are you all right?" She leaned closer to him, her pretty face full of concern.

"Ya, I'm fine." He cleared his throat. "We're just going up the road a mile or two. There's a pond up there I think you may like." He halted the horse at a stoplight. He felt the tension in his stomach relax slightly.

Jason had finished his work ahead of schedule and then asked his father if he could leave early. It was unusual for his father to grant him the afternoon off, but he'd caught him in a good mood. Jason rushed home to change his clothes, and when he told his mother his idea, she pulled together a lunch for him and gave him an old quilt. Once the basket was packed, he rushed to Veronica's house, hoping she was home and available for an impromptu date.

Veronica had looked positively adorable when he arrived and found her covered in soil from the neck down. He almost wished he had one of those fancy phones with a camera just so he could take a photo and keep it forever. Instead, he'd keep the mental picture in his mind. He certainly would treasure it.

She craned her neck and looked into the bed of the buggy again. "I see you brought a nice *big* basket."

"I did." Jason nodded. "My *mamm* had made chicken salad, and she put a few other things in there for us. She sent an old quilt for us to sit on too."

"So your *mamm* knows about me. I mean, we met at the church service that day, but she knows we are seeing each other now?"

Jason recalled how he'd panicked when his *mamm* told him she'd met Veronica in the kitchen that day. What if one of the other women had made a Lancaster Sheds connection with her and pointed Veronica out as Seth's fiancée? But all she said was that she complimented Veronica on the raspberry pies he'd been bringing home.

He didn't want to think about that now.

"Ya, she does."

Veronica settled back in the seat, appearing satisfied with that information.

Jason guided the horse to the road leading to the pond and then halted it near the spot where he wanted to have the picnic. He climbed out and grabbed the picnic basket. Veronica laid out the quilt on the ground next to the pond, and he sat down beside her.

While he made their chicken salad sandwiches, she retrieved the plates, utensils, napkins, and bottles of water.

"This is perfect," she said, heaving a deep sigh. "What a beautiful place to have lunch and relax. This is just what I needed today."

"*Gut.*" Jason handed her a sandwich, and she thanked him. "You were doing a nice job in the garden when I arrived."

"*Danki.*" She looked embarrassed. "I know I was a mess."

"I thought you looked cute," he admitted, and she blushed. He enjoyed how she looked with her cheeks bright pink.

"My family and I have been working so hard all week," she explained while pulling a bag of pretzels from the basket. "We're having church at our *haus* on Sunday. There's so much to do, and it seems like we never have enough time to do it. We haven't even started cleaning out the barn yet. That's what we're doing all day tomorrow and Saturday. I won't even have time to open my bake stand. I haven't had time at all to bake this week."

Jason gave her a knowing looking, then scooped chicken salad onto bread for his sandwich. "*Ya,* it is a lot of work to host church. Do you need me to come over and help?"

"Oh, no, *danki.* We'll get it done. You should come to service Sunday, though." She wiped her mouth with a napkin. "This is the best chicken salad I've ever had. I'd like to get the recipe from your *mamm.*"

"I'll ask her for it." He bit into his sandwich.

"So, will you come on Sunday?" she asked.

He cleaned his mouth with the napkin and nodded. "*Ya*, I'd love to come."

"Great. I won't be able to visit with you before Sunday, so I was hoping to get a chance to invite you. You should give me your phone number so I know how to reach you."

"I will. And I'd love to come on Sunday. After we're finished eating, let's go for a walk around the pond," he suggested.

"Okay."

Veronica talked about her garden and then baking while they finished their sandwiches and pretzels. As he listened to her, he kept thinking about Seth. He wondered if Seth had enjoyed Veronica's smile as much as he did. Had Seth loved how adorable she looked when she was embarrassed? Did Seth ever get the chance to see her covered in dirt after working in the garden? Had Seth ever brought her to this same pond for an impromptu picnic?

You need to tell her the truth.

The voice that had warned him so many times before resounded in the back of his mind. It was time. He couldn't wait any longer. He was already deeply attached to Veronica, and he needed to be upfront and honest with her. Veronica deserved his honesty.

"Are you ready for pie?" she asked.

"*Ya*, I'm always ready for your pie. *Mamm* will understand if we don't eat the cookies she gave me."

She cut each of them a piece, and they both started eating.

"You were right about the weather this week," she commented. "It hasn't rained yet."

He brushed his napkin across his mouth. "That was more a comment about how I feel lately rather than about the weather."

"What do you mean?" she asked.

"Lately I've been in such a *gut* mood that I wouldn't care if it rained." Jason forked another bite of pie into his mouth.

Veronica smiled as she pushed her fork through her piece. "I know what you mean."

He felt elated as he finished eating.

"Do you still want to go for a walk?" Veronica asked.

"Yes, I do." Jason packed up the food and stowed the basket and quilt in the buggy. "Are you ready?"

"*Ya.*" Veronica brushed her hands down her apron.

"You look perfect," he told her.

She gave him a shy smile. "*Danki.*"

"Let's enjoy this *schee* day." He held out his hand, and she hesitated for a short moment. But then she took it, and they walked side by side around the pond. He enjoyed the warm, soft feel of her small hand in his. The day couldn't be any more perfect.

"Remember how I told you I dreamed about Seth a lot?" she asked, looking out over the pond.

Jason's shoulders tensed at the sound of his friend's name. "*Ya,* I do."

"I used to dream I was trying to save him or I was cemented in one spot while he was falling. I'd wake up sobbing and feeling guilty for not being able to save his life. Those nightmares have stopped." Veronica smiled up at him. "I think it's because of you."

Guilt squeezed at his chest. "I need to tell you something."

"What?" Her eyes sparkled with curiosity in the afternoon sun.

"I know how you feel."

"What do you mean?" She searched his eyes.

He had to tell her. But what would she think of him after she knew the truth? Would she ever trust him again? He studied her. He couldn't stand the thought of losing her, not after their friendship had progressed this far.

Her expression crumpled. "Is something wrong?"

"No." He spotted purple asters growing next to a nearby tree. He picked four of them and handed them to her. "You've taken away my nightmares too."

Veronica held the flowers gingerly, as if they were made of glass, and smelled them. "They are so *schee. Danki.*"

Why was he such a coward? She deserved to know the truth. He opened his mouth to tell her.

Veronica looked up at him again. "I've had a wonderful time this afternoon, but I need to get back and help with the chores."

"I understand," Jason said. "I've kept you away long enough."

Veronica held on to the flowers as they walked back to the buggy together. She climbed into the passenger side and smiled over at Jason as he took the reins. Jason kept his eyes on the road, and his expression remained pensive. Was something bothering him?

But then he reached over and squeezed her hand. "*Danki* for letting me steal you away this afternoon."

"*Danki* for rescuing me from my chores." Veronica looked out the window and breathed in the warm, fresh air. "I can't believe next week will be September. The summer went by quickly."

"*Ya*, it did," he agreed.

Veronica smelled the beautiful purple flowers and closed her eyes. The afternoon had been perfect. Her heart was bursting with . . . love?

Was she falling in love with Jason?

The question gripped her heart. Was it too soon to feel this way? Should they know each other longer before feeling this deep connection? Could he possibly love her too? He'd told her the weather always seemed sunny to him now. Did he say that as a way of telling her he loved her?

Veronica stole a quick glance at Jason and found him staring at the road in front of them. She longed to ask him how he felt about her, but her intuition told her he felt the same way. After all, he'd brought her gifts, and he even left work early today to see her. Of course he loved her.

The thought settled in her soul, and she felt euphoric. Veronica had managed to find love again after a tragedy that rocked her to the core. Her mother was right when she said she would, but Veronica had never imagined that she'd find love so soon after losing Seth.

"We'll have to go back there," Jason said as he guided the buggy onto her street. "We didn't get a chance to skip stones."

"*Ya*," Veronica agreed. "We'll have to be sure to do that next time."

"You still need to teach me to skip them like you do."

"Oh, that takes a lot of practice," she teased. "We'll have to visit that pond a few more times if you want to become an expert like me."

He grinned at her. "That sounds like a plan then. You'll owe me three more picnic lunches with time set aside for stone skipping."

"That's a date—or rather three dates," she promised.

Jason guided the horse into her driveway, and she frowned. The time had gone by too quickly.

"Please tell your *mamm* thank you for the delicious chicken salad."

"I will." He halted the horse in front of the barn.

"Would you like the rest of the pie?" she offered.

"I'll take it if you don't want it," he said.

Veronica placed the pie on the passenger seat. "And you'll come to church on Sunday?"

"*Ya,* I'll be here."

Jason leaned across the seat toward her and touched her cheek. His light-brown eyes were intense, causing her mouth to dry and her breath to hitch in her chest. Was he going to kiss her? Was she even ready for him to kiss her? It seemed too sudden and too soon, but at the same time, she wanted him to kiss her.

"I'll see you Sunday," Jason whispered before turning his attention back to the reins.

"Good-bye," Veronica whispered in return, her voice stuck in her dry throat. She climbed from the buggy and carried her flowers to the house, stopping to wave as the buggy made its way back down the driveway.

Veronica found her mother and Emily in the kitchen, wiping down the stove and the cabinets.

"Veronica!" Emily rushed to her. "How was it?"

"I had the best time." Veronica sighed as she pulled a vase from the cabinet and filled it with lukewarm water before placing the flowers in it. "We had chicken salad sandwiches and raspberry pie. Then we walked around the pond and talked." She held up the vase. "And he picked flowers for me."

Emily smelled the flowers with a dreamy expression. "That's so romantic. I hope I can find someone romantic like that someday."

"You will, Emily." Veronica set the vase on the window sill above the sink and then looked at her mother. "*Mamm,* I think I'm falling in love with Jason." Her smile deepened as she revealed her thoughts out loud. "I can't believe it. It feels like a dream, but I really think I've found love again, just as you said I would."

Mamm's eyes shimmered with tears as she smiled. "I'm so *froh* for you."

2">

"Danki." Veronica turned to Emily, who hugged her. "I'll never forget Seth, but I realized I can love Jason too."

Mamm hugged her. "That's how it should be."

Veronica looked at the flowers and smiled. She was thankful, not only that her soul was healing, but that she had found love again.

CHAPTER 16

JASON CLIMBED OUT OF HIS BUGGY SUNDAY MORNING AND nodded greetings to some familiar faces, people he recognized from youth gatherings and businesses in town. He scanned the packed yard looking for Veronica, but he imagined she was with friends, greeting them before the service.

"Jason!" Leroy stepped away from a group of men and shook Jason's hand. "I'm so *froh* you made it. Veronica said you were going to join us for church today."

"*Danki.* I'm glad to be here."

Leroy glanced behind Jason's shoulder. "Did your family come with you?"

"No, they didn't. I invited them, but my *mamm* promised she and *Dat* would go to her sister's district today, and my *bruder* wanted to stick with ours to be with his girlfriend. They send their regards."

"Well, be sure to bring them sometime when they're available."

"I will. *Danki,*" Jason said, touched by Leroy's hospitality.

"Jason!" Hank Ebersol joined the two men. "It's *gut* to see you."

Jason shook Hank's hand and greeted him, then said hello to a few of the older men's friends, all older, married members of the district.

He was discussing the rising cost of lumber with the group when he felt a hand touch his shoulder. Turning, he found Veronica smiling at him.

Clad in a forest green dress and black apron, her eyes were bright and her smile was warm. "You made it."

"I promised you I would." Jason took in the sight of her dress, and it suddenly occurred to him that she wasn't wearing black this Sunday. She was no longer in mourning. His spirits soared.

"Veronica!"

Rachel called to her from the porch steps.

"I need to go, but we'll talk later. Stay after the service, okay?" Veronica asked.

"Of course I will." Jason planned to ask her if he could see her tonight. He'd spent the evenings during the past week working in his father's shop late at night, making her a gift. He couldn't wait to give it to her, but he had to wait until they were alone.

"I'll see you later," Veronica said before hurrying off to join her sister.

Rachel smiled and waved at Jason, and he returned the gesture. Both her sister and her father had already made him feel welcome this morning. He was thankful for their acceptance, but he worried their feelings toward him would change once they found out the truth about his knowing Seth.

"So, Jason," Hank said. "How far do you live from here?"

"I'm in Gordonville." Jason talked to Hank about traffic and shortcuts while they waited for the time to file into the barn. Soon it was nine o'clock, and Jason made his way inside. The familiar aroma of animals, hay, and dust settled over him as he sat with the other unmarried men. Jason was talking to another young man when he noticed the young, unmarried women coming into the barn.

His eyes settled on Veronica as she walked with her sisters. She met his stare, and when she gave him a little wave, he felt exhilarated. He knew at that moment that he loved her. His feelings for her were much stronger and deeper than anything he'd ever felt for Arie. The urge to tell her how he felt overwhelmed him. He would tell her later today when they were alone. The thought both excited and terrified him. He could only hope she felt the same for him.

Once all the members of the congregation were seated, the service began with a hymn, and he joined in as the congregation slowly sang the words. Jason concentrated on his feelings for Veronica as he sang. He recalled how close he was to telling her the truth during their picnic on Thursday. He needed to find a way to harness his courage tonight. He couldn't afford to be afraid any longer. Their love couldn't thrive if he continued to keep such a tremendous secret from her.

Jason was still deep in thought when the ministers returned during the last verse of the second hymn. One of them began the first sermon, and his message droned on like background noise to the thoughts swirling in Jason's head. Although he tried to focus on the service, he couldn't stop looking across the barn. Veronica caught his eye, and a smile formed on her pink lips. Butterflies fluttered in his stomach as he smiled back at her.

The first sermon ended, and Jason knelt in silent prayer along with the rest of the congregation. He closed his eyes and prayed.

Lord, thank you for bringing Veronica into my life. Please help me explain to her how I found her and why I kept my friendship with Seth a secret from her. I know I should've been honest from the beginning, but now I fear losing her when I tell her the truth. Guide my words, and when she learns the truth, please soften her heart toward me. In Jesus' holy name, amen.

When the service was over, he helped a few of the other men convert the benches into tables and then sat and talked with them while they waited for their lunch. He looked up as Veronica moved past him and nodded a greeting. He couldn't wait to talk to her later.

"I saw Jason during the service," Emily said as they filled trays with food in their kitchen. "That's nice that he came today."

"*Ya,*" Rachel chimed in as she picked up a coffeepot. "You got to see him Thursday and then again today. You must be excited."

"I am." Veronica nodded and lifted a tray filled with bowls of peanut butter spread. "I've asked him to stay after lunch too. I thought he could spend some time with the family."

"You don't want to go to the youth gathering?" Emily asked, looking surprised.

"No, I'd rather be with him," Veronica said with a shrug. "We'd better get the food out there before the men start complaining."

Veronica smiled at Jason as she delivered food to his table. She couldn't wait to talk to him later.

After lunch, with the help of some of their guests, the Fisher women cleaned up the kitchen. Then Veronica walked outside to find Jason. She had seen him talking to her father earlier. She spotted Tillie, Hank's wife, and walked over to the woman with graying brown hair and kind, deep-brown eyes. She and Hank had lived next door to Veronica's family for as long as she could remember. *Dat* and Hank had grown up together, and they both worked as apprentices for the same leatherworker in Ronks when they were teenagers. They saved their money and opened their own shop when they were in their twenties. Since Veronica and her siblings had known Tillie and Hank all their lives, they considered them to be like an aunt and uncle instead of only their neighbors.

"*Wie geht's?*" Tillie asked, touching Veronica's hand. "How are you doing?"

"I'm doing fine, *danki*." Veronica smiled. "How are you today?"

"I'm *gut*." Tillie's attention moved to Veronica's dress. "I noticed that you're wearing color today instead of dressing in black. Does that mean you're feeling better?"

"I am, *danki*," Veronica said. "I still miss Seth, but it's getting a little easier."

"*Ach*, Veronica." Tillie's eyes brightened. "I'm so glad to hear you say that. Hank and I have been so worried about you. You've been through so much."

"I appreciate your concern." Veronica's thoughts turned to Jason. "I've actually met someone."

"You have?" Tillie said with obvious curiosity. "Who is he?"

"His name is Jason."

"I had no idea. Your *mamm* hasn't told me. How did you meet him?"

"He visited my bake stand, and we became *freinden*. He came to service today. He's tall and has brown hair and eyes. He was talking to my *dat* earlier." She looked around the yard, finding only Hank talking to David. She would have to ask Rachel about that later.

"Now that you mention it, I think I saw Jason with your *dat*," Tillie said with a smile. "He's handsome."

Veronica nodded. "*Ya*, he is, and he's very sweet and easy to talk to. I feel like God sent him to help me through my grief. I'm so thankful."

"That's *gut* to hear."

"Did you happen to see where they went?"

Tillie pointed toward the store. "I think they went into the shop. I heard them talking about tools or something. You know how *buwe* get."

"*Danki.* I'll talk to you later."

Veronica surveyed the driveway, which had been clogged with buggies earlier, and found it empty. The members of the congregation had left for the day, and the youth, including Emily, probably by now had left to go to another farm for their gathering. Rachel must be somewhere waiting for David. The bench buggy, which had transported the benches they used for the service, sat parked by the open barn door. Since no work was allowed on Sundays, her *dat* and Hank would load them up tomorrow and take the buggy to the next home that would host the service in two weeks.

Veronica walked over to the store, her shoes crunching on the rock path that ran from her house to the front door of the store. She moved up the path and opened the door, causing the bells attached to it to jingle. She breathed in the familiar scent of leather and walked past the displays of bags, leashes, and blankets on her way to the workroom. Veronica found Jason and her father deep in conversation as they sat on stools next to the long workbench. They were oblivious of her presence, despite the loud bells that had rung when she'd entered the store.

She leaned against the doorway that separated the store from the workroom and watched them, enjoying their discussion of leatherworking and tools. She admired Jason, taking in his handsome face and serious eyes while he talked to *Dat*. He looked like he fit in with her family, like he belonged there. Was Jason her future? Would she take his name and build a home and family with him?

The thoughts swept through her and sent goose pimples down her arms. She knew her feelings were growing for him, but she hadn't thought about marriage yet. Was she pushing herself too quickly into those feelings, or were they genuine?

Jason turned toward her, and his eyes widened. "Veronica?"

Dat looked over his shoulder. "How long have you been standing there?"

Veronica shrugged. "A few minutes."

"Are you spying on us?" Jason's face formed a mock frown. "You do realize we were discussing top-secret men topics."

Veronica rolled her eyes. "Trust me when I tell you that I am not interested in your top-secret men topics."

Dat laughed. "She's never had the slightest interest in this store. Emily is my *dochder* who wants to come out here and work."

"You know I'd rather bake than run a cash register." Veronica ran her fingers over the doorframe.

"I'm sorry for stealing Jason from you," *Dat* said. "He asked me about one of my projects, so I thought I'd show it to him."

"Oh." Veronica smiled. "I just was wondering where you were. I was hoping you hadn't left."

"I told you I wouldn't." Jason glanced over her.

"I'm glad you didn't leave." She gestured town the door. "*Mamm* and I will be putting supper together in a while. Can you stay that long?"

Jason nodded. "Yes, I'd love to."

"All right. You two have fun. I'll see you later." Veronica smiled as she walked back toward the house. Jason fit in so well with her family. Was she ready to give him her heart?

LATER RACHEL PLACED THE TUNA CASSEROLE VERONICA made into the oven to warm.

"Rachel," Veronica said, "I saw David out there talking to Hank earlier. Is David staying for supper?"

"*Ya.*" Rachel set the timer on the stove and smiled. "I took your advice, and we talked the other night. He told me he was feeling distant from me too. We worked things out, and I feel better about our relationship now."

"Oh, that's *gut.*" Veronica washed her hands at the sink. "I'm so glad it worked out for you. I thought you were going to the youth gathering with Emily tonight. I was surprised to see David here."

Rachel began pulling dishes out of the cabinets. "It was David's idea to stay. He said he wanted to spend more time alone with me. He feels like we have too many other *freinden* around us all the time, and we don't have much time to talk in private."

"That's really nice that he wants to spend more time alone with you," Veronica said. "I'll help set the table. Jason is staying for supper too."

"This will be fun." Rachel beamed. "Our boyfriends can get to know each other."

"Right." Veronica let the word reverberate through her mind—*boyfriend.* She hadn't called Jason that, but he seemed to have already earned that title. Did he consider himself her boyfriend?

Veronica let that question filter through her mind while she and Rachel prepared the table for supper. Rachel put out the plates and utensils, and she set out a pitcher of water and glasses.

Once the tuna casserole was warm, Rachel and Veronica called the men into the kitchen for supper. Veronica sat with Jason, and Rachel and David sat across from them. *Dat* and *Mamm* sat at their usual spots on either end of the table. David and Jason talked about woodworking while Veronica and Rachel discussed their plans for the week.

When supper was over, Rachel and Veronica washed and dried the dishes and *Mamm* wiped the table and swept the floor.

"David and I would like to sit on the porch," Rachel told Veronica as she wiped her hands on a dish towel. "Is that okay? I know you and Jason like to sit there, but I was hoping to have some more time to talk to David alone."

"It's fine," Veronica insisted. "I'm sure Jason and I can find somewhere to go. Maybe we'll go for a walk."

"*Danki.*" Rachel hugged her. "You're the best *schweschder.*"

"I'm going to tell Emily you said that," Veronica teased.

Veronica and Rachel found Jason and David standing out by the barn.

"David," Rachel said, walking up to him. "Would you like to sit on the porch with me for a while?"

"Sure," David said. "I'll talk to you later, Jason."

As Rachel and David walked around the house, Veronica let Jason know they had a decision to make. "We lost our spot. Where would you like to go?"

"I haven't seen your *dat's* pasture," Jason said. "Do you want to walk over there?" He pointed toward the fence around the perimeter of the small pasture.

"That sounds nice." Veronica fell in step beside him, and he took her hand in his. They walked the length of the fence and discussed their plans for the week.

Just as the sun was starting to set, they made their way back to the driveway. Jason retrieved his horse from the barn, hitched him to the buggy, and said, "Let's talk a little longer."

Leaning against the buggy, his focus moved down to the pasture, and he seemed to be deep in thought.

He turned toward her. "I had a nice time with your *dat* today."

"*Gut.*" She sidled up to him. "You two were so busy talking that you didn't even hear the bells on the door when I came into the store."

"Your *dat* is so *schmaert*. I could learn a lot from him."

"I can tell he likes you." Veronica smiled. "I think he wishes he'd had a son, too, so he enjoys when young men show an interest in his work."

Jason nodded. "I can see that. Veronica, I have to tell you something." He paused, and she felt anticipation rushing through her. "I'm falling in love with you." His voice was hoarse, and his expression was wistful.

Her mouth dried.

"I know it's too soon, but I have to tell you how I feel. I can't keep it inside any longer." Jason's eyes were intense. "I think about you all the time. You're my first thought in the morning and my last thought as I fall asleep at night. I'm crazy about you."

He paused as if awaiting her response, but she felt as if her shoes were fused to the ground. A lump choked her throat, her tongue wouldn't budge, and she lost her ability to speak.

"I made you something," Jason continued while reaching into the back of his buggy. "I brought home some scrap lumber, and I made you this." He lifted a small shelf that was stained a light brown. Four hooks were attached to the bottom. "I thought you could hang this in the kitchen. The hooks are for you to hang your favorite cooking tools, like your spatulas or measuring spoons."

Jason handed the shelf to Veronica, and she absently ran her fingers over the smooth wood and hooks.

He loves me.

The words repeated in her mind as she continued to inspect his gift.

"Do you like it?" he asked.

"*Ya.*" She smiled at him, her eyes misting with tears. "It's perfect. It's *schee.*" *You love me! You love me!*

"I wanted to give you something special," Jason continued. "Something I made for you, and something you could use every day and think of me. I hope you like it." His brown eyes pleaded with her, nearly begging for her approval.

"I know just where I'm going to hang it. *Danki,* Jason. It's *wunderbaar.*" She held the shelf to her chest. She wanted to tell him that she loved him, too, but she couldn't bring herself to form the words. Something intangible was holding her back, strangling the words in her throat.

"It's getting late. I better go home."

"I'm so glad you came over today."

"I am too." Jason touched her shoulder.

Veronica's body trembled as he leaned toward her. She closed her eyes, trying to stop herself from quaking as he moved closer. She could feel his breath on her face, and she was positive he was going to kiss her. She wanted him to kiss her, but it didn't feel like the right time. Was he moving too fast? Suddenly his lips brushed over her cheek, as faint as a whisper on the wind.

"*Gut nacht,*" he whispered before climbing into the buggy.

"*Gut nacht,*" she breathed, her body still vibrating from the feel of his tender kiss and the news that he loved her.

Veronica stood mesmerized as his buggy moved down the driveway. Then, as she made her way into the house, emotions swirled inside her. She found her mother sitting in the family room, reading her Bible by the light of a propane lamp.

"*Mamm,*" Veronica said, her voice thick. "He told me he loves me." She lowered herself into the chair beside her mother. "He loves me, *Mamm.* He loves me." Her eyes clouded with tears.

"Oh, Veronica." *Mamm* placed the Bible on the table beside her. "That's *wunderbaar.*"

"I didn't know what to say." Tears streamed down Veronica's cheeks. "I was so stunned that I couldn't speak. I had thought he might feel that way, but I never thought I'd hear him say it so soon."

"How do you feel about it?" *Mamm* asked.

Veronica breathed a deep sigh. "I'm *froh*, I'm overwhelmed, and I'm scared. It's just so soon." She examined the shelf in her lap. "He made me this beautiful shelf to use in the kitchen. He said I should hang my favorite cooking utensils on it." She held up the shelf, and *Mamm* smiled.

"That's so *schee*. What did you say?"

"I thanked him." Veronica's bottom lip quivered. "*Mamm*, I'm terrified. I'm positive that I love him, too, but I couldn't say the words out loud." She paused as fear gripped her. "I'm afraid of losing him like I lost Seth," she whispered.

"Oh, Veronica." *Mamm* took her hand in hers. "Don't let that fear paralyze you. If this feels right, then follow your instinct. Don't let yourself be too afraid to fall in love. You lost Seth, and it shattered you. Now it's time for you to start over. This is a new relationship and a new chance at love. Embrace it and enjoy it."

Veronica stood and wiped her eyes. "*Danki, Mamm.* I know you're right. I'm going to go to bed."

"*Gut nacht*," *Mamm* said. "Sleep well."

"You too." As Veronica walked past the front door, she heard muffled voices and hoped her sister was having a good visit with David.

She went into the kitchen and placed the shelf on the counter. She ran her fingers over it and recalled the electricity in Jason's eyes when he told her he loved her. She closed her eyes and held her breath while she concentrated on her feelings.

Jason loved her.

Veronica loved him.

Jason was the answer to the fervent prayer her family had sent up to God. Jason was her future, and she was ready to embrace him. She was ready to tell him she loved him too.

CHAPTER 17

JASON ROLLED ONTO HIS SIDE IN BED AND LOOKED AT THE open window where a faint breeze brought a tiny, teasing hint of cool air into his hot, stuffy bedroom. He'd tried counting sheep and praying. He also tried to turn off his thoughts, but he couldn't fall asleep.

When Jason closed his eyes, he only saw Veronica's beautiful face with her eyes wide after he'd told her he loved her. He saw the awe in her expression when he gave her the shelf. Did she love him, too, or had he pushed too far too soon yet again?

Now there was no going back. He'd opened his heart and let her in. Yet he still had one problem—he hadn't told her the truth about Seth. The guilt was suffocating him, tearing at his soul and keeping him awake. He had to tell her. But how?

He suddenly missed Seth more than ever. He and Seth used to enjoy long talks at work. They discussed everything from building techniques to their hopes and dreams. Right now Jason longed to be able to talk to his best friend and share his confusing feelings for Veronica.

Jason covered his face with his hands as he realized the irony in that thought. How could he have ever shared his feelings for Veronica when she was supposed to have married Seth?

Jason needed someone to talk to right now. He needed Stephen's advice. His younger brother always seemed to know what to do in difficult situations, and he knew for sure that Stephen would be honest with him.

He popped out of bed and padded down the hallway, his bare feet slapping against the hardwood floor. He gingerly turned the knob on Stephen's door and then pushed it open, the door moaning in protest. His eyes adjusted to the dark, and he spotted his brother lying on his back, a soft snore growling from his throat.

"Stephen," Jason hissed. "Stephen!"

Stephen snorted loudly and sat up. "Huh?"

"Stephen," Jason said again, stepping softly into the room and closing the door behind him. "Are you awake?"

Stephen rubbed his eyes and yawned. "I am now. What do you want?"

"I need to talk." Jason pulled a chair over to the side of the bed.

With a groan, Stephen flopped onto his side, burying his face in his soft pillow. He raised his head again, and the bright green numbers on his battery-operated digital clock reflected against his face. "Can't this wait until tomorrow? It's nearly two o'clock in the morning."

"No, I need to talk to you now. It's about Veronica."

Stephen groaned again. "What now?"

"I need your advice. You know I went to church at her parents' *haus* today." He recounted how he'd spent the day with her family, took her for a walk around the pasture, gave her the shelf, and told her he loved her.

"So you love her," Stephen said through a yawn. "I'm *froh* for you. Now may I please go back to sleep?"

"That's not all," Jason said, and his brother blew out another frustrated moan. "Please, Stephen, just listen. The problem is that I haven't told her how I found her. I haven't told her I knew Seth. Really, the truth is that Seth was my best friend."

Stephen sat up straight in the bed and flipped on the Coleman lantern on his nightstand. His face was ghostly pale in the sudden light. "Wait a minute," he said in clear, alert tones. "Let me get this straight. You've been seeing Veronica for a couple of weeks now, right?"

Jason nodded. "That's right."

"You've told her you love her, but you haven't told her you knew Seth?"

Jason nodded again.

Stephen glowered. "Why haven't you told her?"

"I'm afraid of losing her."

Stephen ran his hand down his face with irritation. "Jay, you do realize this will change everything. She's going to think you're a liar because, essentially, you've been lying to her since the first time you met her. You acted as if you'd never seen her before you went to her bake stand, and you've kept acting like that was the first time you ever saw her. You can't base a successful relationship on lies."

Jason's throat dried as renewed apprehension took hold of him.

"You know I'm right, Jay. You have to tell her, and you need to tell her as soon as possible."

Jason nodded and shoved his hands through his hair. "This is going to crush her faith in me."

"You knew that all along," Stephen insisted. "I told you from the beginning to be honest with her."

"*Ya*, I know." Jason shook his head. "Now I have to face the consequences."

"Right." Stephen yawned again. "We'll talk more tomorrow. Go to bed."

"All right." Jason stood and pushed the chair back to the wall. "*Danki. Gut nacht.*"

"You mean *gude mariye.*" Stephen flipped off the lantern. "Go to sleep."

Jason pushed the door open and stepped into the hallway.

"Jay," Stephen called to him.

"*Ya?*" Jason stuck his head into the doorway.

"It will be okay. Just be honest with her and have faith that she'll understand. Keep reminding her that you love her."

"Right." Jason rested his hand on the doorframe. "Thanks, Stephen." He softly closed the door and then shuffled back to his room. When he flopped down on his bed, he didn't feel much better, but he knew what he had to do. It was time to stop procrastinating and face the truth. He had to do it if he truly wanted to have a future with Veronica.

THE FOLLOWING MORNING JASON STOOD IN THE MIDDLE OF the shop with his fingers gripping a cold bottle of water and watching Stephen help another worker build floor joists for a large shed. He'd slept barely an hour last night, and the weight of his guilt, worry, and exhaustion made his legs feel like blocks of lead. His brother's advice and his fear of losing Veronica kept his mind and stomach churning throughout the night.

"Jason?" *Dat* came up behind him. He was holding a clipboard, and a look of concern clouded his face. "Are you ill?"

"I didn't sleep last night." Jason cupped his hand to his mouth to stifle a yawn.

"Why?" *Dat* asked.

Jason gave his father a brief overview of his concerns, and his father scowled while he listened. "I can't concentrate on anything. I need to take care of this."

Dat hugged the clipboard to his wide chest. "You've made yourself ill over this, haven't you?"

Jason nodded as another yawn gripped him.

"This *maedel* means a lot you."

"More than I can express in words."

Dat paused for a moment. He lowered the clipboard and then released a long breath through his nose. "I don't think you're well enough to operate the tools," he finally said.

"What do you mean?" Jason asked.

"Accidents happen when employees aren't at their best physically or emotionally." *Dat's* eyes studied him as if trying to convey something other than the words he was speaking. "I think you need to go home and rest." He enunciated the words, as if speaking in code.

"You think I should go," Jason repeated the words.

"*Ya.*" *Dat* pointed the clipboard toward the door. "Go now before I change my mind."

"*Danki!*" Jason rushed to the front of the shop and breathed a sigh of relief when he spotted one of the shop's drivers in the office. "Joe," he called. "Would you please take me to Bird-in-Hand?"

"Sure thing, Jason," Joe said. "Hop in the Tahoe."

VERONICA HUMMED TO HERSELF AS SHE HUNG A PAIR OF HER father's trousers on the line that ran from the back porch to the barn. After spending all morning washing clothes in the wringer washer, she breathed in the fresh air and smiled. With the humidity almost gone, it was starting to feel like fall. She loved the fall, especially seeing the leaves change color. She looked forward to wearing a sweater and lighting a fire in the old stove in the kitchen.

As she hung a second pair of her father's trousers on the line, she heard the hum of an engine moving up the rock driveway. Veronica descended the porch steps and stood in the driveway, where she spotted an unfamiliar large, black SUV approaching the back of the house. She tented her hand over her eyes and tried to focus on the driver and passenger, but she couldn't see anything through the fancy tinted windows.

The truck came to a stop, and a few moments later a man climbed from the passenger seat. He leaned into the truck and said something to the driver before slamming the door and walking toward the house. The truck then slowly backed out of the driveway.

As the man in the straw hat came into view, Veronica realized it was Jason. She rushed to meet him.

"Jason!" she called. "What a surprise." Her smile dissolved into a frown when she noticed the dark circles under his dull eyes. "Jason? *Was iss letz?*"

"We need to talk." His voice was flat. "Alone."

Worry coiled her in stomach, and her hands trembled.

"Come in." She led him inside, and Jason lingered by the back door. He hung his hat on a peg on the wall.

When Veronica stepped into the kitchen, Jason followed her. Emily was washing the breakfast dishes.

"Hi, Jason." Emily smiled, but then looked confused when she saw his face.

"Emily, would you please finish hanging out the laundry for me?" Veronica asked, giving her sister a pleading expression. "Jason needs to talk to me."

"Sure." Emily dropped the dishcloth, dried her hands, and hurried out the door.

Emily glanced back at Veronica once, lifting her eyebrows and hands in concern to ask if she was okay. Veronica shrugged, and Emily disappeared through the mudroom.

"Would you like *kaffi*?" Veronica asked, setting the percolator on the stove and turning on the burner.

"*Ya*," Jason said, lowering himself into a kitchen chair. "*Danki*."

Veronica busied herself by pulling out a tin of cookies and two mugs. Jason kept his eyes trained on the tablecloth, and he seemed as if he were waging a silent war inside of himself. In the two months she'd known him, she'd never seen him so distraught, not even when she'd first turned down his offer to date her. What could possibly have upset him so much?

She sat down across from him, but he didn't look up.

"Would you like a *kichli*?" She pushed the tin closer to him and removed the lid. When he didn't respond, she placed two in front of him on a napkin. "I made your favorite, peanut butter."

His attention moved to the cookies and then back to the tablecloth.

"Jason, please look at me," she pleaded softly as her stomach roiled with apprehension. "Please tell me what's wrong."

He kept his eyes focused downward, and her anxiety deepened.

"You're scaring me," she admitted. "I can't stand this anymore. You look as if your horse dragged you across town. Please tell me what's wrong."

He took a deep, trembling breath and leveled his gaze at her. The anguish in his brown eyes sent worry rippling through her. "I didn't sleep last night."

"Why?" she asked.

"Something has been bothering me for a long time, and last night I realized I finally have to face it."

"Jason, I can't stand seeing you like this." Veronica reached across the table for his hand, but he pulled it back. The rejection caused her to wince. What had she done to push him away?

"I haven't been completely honest with you." His voice was

thin and shaky. "Do you remember when I came to see you at the bake stand that very first day? My *mamm* had asked Stephen to find the bake stand and buy some of the raspberry pies she heard about."

She nodded. "*Ya*, I do. You were very quiet. You made me nervous, actually." She tried to give a little laugh to lighten the mood, but he didn't crack a smile. Instead, his frown deepened.

"That wasn't the first time I'd seen you."

Veronica tilted her head. "I don't understand."

"I saw you in April." Jason absently drew circles on the table-cloth with his finger.

"You're not making sense." She was growing weary of his evasiveness, but she kept her frustration in check. "What do you mean?"

"I saw you at Seth Lapp's visitation," Jason said. "You were sobbing on the porch. Your *schweschdere* had to hold you up because your legs were giving out beneath you."

Veronica vaguely remembered being on the porch at Margaret's house, but that felt as if it had happened years ago. Her mouth dried. "You were there?"

"*Ya*, I was." He slumped back in the chair.

"I don't remember seeing you." She didn't remember seeing anyone, except for Seth's family and Seth's body. "I thought you didn't know Seth."

"I never said I didn't know Seth." His voice was matter-of-fact, but his eyes remained afflicted.

Icy fear prickled her spine. "Why didn't you tell me you were there?"

"There's more that I haven't told you."

Veronica braced herself as the warm smell of coffee over-took the room, the comforting aroma conflicting with the dread growing inside her.

"I work at the Lancaster Shed Company."

Veronica blinked as his words came into focus. "I thought you worked in construction."

"I do work in construction. I build sheds." He paused for a moment. "Actually, my *dat* and my *onkel* own the company."

"Wait a minute." She held up her hand to stop him. "Your family owns the Lancaster Shed Company, and you work there. And you were at Seth's visitation." The connection became clear in her mind, and she gaped. "You knew Seth."

"*Ya,* that's right." Jason nodded, and his expression was pained. "I trained him when he first started, and we hit it off immediately. He was my best friend."

This can't be true! It can't be! Veronica couldn't breathe. She gasped and placed her hand on her chest, trying to calm herself. Then she remembered Seth had mentioned a friend at work named Jason. Seth said Jason had trained him when he started at the Lancaster Shed Company, and Jason was also a good friend to him. She shook her head as the details clicked in her mind. If Seth had ever mentioned Jason's last name, it didn't sink in, though it had seemed a little familiar when Jason told her his name. But why hadn't she made the connection before today?

"He talked about you all the time, so I felt as if I knew you." Jason spoke quickly, as if he wanted to get the words out before she kicked him out of her parents' house. "When I saw you at the visitation, I couldn't get you off my mind. I wanted to meet you. I wanted to visit and offer my condolences, but when I met you that day at the bake stand, I couldn't bring myself to tell you I knew Seth. I wanted to apologize to you and tell you how sorry I was that he died. I was there the day of the accident. But I didn't want to upset you."

"You were there?" Her voice pitched higher on the last word

as her world spun. "You were there when Seth died?" Tears stung her eyes.

"*Ya*, and I'm so sorry." Jason came around the table and sat beside her, angling his body toward her. "We were working on a shed together. He was up in the rafters, and I walked away to get us some water. In that short span of time, he fell, and there was nothing I could do."

The floor seemed to drop out from under Veronica. She gasped again as the image crept into her mind. Tears rushed down her hot cheeks, and she choked back a sob. Why was he doing this to her? Why was he making her relive Seth's death?

"We tried to resuscitate him while we waited for the ambulance, but it was too late," he continued, reaching for her hand. "I'm so sorry, Veronica. It was my fault. If I hadn't walked away, I could have prevented his fall or possibly even saved him."

Veronica pulled her hand away and brushed away her tears. She couldn't keep herself from crying. This was too much. Her heart couldn't take it.

"When I met you, everything changed. My feelings for you were strong from the beginning, and I meant it when I told you I love you. I want to be with you. I just had to tell you the truth. I should've told you from the beginning, but I—"

"Stop!" Veronica said it more forcefully than she'd meant to. She stood up and backed away from him, stumbling over the chair as she moved to the opposite side of the kitchen. She had to get away.

"Veronica, please." Jason walked toward her. "Please let me explain. I never meant to keep this from you. I wanted to tell you from the beginning, but I was terrified of losing you."

"Don't come any closer." She held a trembling hand out toward him. "You lied to me, Jason. You made it seem like you had no idea I'd lost Seth, but you knew all along."

"I'm sorry." Jason's eyes pleaded with her. "I never meant to deceive you. My feelings for you are pure."

Veronica eyed him while contemplating all he'd said. Suddenly everything clicked into place, and betrayal slammed through her. "That's how you knew I liked pretzels, books, and vanilla candles."

Jason nodded. "*Ya*. That's true. Seth talked about you all the time. He told me about how you used to go over to his *haus* and play games with him and his *schweschder*. He told me about how you'd take long walks and sometimes watch thunderstorms on the porch. He shared how nervous he was when he proposed to you. He was so excited about your wedding. He couldn't wait to start building a *haus* for you."

"Stop talking!" Every detail Jason shared rocked her to her very core. She was losing Seth all over again. "You had no right to use that information against me. That was personal and private. Those were memories special to me." Her tight voice broke. She crossed her arms over her trembling body in a failed attempt to steady herself.

"I'm so sorry. When he died, I felt so lost without him, but I felt like I already knew you. I thought I could talk to you and we could grieve together. I never meant to keep that from you." Jason reached for her, and she took another step back, hitting her spine hard against the wall with a thud. "I never meant to hurt you. I only wanted to get to know you. I wanted to be with you. *Ich liebe dich*, Veronica."

"How could you lie to me? How could you act as if you'd never seen me?" The reality of his lies weighed heavily on her, crushing her soul. She cupped her hand to her mouth. "You used me." She shook her head with emphasis as the situation suddenly came into focus in her blurry mind. "No, you *manipulated* me.

You preyed on my grief and wormed your way into my life and into my family."

"No, no, no." Jason emphasized the words. "I fell in love with you when I saw you, Veronica. I never used you or your grief. I meant it when I wrote you that letter and said I wanted to be your *freind*. I'm willing to wait for you for as long as you need me to."

"Get out," she said, tears flowing from her eyes. Rage mixed with grief bubbled up inside of her. It really was as if she were losing Seth all over again. She couldn't take the pain. It stole her breath and crushed her spirit.

"Veronica, please," Jason said, folding his hands as if praying. "Please listen to me. I love you, and I never meant to deceive you."

She pointed toward the door. "Get out!"

The back door banged shut, and Emily appeared in the doorway holding a wet apron. "What's wrong?" Her blue eyes were wild with alarm.

"Get out, Jason," Veronica seethed through gritted teeth. "Don't make me go and get my *daed*."

Emily's eyes widened as she looked at Jason and then back at Veronica. "What's going on?"

Footsteps sounded from the family room, and *Mamm* suddenly stood in the doorway. "What's happening? Veronica?"

Veronica rubbed her hands over her cheeks. "I need to get out of here." She turned and rushed up the spiral staircase to her room. She slammed the door closed behind her and collapsed onto her bed, her sobs choking her as her face hit the pillow.

CHAPTER 18

As Veronica rushed out of the kitchen, Jason teetered on his legs, and he grabbed the kitchen table for support. His heart splintered into a million pieces when he heard a door on the second floor slam, echoing through the quiet house. The smell of coffee penetrated his senses as the percolator hissed and gurgled, taunting him from the far side of the kitchen. This was not how he'd hoped this discussion would go. He imagined she might understand and forgive him. He'd tried to tell her how much he loved her, but it wasn't enough. He'd pushed her away. He'd managed to do the one thing he feared the most—lose her.

"I'll go after her," Emily offered before disappearing.

"Jason," Mattie said, her eyes scrutinizing him. "What happened?"

"I finally told her the truth." Jason's voice was muted and quaky. He sank into the closest chair.

Mattie sat beside him. "What do you mean?" she asked, her blue eyes drilling into him and demanding an explanation. "What did you tell her? I haven't seen her this upset since she lost Seth."

Jason closed his eyes, and his chest ached. He'd been afraid to hurt Veronica, but now he'd caused her more pain than he'd ever intended to. Why had he been such a coward?

He covered his face with his hands, then told her the same things he'd told Veronica.

Mattie's eyes widened as she listened.

"When I first met Veronica, I thought I was doing the right thing by not telling her I knew Seth," Jason explained. "I was afraid of scaring her away. My *bruder* and my *dat* warned me I should tell her the truth, but it never felt like the right time. The deeper my feelings for her became, the harder it was to tell her."

When Mattie didn't speak, he rambled on, pouring out his feelings, her eyes boring into his with such intensity that he felt as if she could see into his soul.

His hands quaked, and his vision blurred. "Last night I told her I loved her, and I meant it. I couldn't sleep because I knew what I had to do." He shook his head, hoping he wouldn't break down in front of her. "Now I've done exactly what I feared I would. I've told her the truth, and I've lost her."

Jason recalled the pain, shock, and betrayal in Veronica's eyes when he'd admitted he knew Seth. A single tear escaped his eye. How could he hurt her this way when he loved her so deeply?

Mattie sighed. "I don't know what to tell you, Jason. This is a shock."

"I know." He cleared his throat, trying to sound more in control of his emotions than he was.

Mattie pressed her lips together, and he could feel her disappointment. His shoulders sagged with the weight of his guilt.

"She trusted you," Mattie said, her voice calm despite the hurt in her eyes. "You have to understand that was difficult for her to do after losing Seth."

"I know, and I've broken that trust." Jason studied the blue tablecloth while contemplating all that he'd lost. "How can I make this up to her?"

"I don't know." Mattie pinched the bridge of her nose. "I really don't know if you will ever regain her trust. She was so *froh*, and now this." She paused, mulling it over in her mind. "You'll have to give her time to heal. This is like losing Seth all over again. She thought she'd never love again after she lost him, but then she met you. She made a place for you in her life. Now she feels betrayed, and that broke her heart a second time."

"I'm so sorry," he whispered, his voice hoarse. "I would do anything to win that trust back."

Mattie gave him a sad smile. "You'll have to give her time to try to find that trust again."

Jason imagined Veronica sobbing to her sister, and he blew out a shuddering breath while closing his eyes. He couldn't bear the thought of her crying like she did at the viewing.

"Should I try to talk to her?" he offered.

"No." Mattie's answer was polite but forceful. "You should go. You need to give her time to calm down and work through this. She's been through too much already."

"Right." He stood. "Please tell her how sorry I am and that I love her."

"I will," Mattie promised.

"*Danki.*" Jason stood slowly and retrieved his hat from the peg by the back door. He peered back into the kitchen and found Mattie watching him. "I'm sorry for putting you through this too."

She nodded and then disappeared from his sight. He imagined her hurrying up the stairs to console her daughter, the daughter who had already been through one tragic heartache. How could he be so careless and thoughtless?

Jason walked down the long rock driveway and found the

Tahoe waiting by the road. He'd asked Joe to come back for him in an hour. He told him he'd call if he didn't need him to come, but perhaps Jason knew all along that this wasn't going to go well. Then why had he let this facade go on for so long? Why didn't he tell her the truth from the beginning? He knew the answer—because he was a coward. He didn't deserve someone as beautiful and wonderful as Veronica. He deserved to be alone.

The thought settled into Jason's chest as he climbed into the truck. He was grateful that Joe didn't ask him what was wrong during the ride home. Instead, Joe hummed along to the rock music spilling from the speakers and tapped the steering wheel with his fingers.

Jason tried to sort through his feelings during the drive. He had to prove to Veronica that he loved her and had never meant to hurt her. But how could he repair this damage? It seemed an impossible task, but he had faith that somehow he could make things right.

VERONICA HUGGED SETH'S QUILT TO HER BODY AND BUR-ied her face in her pillow as her tears flowed. Betrayal and anguish rioted within her. How could she have been so blind? Why did she allow herself to fall in love so quickly after losing Seth? She'd gotten exactly what she'd deserved after dishonoring Seth's memory so soon after losing him. She should have followed her first instinct when she'd met Jason and stayed away from him.

If only Seth had lived after that terrible accident. They had argued in the past, but he'd never lied to her. He'd never made her feel like a naive little girl. Seth had been her perfect match. She would never trust anyone the same way she trusted him.

Why did you have to leave me, Seth? I need you here with me now!

"Veronica?" Emily's sweet voice sounded from the doorway. "Veronica, may I come in?"

Veronica rolled to her side and shook her head. "Please go away, Emily. I know you mean well, but I really need to be alone right now."

"No, you don't, and I won't let you be alone." Emily crossed the room and sat down on the opposite side of the bed from Veronica. Then she climbed to the middle and rubbed Veronica's back. "I'm not leaving." Emily's voice was warm and comforting. "It's not healthy for you to keep all your feelings inside. You need to talk about it. I'm not leaving until you talk to me. What happened?"

Once Veronica shared what Jason had told her, she was grateful Emily forced her to talk about what had happened. She felt her shoulders ease. Her sister knew when she needed someone to listen.

Emily gasped more than once as Veronica tearfully told her Jason had not only known Seth and never told her, but had been there when Seth fell.

"*Ach*, Veronica. I'm so sorry he didn't tell you the truth from the beginning." Emily touched Veronica's arm.

Veronica sniffed and brushed the back of her hand across her wet cheeks. "I was naive to trust Jason so quickly, and I got what I deserved."

"No, you didn't," Emily said emphatically. "You didn't deserve this, and you did nothing wrong."

"*Ya*, I did." Veronica sat up, still holding the quilt against her body. "I let Jason into my life too soon."

Emily touched Veronica's hand. "You weren't wrong for trusting him. He was wrong for not telling you the truth the first time he met you. He should've told you that very first day he came to the bake stand that he knew Seth."

Veronica nodded and sniffed again. "I feel so stupid."

"Don't feel stupid. We all believe the best in people, and sometimes they let us down even when they have the best intentions in mind."

Mamm appeared in the doorway. "*Ach*, Veronica."

At the sight of her mother, Veronica's tears began to flow anew. There was something about seeing *Mamm* that made her fall apart all over again. She needed her mother to make it all okay again. *Mamm* pulled up a chair beside her and held her as if she were a young child.

"Why did I trust him? Why did I allow him to trick me into loving him?" Veronica asked between choked sobs. "I promised myself I was going to allow myself time to grieve. I was going to hold on to Seth's memory and guard it with all my might. I broke that promise too quickly. I let Jason in, and he shattered me all over again." She sobbed again, her body quaking.

"Shh, *mei liewe*," *Mamm* cooed in her ear. "Stop punishing yourself. You're only human."

Veronica wiped her eyes and willed herself to stop crying. "It hurts, *Mamm*. I feel like I'm losing Seth all over again."

"I know, I know," *Mamm* murmured. "It will get better. I promise you."

Veronica's vision clouded again. "It all makes sense now. How Jason knew my name before I asked him what his name was. How Seth talked about me all the time, so Jason knew all about me. He knew I loved picnics. He knew I'd love the gifts he gave me." Her voice caught. "Why didn't I see through all of that? Why was I so blind to all of it?"

Mamm touched her cheek. "Stop blaming yourself."

"I was so naive," Veronica repeated. "I thought he meant it when he told me he loved me last night. He seemed so honest, and his eyes were so intense. I thought he was like Seth. In my mind, I believed Jason was just as warm and thoughtful as Seth was. I thought Jason was genuine."

"I think he is." Emily's words were soft but firm.

Veronica turned toward her sister. "What did you say?" She was sure she hadn't heard Emily correctly. Her own sister couldn't possibly be taking Jason's side. Was she teasing Veronica, or maybe trying to make light of this grave situation?

"I think he was being honest with you." Emily's mouth was set in a serious frown, and there was no sign of frivolity in her manner. "He looked as if he was just as upset as you were."

"He lied to me," Veronica said, hugging Seth's quilt closer to her chest as if it could somehow shield her raw emotions.

"No, he didn't lie to you," Emily corrected. "He omitted the truth."

"Em, that's the same thing." Veronica shook her head. "He knew finding out the truth would upset me, so he didn't tell me. That's the same thing as lying, and it's wrong. It's a sin to lie." Why was Emily always such an optimist?

"I think he meant it when he told you he loves you." Emily shrugged. "I think you should forgive him and give him another chance."

Veronica glowered. "Why should I believe him now if he couldn't tell me the truth when we first met?"

"He made a mistake," Emily said. "I know you're hurt now. I'm sorry he hurt you, but I think he meant it when he said he was afraid of losing you. I'm not saying what he did was right, but I believe he was sincere when he said he cared about you and didn't want to hurt you."

Veronica turned toward her mother, who seemed to be deep in thought. "Did you talk to him, *Mamm*?"

Mamm sighed. "Yes, and he seems genuinely upset to me too. He wanted to know how he could get you to forgive him, and I told him to give you space." Her eyes were full of sympathy. "I don't think he meant to hurt you. Your emotions are still tender after losing Seth. You wanted to trust him, but he let you down. I'm so sorry, Veronica. I can't stand to see you suffer like this."

Veronica nodded. She could see the pain in her mother's eyes.

"You know you have to forgive him," *Mamm* added. "The hurt will get better. I promise you."

Veronica considered her mother's words. Of course she had to forgive him. That was their way. Her thoughts moved to Jason's handsome face, gorgeous caramel eyes, and adorable crooked smile. He'd stolen her heart with his warm laugh and sweet personality. She'd trusted him with her deepest secrets and most precious memories of Seth. Now she'd have to find a way to get past this hurt along with her grief over losing Seth. Lying in bed and wallowing in self-pity wasn't the way to do it.

She rubbed her hand across her face again. "Are you done hanging out the laundry?" she asked Emily.

Emily shook her head. "No, but I'll get it done."

"Let me help you." Veronica stood up. "I think the fresh air is the best thing for my mood. I need to get outside."

Mamm gave her a sad smile. "*Ya*, you're right. But, Veronica, Jason also asked me to tell you he loves you. And I believe him."

Veronica sniffed and her lips trembled as she let her mother's words take root. Then she blew out a deep sigh and followed her mother and sister downstairs. She needed to find her strength. Somehow she would overcome this emotional pain.

But how would she ever erase her feelings for Jason Huyard?

JASON FOUND HIS FATHER IN THE OFFICE, STARING AT ONE OF his accounting books. "*Dat?*" His voice was raspy with emotion. "Do you have a minute?"

Dat pulled off his half glasses as he looked up. "Jason?" His eyes widened with worry. "What happened?"

"Things didn't go the way I'd hoped." Jason pulled the office door closed and dropped onto the chair in front of his father's desk. A skylight provided enough light to give the office a warm, sunny glow that seemed to mock his bleak mood. "I told Veronica the truth, and she was crushed. I tried to apologize and explain that I love her, but she told me to leave." He detailed his conversation with Veronica as his father listened with a sympathetic expression.

Jason absently ran his fingers over his father's wooden desk while he recalled the pain in Veronica's eyes. "I've really messed this up, and I don't know how to make it better. I love her, *Dat*. I love her more than I've ever loved anyone. How can I possibly make her see how sorry I am? How do I make this up to her? How do I prove my love to her?"

Dat leaned back in his chair and steepled his fingers while considering his response. "Don't give up on her."

"What do you mean?" Jason asked. "I've already begged for her forgiveness and explained how wrong I was."

"You need to keep telling her that. You need to remind her every day if you have to. Show her you know you made a horrible mistake, but you're not going to rest until she really sees how sorry you are." *Dat* folded his arms over his chest. "If you love her, you'll have to fight for her."

Jason nodded. "I will." He stood and started toward the office door.

"Jason," *Dat* called to him, and Jason looked back over his shoulder. "If she's as special as you've said, she will forgive you. It just might take her some time to realize you didn't mean to hurt her."

"*Danki, Dat.*" Jason walked slowly from the office, and the burden of his emotional and physical exhaustion weighed heavily on his shoulders. He hoped his father was right. He vowed not to give up until he convinced Veronica he loved her and was truly sorry.

CHAPTER 19

"You were quiet during supper," Mamm said as she carried dirty dishes to the sink.

"I have a lot on my mind." Jason gathered up the glasses and placed them on the counter while she filled one side of the sink with hot, frothy water. "Could I possibly take some flowers from your garden?"

Mamm turned toward him. "What do you mean take some of my flowers?"

The idea had popped into his mind as he helped his father with paperwork earlier at work. He had been trying to think of something he could give Veronica to try to show her how much he loved her. Flowers seemed to always brighten a *maedel*'s day.

"I'm going to see Veronica tonight, and I want to give her something."

"You're going to see her tonight?" Mamm eyed him. "You look like you haven't slept in days. I think you need to stay home and get some sleep. You'll see her over the weekend."

Jason had to tell her the truth. "It's more complicated than just going to visit her and bringing her a bouquet of flowers. We broke up today, and I need to find a way to win her back."

"*Ach*, no." Mamm frowned. "What happened?"

The water was nearly to the rim of the sink and still running. Jason reached past her and turned off the faucet before it flooded the kitchen. He explained what happened when he told Veronica the truth, and *Mamm*'s hazel eyes sparkled with sympathy.

"I love her," Jason said, his voice thick with anguish. "I just don't know how to prove it to her. I know I was wrong to not tell her about Seth from the beginning, but I can't accept that I have to lose her for the rest of my life because of it. I need to find a way to get her not only to forgive me, but also to give me a second chance."

"*Ach*, Jason." *Mamm* touched his cheek. "You're on the right track." She retrieved a vase from the cabinet beside her. "Help yourself to any of my flowers. Let me get you a box to transport them." She disappeared into the mudroom and returned with a small cardboard box. "You're a *gut* man, Jason. Don't lose your faith."

"*Danki*." Jason added warm water to the vase, went to the garden, and cut a handful of bright-purple lavender, white daisies, blue lily of the Nile, yellow black-eyed Susans, white begonias, orange dahlias, and purple petunias. Then he climbed into his buggy and began the trek to Veronica's house. His hands trembled and his chest constricted at the thought of losing her forever. He prayed for the right words to convince her he loved her and wanted to make things right.

VERONICA WASHED A GLASS AS RACHEL DRIED A PLATE after supper that evening. *Mamm* and Emily had gone to the harness shop to help *Dat* clean and to balance the books, and Veronica and Rachel had stayed behind to clean up after the meal.

"Emily told me what happened with Jason earlier today," Rachel said.

Veronica nodded and kept her eyes focused on the glass while she rinsed it. She didn't have the strength to respond to Rachel's comment.

Veronica didn't want to discuss Jason. Emily had analyzed the situation at least a dozen different ways while they finished hanging out the laundry. While Veronica remained silent, Emily discussed how genuine the look in Jason's eyes was and how she believed he loved her. Emily insisted she had broken Jason's heart when she'd first rejected him, and that proved he never meant to hurt her by keeping the secret.

Veronica was thankful for her sister's emotional support, but she didn't want to hear it anymore. She just wanted to get over him and move on. She'd hoped that would be the last of her family's discussion about Jason for the day.

Then during lunch, *Mamm* had brought up the subject of Jason again. This time, to Veronica's dismay, the discussion had included her father. Veronica wanted to eat her roast beef sandwich in peace, but Emily and *Mamm* talked on and on about Jason and the power of forgiveness while they ate. *Dat* kept his eyes focused on his sandwich, seeming to share Veronica's uneasiness with the conversation. She appreciated that he didn't chime in while *Mamm* shared her feelings, telling Veronica again that she would recover from this pain and find love again.

Veronica was tired of talking about Jason, tired of thinking about Jason, and tired of wrestling with feelings for him.

"I'm sorry he hurt you," Rachel continued.

Veronica braced herself for more platitudes and advice that would only make her doubt her instinct to push him away. Why was this so difficult? She placed more drinking glasses in the hot, soapy water and began to wash another one with her dish cloth.

"Emily told me Jason and Seth worked together and were best *freinden*. I would imagine he's missing Seth too," Rachel said nonchalantly while drying the glass Veronica had placed in the drain board. "He probably thought you could grieve for Seth together."

Veronica stopped washing the glass and turned to look at her sister. No one had mentioned Jason's own grief over losing Seth before. "What did you say?" she asked, wondering if she'd misunderstood.

Rachel placed the glass in the cabinet. "I said he must really miss Seth. I imagine that was why he came to see you in the first place. I can't imagine what it would be like to lose Sharon. We've been best *freinden* since first grade." She picked up a handful of utensils. "I'm sure he's really hurting."

Veronica's hand shook and her stomach twisted. Had she been so engrossed in her own grief that she hadn't given any thought to his? Was she wrong to not even consider how Jason felt after losing Seth?

But he lied to me!

Veronica's thoughts and confusing emotions swirled together as she peered out the window over the sink. How could she allow herself to feel an attachment to a man who had lied to her?

A horse and buggy steered up the driveway, and Veronica turned to Rachel. "Are you expecting someone?"

"No." Rachel brushed her hands on her dish towel. "I'll go see who it is since everyone else is in the store."

"*Danki.*" Veronica peered out the window as the buggy came to a stop.

The back door clicked shut as Rachel strode outside. Veronica dried her hands on a towel as an uneasy feeling washed over her.

Rachel returned a moment later. "Jason is here. He wants to talk to you." Her brown eyes pleaded with Veronica. "I think you should give him a chance. He seems really sincere."

"No." The word was more forceful than Veronica had intended, and her sister took a step back. "I don't want to see him." She kept her tone even, despite her rioting emotions. "Tell him I'm not feeling well."

"But he—" Rachel began.

"Please, Rachel." Veronica rubbed her forehead. "Please respect my wishes. I've spent all afternoon and evening listening to lectures from everyone about how I need to forgive him. Right now all I need is some time alone to think. I need you to consider how I feel right now."

Rachel's expression softened. "All right. I'll tell him."

Veronica breathed a sigh of relief. She couldn't face Jason right now, no matter how much she longed to see him. The thought surprised her. Why did she long to see him? How could she even consider giving him a second chance after he'd stung her to her very core?

She really did need some time alone with her thoughts. After the dishes were done, she would retreat to her room and avoid her family for the rest of the evening. She didn't need their sympathetic expressions and unsolicited advice. And most of all, Veronica didn't need to hear how sorry Jason was. She just needed time to sort through her feelings without worrying about his.

Veronica quickly washed the rest of the dishes, cleaned the table, and then went up to her room. She sat down on her bed and looked at the candle on her nightstand. It was the sweet candle Jason had given her—the candle she had enjoyed and that reminded her of his friendship. Part of her wanted to throw it out the window. Yet another small part of her wanted to keep the candle and light it every night while remembering how happy she'd been when she was picnicking with Jason at the pond.

Why is this so difficult?

Veronica turned her attention to the window and wondered

what Jason had planned to say when he visited tonight. What could he possibly say to make things right between them? It didn't matter. She was going to close off her emotions for him—and anyone else who wanted to try to take Seth's place. Her mother had told her she needed to take time to grieve, and she intended to start right now.

Hugging Seth's quilt to her chest, she leaned back on the headboard. The quilt brought her comfort, but somehow it wasn't enough to stop the turmoil writhing in her soul. How would she ever find relief? She closed her eyes tightly.

Please, God. Please heal my broken heart.

JASON CLUTCHED THE VASE OF FLOWERS SO TIGHT HE feared he might shatter the glass. He leaned back against the buggy as Rachel made her way down the porch steps toward him. Her frown indicated the answer he'd both expected and feared—Veronica refused to see him. The trip to her house was wasted, as were the flowers he'd plucked from *Mamm's* garden.

Rachel grimaced as she approached him. "I'm sorry, Jason. Veronica said she's not feeling well." She shook her head. "Who am I kidding? She told me to tell you she's not feeling well, but honestly, she doesn't want to see you."

"I had expected that." Jason's hands shook as he held out the flowers. "Would you please make sure she gets these?"

"Of course I will." Rachel breathed in the smell of the flowers. "These are lovely." She studied the bouquet but seemed to be contemplating something else. Then she met his stare, and her expression softened. "Emily told me what happened when you came to see Veronica this morning."

Jason's stomach clenched, anticipating what Rachel might say to him.

"I understand why you didn't tell Veronica the truth when you met her," she said simply, and the tension coiling inside of him eased slightly. "You were grieving for Seth, too, and you were worried that you would scare her away if you mentioned something that was so painful. By the time you were ready to tell Veronica the truth, you cared about *mei schweschder* so much that you were terrified of losing her."

He nodded with emphasis, stunned that Rachel understood him so well. "That's exactly it. How can I make Veronica understand that?"

Rachel's frown was back. "She's very stubborn."

Jason gave a wry smile. "I've already figured that out."

"If you really love her, then you shouldn't give up on her," Rachel said. "She's upset now, but I think she still has feelings for you."

A tiny spark of hope seemed to ignite inside of him. "You think so?" he asked.

"*Ya*, I do." Rachel smelled the flowers again. "I'll make sure she gets these, and you make sure you keep reminding her how much you care about her. I have a feeling things will work out between you and Veronica."

"*Danki.*" Jason told her good-bye and climbed back into the buggy.

Rachel waved before disappearing into the house.

As he guided the horse down the driveway, Jason considered Rachel's words. Was she right about Veronica? Did he still have a chance with her? He didn't know what to believe. All he knew was that he was overwrought with emotion—grief over losing Seth, anguish over losing Veronica, and confusion over what to do to make things right with the woman he loved.

Jason guided the horse down a side road and found his way to the cemetery where Seth was buried. His heart squeezed when he spotted Margaret Lapp standing by Seth's grave. She must have walked here to visit Seth, too, maybe even to talk to him.

Jason took a deep breath, hopped out of the buggy, and after tying the horse to the fence outlining the cemetery, stepped through the open gate. His boots moved through the lush, green grass as he found his way to the small, gray, cement gravestone that marked the final resting place of Seth A. Lapp. The stone was identical to the rest of the grave markers in the small, private cemetery, but the name on it was significant to everyone who knew Seth.

Margaret glanced over her shoulder as Jason approached. "Jason?" She smiled. "How nice to see you. How are you?"

"I'm all right." Jason slipped his hands inside his trouser pockets, relieved she not only remembered him from such tragic days but seemed cordial. But of course she would remember him; it was his fault Seth was dead. How could she be so gracious to him now?

Suddenly he thought about how she and Seth's sister, Ellie, could have been at the church service the day he visited Veronica's—and Seth's—district. Or Ellie could have been at that combined youth group gathering where he talked with Veronica by the pond. He had been so focused on Veronica that he hadn't even thought of either possibility.

What would have happened if Veronica had discovered through Margaret the secret he was keeping?

"How are you?" he said, trying to push away that thought.

Margaret sighed. "Prayer keeps me going. And Ellie and I have been spending most Sundays visiting an elderly aunt of mine. She lives a few miles from here, but she's lonely. Thinking about someone else's problems instead of our own helps too."

That explained it. But he felt shame for focusing on himself, on what-ifs, while Seth's mother was helping others despite her grief.

Margaret was studying him. "What brought you out here today?"

"I've been having a rough time, so I thought I'd stop by to see him." He pointed toward the gravestone, taking in Seth's name, date of birth, and date of death etched in the cement.

"I'm glad you came." Curiosity sparkled in her green eyes. He hadn't realized Seth had gotten his eye color from her. "Seth thought a lot of you. He mentioned you often."

A lump swelled in Jason's throat. He felt he had to apologize to her once more, but he feared his threatening tears.

I have to. She deserves this.

"I'm so sorry about the accident. If I hadn't left to get water, I could've broken Seth's fall. I never should've walked away from him. I heard the board snap . . ." A single tear slipped from his eye, and his voice thickened. "I ran back as fast as I could, but it was too late. He was already . . . gone."

"Shh." Margaret reached up and cupped her hand to Jason's cheek. "Stop right now. You don't have to say anything else. No one ever blamed you for the accident. Your *dat* was honest with me. He said Seth never should've been in the rafters without a worker standing nearby. You told him you were stepping away, and it was his choice not to move to a safer area. You need to let go of that guilt and allow your heart to heal. It was never your fault."

Jason nodded and cleared his throat while willing his tears to stop flowing. "I miss him," he whispered.

Margaret gave him a sad smile. "*Ya*, I know. Ellie and I miss him every day."

"I've done something Seth would not like," Jason blurted out.

"What did you do?" Margaret asked.

"I fell in love with Veronica Fisher." Jason frowned,

embarrassed. "Seth talked about her all the time, and I felt as if I knew her even though I had never met her. After Seth died, I wanted to express my condolences to her. I met her, and then I fell in love with her." He paused and shook his head again. "I know it was wrong, but I didn't mean to develop feelings for her."

"Jason, I think that's wonderful," Margaret said. "Oh my goodness. I didn't know it was you Veronica was talking about when she told me she was interested in someone. She came to visit me a few weeks ago and told me, but she didn't tell me who it was. I'm *froh* that it's you."

"Veronica told me your blessing made all the difference to her in deciding to date me. You really don't think I've hurt Seth's memory with Veronica?" Jason asked. Even though his relationship with Veronica hadn't worked out, Jason wanted Margaret's approval. He wanted her to say he hadn't been a terrible friend by falling in love with Seth's fiancée.

"I think it's nice that Veronica found someone who was close to Seth." Margaret smiled. "I think Seth would approve, and I'm *froh* for you both. I know you'll be *gut* to her and treat her right. She needs a nice, thoughtful man who will take *gut* care of her. Seth loved her very much, and I think they had a *gut* relationship."

"It's more complicated than that." He grimaced. "We broke up yesterday."

"Oh dear." Margaret clucked her tongue. "I'm sorry to hear that." She tilted her head in bewilderment. "What happened?"

"It's my fault," Jason explained, kicking a pebble with the toe of his boot. "When I first met her, intending to offer my condolences, I didn't tell her I knew Seth. I was immediately attracted to her, and I didn't want reminding her of her pain to ruin any chance I had of getting to know her. And then as time went on, I was afraid telling her would mean losing her."

He focused on the grass to avoid Margaret's eyes. "I was wrong to keep my friendship with Seth a secret. I listened to her when she talked about how much she missed him, and I told her I understood without confessing the truth. I finally told her yesterday, and it was too late. She thinks I deliberately lied to her to take advantage of her grief and manipulate her."

He rubbed his chin. "I don't know what to do now. I can't imagine losing her, but I don't know how to get her back."

"Veronica is a strong and stubborn *maedel*."

"I know." Jason nodded. "I just had the same discussion with her *schweschder* Rachel."

"Veronica will change her mind and forgive you." Margaret folded her arms over her small frame. "She seemed very *froh* the day she told me about you. She was struggling with her feelings because she felt as if she was betraying Seth by allowing herself to have feelings for you. I think both you and Veronica need to realize that Seth is gone now. You both miss him, but you both deserve to move on with your lives. I believe Seth would bless your relationship. You both loved Seth. You'll never forget him, but you don't have to worry about hurting him by loving each other."

"*Danki*, Margaret," Jason whispered as her words sank in.

They talked for a few more minutes, and then he said goodbye and padded through the grass to his buggy.

Margaret's words occupied his thoughts throughout the evening. Seth's mother was right, but he had to make Veronica believe Seth would be thankful that he and Veronica had found each other. He hoped Veronica would see that his love for her was pure and he only wanted to make her happy.

THAT NIGHT VERONICA TOSSED AND TURNED IN BED. SHE couldn't stop the stabbing pain in her heart. How could Jason betray her like this? How could she have allowed herself to fall for him so quickly? Questions continued to assault her mind, driving the knife deeper into her soul.

Finally, she sat up and flipped on her Coleman lantern. She needed something to take her mind off her anguish. Her thoughts turned to the hope chest in the attic. Maybe she could find more forgotten recipes that would take her mind off Jason and Seth and keep her distracted. Even though *Mammi's* raspberry pie recipe had started her on a path that allowed Jason to find her—and break her heart—she wouldn't have had her bake stand without it. She enjoyed a business she could operate from home on her own.

With the lantern illuminating the way, Veronica padded out to the hallway and up the stairs to the attic, her bare feet quietly slapping the cool wooden floors. She climbed over the boxes and made her way to the hope chest. She pulled on the lid. When it didn't open, she looked for the same brass key she'd found before, but it wasn't there.

"Did *Mamm* lock the hope chest again and take the key?" Veronica whispered.

"Veronica?"

Turning, Veronica found her mother standing behind her, holding up a lantern. "*Mamm.* I didn't hear you come in. How did you know I was up here?"

"I thought I heard the stairs creak." *Mamm* had a suspicious look in her eye. "What are you doing up here so late?"

"I couldn't sleep so I thought I'd come up here." Veronica pointed toward the chest. "I can't open it. Did you lock it?"

Mamm hesitated, her expression almost nervous. "*Ya,* I did. Why do you want to look in there again?"

Veronica blinked, wondering why her mother was acting so anxious. "I just want to look for more recipes. Is that okay?"

Mamm pressed her lips together. *"Ya,* it's okay. How about I look for you?"

"Okay." Veronica shrugged.

Mamm padded to the other side of the attic, opened a small wooden box, and held up the key. Then she unlocked the chest and lifted the lid.

Veronica opened her mouth to ask her mother why she'd locked it, but then let the words disappear. She didn't want to pry. After all, the hope chest belonged to her, and it was her prerogative to lock it.

After placing the lantern on a box beside the chest, *Mamm* carefully moved items around, digging a little deeper than before.

Veronica spotted a small plastic box at the bottom and reached for it. "Are these more recipes?"

"I'm not sure," *Mamm* said, quickly picking it up herself.

"May I open it?"

"Ya," *Mamm* said, though she seemed hesitant as she handed it to Veronica.

Maybe Mamm *just wishes she could look over all her treasures without company. I'll suggest we go soon, especially if we don't find recipes in this box.*

Veronica smiled, hoping she really would find more of her grandmother's recipes inside. She needed to feel that strong connection to her grandmother again, and the recipes were the best way to find it. The season for her raspberry pies was coming to an end, and she would love to find something just as special to bake in the coming weeks and months.

She sank down onto a nearby cardboard box marked "Books," opened the small plastic box, and found a folded piece of yellowed paper. Veronica turned over the paper and realized it was a letter her grandmother had written to her grandfather.

"*Mamm*, this is a letter *Mammi* wrote. May I read it?"
"*Ya*. Why don't you read it aloud?"

Dear Mose,

As I write this letter, I'm watching the sunset outside my bedroom window. The sky is bathed in *schee* shades of purple, orange, magenta, and yellow, reminding me of that walk we took around your *dat*'s pond a few months ago. That was the perfect evening. The air was warm, and the birds were chirping their *froh* songs as we talked.

I've done a lot of thinking since our argument yesterday. I've realized now that you were right when you said bad things happen but we can't let them tear us apart. This has been both a terrible year and a *wunderbaar* year. I never imagined I would lose my *bruder*, and I had no idea his death would take such a toll on my parents. Yet I also never imagined that you and I would fall in love. For years you only saw me as Elias's younger *schweschder*, and I never expected to become more than that to you. You surprised me the day you asked me to go for a ride in your buggy so we could talk alone.

When you said I shouldn't let my grief stop me from marrying you, I was hurt. At first I thought you didn't understand how I was feeling. I was angry since you and Elias had been best *freinden*, and I thought you didn't care about Elias and were disrespecting his memory. Then I realized you do care about Elias. You were trying to tell me that even after we're married we will always keep Elias's memory close to our hearts. And Elias would want us to be *froh* together. He would bless our relationship.

Mose, I'm writing you tonight to apologize to you and to

give you my answer. *Ya*, I will marry you in the fall. I always have loved you. I even loved you when you used to tease me and tell me I was nothing but a *gegisch maedel*.

Danki for not giving up on me. I can't wait to see you again. I'm going to make you another raspberry pie so we can share it while we discuss our wedding plans.

Love always,
Ruth

Questions swirled in Veronica's mind. Her *mammi* had lost a brother? And the grief of losing him had almost cost her grandparents their marriage?

"Have you ever seen this before?" she asked her mother as she handed the letter to her.

Mamm scanned it, and her eyes shimmered in the light of the lantern. "I remember reading this years ago. I had forgotten I'd put it in here."

"What happened to *Onkel* Elias?" Veronica cleared her throat as her eyes stung with tears.

"He died in a farming accident when *Mammi* was only twenty." *Mamm* shook her head. "It was terrible. The farm was having a bad year, and it was just devastating for the family. They went through a really rough time." She handed the letter back to Veronica.

"Why didn't *Mammi* ever tell us about *Onkel* Elias?"

Mamm shook her head. "I guess it was always too painful for her to share. I thought I had told you about him."

Veronica shook her head. "No, you never did."

"I'm sorry." *Mamm* frowned. "It was never easy for *Mammi* to talk about him."

"*Mammi* almost didn't marry *Daadi* because of what happened to Elias?" Veronica asked.

"That's right. *Daadi* was best friends with *Onkel* Elias. In fact, that's how your *daadi* and *mammi* met." *Mamm* smiled with a far-away look in her eyes. "*Mamm* said *Dat* used to tease her, but it was really his way of flirting with her. He liked her, but it took him a long time to ask her to be his girlfriend." Her smiled collapsed. "And then Elias died, and *Mamm* had a difficult time coming to terms with her grief. They were very close."

"But in the end she learned to move past it." Veronica ran her fingers down the letter. "*Mammi* realized she would keep her *bruder*'s memory close to her heart, but she could still move on with her life."

As her mother's thoughts seemed to go somewhere beyond the attic, Veronica contemplated her grandmother's words and thought about Seth and Jason. Was this the sign she needed? From her grandmother? Was *Mammi* trying to tell her to forgive Jason and move on—giving her the recipe for happiness her own heart seemed to have forgotten? Her thoughts were a jumbled mess. She couldn't make sense of any of it. Maybe she needed some rest to help her sort through all her confusing emotions.

She glanced up at *Mamm*, who was now looking at her. "May I keep this letter?"

"Of course." *Mamm* stood and touched Veronica's arm. "You need to try to get some sleep."

"*Ya*, I think you're right." Veronica nodded.

Mamm locked the hope chest and then slipped the key back into the pocket of her robe. Veronica again wondered why *Mamm* had decided to keep the chest locked, but she shrugged it off.

As she followed *Mamm* down the stairs, more questions about her grandmother came to mind. How did *Mammi* overcome her grief after losing her brother? Could Veronica also learn how to move past her grief for Seth and find a way to go forward in her life?

After saying good night to her mother, Veronica climbed

into bed and read the letter again. She eventually put it next to her on the bed and fell asleep.

VERONICA AWOKE WRAPPED IN SETH'S QUILT WITH HER grandmother's letter still beside her. She was thankful she'd finally fallen asleep, but the worry and frustration that had clouded her thoughts the previous evening were still present in her mind. She needed to stop dwelling on her confusing feelings, and baking had been her escape from her grief in the past. She would pour herself into baking raspberry pies and preparing her items for her bake stand on Saturday. She also had to help coordinate the menu for the next group of *Englishers* who planned to come for a meal.

Veronica changed into a fresh dress and apron and then made her way down the stairs to the kitchen. She found her sisters and mother eating breakfast, and the fragrance of eggs, warm bread, and hash browns caused her stomach to growl.

"*Gude mariye*," Veronica said. The three women greeted her as she sat down beside Emily. She bowed her head in silent prayer and then filled her plate. "I didn't realize I had overslept."

"We thought you needed your sleep, so we didn't wake you." *Mamm* brought her a cup of coffee.

"*Danki*." Veronica poured cream into the brew and took a sip. Her attention moved to the center of the table, where she found a vase overflowing with colorful fresh flowers. "Where did those *schee* flowers come from?"

Rachel and Emily shared a knowing expression before Emily pushed the vase toward Veronica.

"Smell them," Emily said with a grin.

Veronica breathed in the sweet aroma of the beautiful flowers and smiled. "Did *Dat* bring them in for *Mamm* this morning before he went out to the store?"

Rachel shook her head. "No, they aren't from *Dat*. We don't even have some of those varieties in our garden. Jason brought them for you last night. That's what I was trying to tell you when you insisted that I tell him you weren't feeling well."

Veronica's stomach plummeted. She touched the leaf on a black-eyed Susan. "Jason brought these for me?"

Rachel nodded. "*Ya*, he did. He really wanted to talk to you."

Veronica smelled the flowers again as the room fell silent. Out of her peripheral vision, she spotted her sisters in a wordless conversation with meaningful expressions. Veronica's stare moved across the kitchen to the shelf Jason had given her. Her father had hung it for her the night she'd received it, and her favorite cooking utensils dangled from the hooks while a decorative ceramic rooster sat on the shelf. Jason had given her so many gifts.

Including a chance to love again.

Her thoughts moved to her grandmother's letter that she'd found in the hope chest last night. Could she also work through grief and make room in her heart for both Seth and Jason?

Veronica could feel her sisters watching her as if they were waiting for her to say something about Jason and the cheerful flowers.

No. She refused to allow herself to give in to their curiosity. She didn't want to discuss Jason anymore. And her grandmother's situation had been entirely different. No one had lied to her.

Jason *had* lied. It was over, and she had moved on with her life. Or, at least, she longed to move on with her life, but it seemed an impossible task.

"What do you have planned for the day, Veronica?" *Mamm*

asked, breaking the silence that hung over the kitchen like a dense fog.

"I was hoping to make some pies for the bake stand," Veronica said before buttering a piece of bread.

"We don't have many raspberries left," Emily chimed before picking up a piece of bread from the basket. "These will probably be your last pies for the season."

"That's exactly what I was thinking," Veronica said. "Hopefully we can sell them all on Saturday."

"That's a *gut* idea," *Mamm* said.

"We can get started after you finish eating," Emily suggested before biting into the bread.

"That's a great plan. We also need to decide on the menu for the next *Englisher* group dinner." Veronica felt her shoulders relax slightly. She was grateful her family agreed she should bake today. If she kept busy, then maybe, just maybe, she could find a way to forget about Jason and all the plans she'd imagined for them. She'd keep baking and remain distracted, and hopefully her heart would find a way to heal once again.

CHAPTER 20

Jason guided his horse into Veronica's driveway on Saturday morning. His breath caught in his throat when he spotted Veronica smiling and talking to a group of five *English* women who were gathered around her stand. He halted the horse across from the bake stand and retrieved a blue gift bag from the passenger side.

Suddenly his confidence in the gifts inside evaporated. What if Veronica hated them or thought they were stupid? Jason had poured hours last night into putting the gift bag together. He'd spent the day thinking about her at work, and he found himself stuck on the scent of her hair. That was when the idea of the gift bag struck him. First, he'd stopped at the drugstore on his way home from work for lavender-scented body lotion. He was thankful that a patient employee had helped him search through endless brands for that specific scent.

At home he'd spent nearly an hour walking around the pond at the back of his father's property, combing the ground for flat rocks that would be suitable for stone skipping. After he'd gathered ten of them, he stored them in a plastic zip-up bag and put them in the powder-blue gift bag he'd purchased at the drugstore. He'd picked that bag because it reminded him of Veronica's eyes.

Later that night, he shut himself up in his bedroom and tried to craft the perfect letter. It had taken him nearly two hours to write. He didn't want to come on too strong, but he had a feeling this would be his last chance to prove to Veronica that he truly loved her. He finally settled on a short letter he hoped would be enough to convey how strongly he felt about her. Then he sealed it in an envelope and slipped it into the bag with the lotion and bag of rocks.

With the gift bag in his hand, Jason climbed from the buggy and tied the reins to a nearby hitching post, then stood beside it as he watched Veronica.

Despite the dark, threatening clouds in the sky, her complexion glowed against the cobalt-colored dress she wore with a black apron. The dress made her eyes a deeper shade of blue than usual. With her gaze trained on her customers, she explained her raspberry pie recipe as they listened with interest. The women handed Veronica money, and Veronica bagged their pies, jars of jam, and jars of relish as she continued to share information about her recipes and the Amish culture.

She didn't seem to notice Jason—or perhaps she was expertly ignoring him. He had expected to be ignored again today, but he refused to give up on her. He could never give up on someone he loved with all his heart.

The women finally thanked Veronica and then piled into a maroon van before driving off. As the van motored down the driveway, the women waved to Jason as if they'd known him his whole life. He noticed one woman holding up a cell phone to take his photograph, and he looked away.

Veronica had turned her gaze on Jason. Her beautiful face clouded into a deep scowl. Her pale-blue eyes shimmered with a mixture of disappointment and bitterness. His confidence sank, and his stomach clenched. He longed to take back all the mistakes he'd made during their relationship, starting with the first day they'd met.

"Hi," he said, trying to keep his tone warm, but his voice sounded strained and nervous. "How are you?"

Without responding, Veronica slipped out from behind the bake stand counter and started toward the house.

"Veronica!" Jason raced after her, quickly catching up to her. "Veronica, please. Wait. Just let me talk to you."

She stopped at the porch steps and spun, glaring at him with fury burning in her eyes. "I don't know what else I have to do to make it clear that I don't want to see you." Her voice was laced with resentment. "Whatever we had is over, and you need to leave me alone. Just go home and forget all about me. Pretend you never knew me."

"I can't do that." He stepped toward her. "I could never forget you. My feelings for you run too deep. Please forgive me and give me a chance to show you how much you mean to me." He took a deep, calming breath and gathered his thoughts. "I made a mistake. I should've told you the truth from the beginning, but I was a coward. We all make mistakes because we're only human. Just give me another chance, Veronica. I'm begging you to listen to me. Don't push me away again."

"I've already forgiven you, but that doesn't mean we can just pick up where we left off. Some things become too damaged to be repaired." She crossed her arms over her chest. "It's too late for us."

"No, it's not. You can't possibly mean that after all we shared. You're my best *freind*." Jason's voice beseeched her, his voice faltering with every word. "I made a mistake, but we can just start over. Please, Veronica."

Veronica shook her head as her eyes glistened with tears. "I can't start over, Jason. I've been hurt once too often, and I don't have the strength to do it."

"It's easy. Let me show you how." He held out his hand to her. "Hi, I'm Jason Huyard. It's nice to meet you."

Veronica studied his hand, and her bottom lip quivered. "I can't do this, Jason. I can't take that risk with you again. It's time for both of us to move on. Mary really likes you. You should get to know her. She could be the right girl for you. I'm sorry, but we're not meant to be."

"You can't mean that," Jason said, his voice shaky with the agony of their breakup drowning him. "We have a deep connection. I know you feel it, too, or you at least felt it at one time. When we sat together at the pond during the youth gathering, you poured out your soul to me without any prompting. You trusted me the same way I trusted you when I told you about Arie. We belong together."

"No, we don't." Tears streamed down her pink cheeks, and he fought the urge to brush them away with the tips of his fingers. He longed to pull her into his arms and console her, but he knew she'd only push him away. "It was a mistake."

"How could you call that bond a mistake?" he asked, taking another step toward her. "Connections like that come along once in a lifetime."

"*Ya*, that's true," Veronica said, her voice almost as quiet as a whisper. "My connection died in April."

Jason blanched as if she'd struck him. She'd wanted to hurt him, and she did. The remark sliced right through him. "I know you miss him. I miss him too."

"You couldn't possibly ever know how I feel." She spat the words at him. "You used Seth to manipulate me."

"Why would I do that?" His voice rose with the frustration that bubbled up inside of him. "Why would I use my best friend's memory to hurt his fiancée? I only wanted to help you, but I fell in love with you in the process. My feelings for you are real and pure, Veronica. The only mistake I made was not telling you the truth in the beginning." His body shook with anger. "I'm sorry for that. I keep telling you I'm sorry, but it's never enough. What do I need to do to show you how sorry I am?"

"There's nothing you can do," she said, seething. "Please leave."

The hum of an engine behind him drew his attention to a blue sedan parking by the bake stand.

"Excuse me," Veronica said. "I need to take care of my customers."

"Wait." Guilt rained down on him, and Jason reached for her hand and then stopped before touching it. Why had he lost his temper? He wanted to convince her to forgive him, not make things worse. "Veronica, I'm sorry. Just wait."

"I have to go." She glared at him.

He held up the blue gift bag. "I have this for you."

Her expression softened for a brief moment and then hardened again. "Please stop bringing me gifts. You have to accept that this is over, Jason. You're wasting your time with me."

"I would never consider time with you wasted." Jason pointed toward the porch steps. "I'll leave this here for you."

Veronica paused and eyed him for a moment. "Have a *gut* day." She turned and started toward the bake stand, lifting her chin as she walked.

"Good morning," she called to the elderly couple who climbed from the car. Her tone was bright and sunny as if she hadn't just had an emotional conversation with Jason. She slipped behind the bake stand counter and forced a smile as she handed the woman a jar of jam and started discussing the recipe.

Jason placed the gift bag on the steps leading to the porch and then folded his arms over his chest while he watched Veronica interact with her customers. He considered standing there all day and waiting for her to take back the words that had sliced at his heart. He had to convince her to give him another chance. She couldn't possibly believe the connection they'd felt had been a ruse. She had felt it, too, but she refused to admit it. He had to make her see they were meant to be. He would fight for her.

He turned toward the harness shop where a red pickup truck was parked out front. The bright-red Open sign was displayed in the window, beckoning him to go in and see Leroy. Maybe Leroy could help him figure out what to do to help Veronica realize his intentions were pure.

Jason glanced over his shoulder at Veronica and her customers once more, then started down the path to the shop, his work shoes crunching on the rocks. He hoped Leroy could help him. He didn't want to give up on Veronica, but without some help, he had no chance of winning her back.

"THANK YOU FOR STOPPING BY," VERONICA TOLD THE ELDERLY couple as she handed the woman her change. "I hope you enjoy the pie and jams."

"Oh, I'm sure I will, sweetie." She smiled and pushed the money into her wallet. "Have a nice day."

The man glanced up and frowned. "It looks like it might rain. Stay dry."

They said good-bye and climbed into their car.

Veronica forced a smile and waved as they drove off. Once they were out of sight, she sat on a stool, and her body wilted as if she'd just helped her father's horse pull the buggy to town and then back home again. She'd never expected Jason to visit today. If she'd known he was going to come, she would've asked Emily to run the stand for her. Her heart had fractured into thousands of pieces when they argued. She hated herself for being so callous toward him, but she had to convince Jason she wanted him to stop coming to visit her. She needed him to stay away from her. It was painful for her to look at him, because every time she saw him, she remembered that Jason was there when Seth died. Jason had witnessed the accident that had taken Seth from her, but he hadn't told her about it. He hadn't shared what Seth's last words were. She couldn't bear the thought that Jason had been one of the last people to see Seth alive.

Veronica turned her attention to his horse and buggy and realized he hadn't left yet. Where had he gone? Had he gone into the house to talk to her mother and Emily? Or had he gone to her father's store?

Tears flooded Veronica's eyes as she recalled the cruel things she'd said to Jason. She told him they were never meant to be together and he belonged with someone else. She told him to see Mary. Why had it hurt her so much to say those words to him again? Why did she feel guilty for causing his wounded expression? Why couldn't she just let go of him?

And why did he keep coming back to her house with more gifts? She looked toward the house and spotted the lonely blue gift bag sitting on the porch steps. She longed to know what he had brought her today.

The front door opened and clicked shut, and *Mamm* started down the porch steps. She stopped and picked up the gift bag, then made her way toward Veronica with a questioning expression.

"I know Jason was here. I saw him out the window."

"*Ya.*" Veronica sighed. How could she be so hateful to him? He didn't deserve that. The guilt weighed heavily on her shoulders.

"What happened?" *Mamm* hopped up on the stool beside Veronica.

Veronica ran her fingers over the counter. "We sort of argued."

"You sort of argued?" *Mamm* leaned forward with a quizzical expression. "What do you mean?"

Mamm listened quietly as Veronica gave her a brief overview of the conversation with Jason, but then disapproval overtook her expression. "I shouldn't have been so cross with him, but I was trying to make him understand that it's over."

"Do you really think it's over?" *Mamm* eyed her with suspicion. "Because I have a feeling it's not over if your feelings are this strong for him."

"I don't know." Veronica shrugged as tears saturated her eyes again. "I'm so confused."

Mamm's stare moved toward the buggy. "Is that Jason's buggy?"

"*Ya*, he's still here. I thought he was going to leave. Do you think maybe he went to see *Dat*? But why would he?"

"I guess he's going to ask your *dat* for advice. I saw his expression when he was talking to you, and he looked desperate." *Mamm* placed the gift bag on the counter, and Veronica studied it. "Did he bring you this?"

Veronica nodded and brushed away a tear that had escaped her eye. A lump expanded in her throat, and she hoped she wouldn't actually sob. She couldn't allow her feelings to spill out uncontrolled. She needed to be strong. She couldn't let Jason upset her. He'd hurt her too much already. Why wouldn't this ache inside of her just go away? She was tired of feeling so conflicted. Why did Jason affect her this way?

Mamm pointed toward the bag. "Open it."

Veronica shook her head. "I told him I couldn't accept it. It's probably something Seth told him I liked, so it's not really a heartfelt gift."

"Please open it." *Mamm* handed her the bag. "He brought it over here for you. The least you can do is open it."

Veronica bit her lower lip as she opened the bag. She pulled out a bottle of lotion and studied it.

"What kind of lotion is that?" *Mamm* asked, craning her neck to read the bottle. "Oh, lavender." She pumped out a small amount, rubbed it on her hands, smelled it, and smiled. "It's lovely. Smell it."

Veronica breathed in the sweet aroma and frowned. "Why did he buy lavender? Seth used to buy me vanilla lotion because he said he loved that scent as much as I did."

Mamm gave her a knowing smile. "He's not Seth, Veronica. He's Jason, and I assume he wanted you to have it." She touched the bag. "What else is in there?"

Veronica reached in to find a bag of flat rocks. She immediately understood the reference to stone skipping, and her breath caught in her throat.

"Rocks?" *Mamm* asked, her nose wrinkling with disgust. "Why would he give you rocks?"

Veronica didn't try to explain. Instead, she peeked in the bag and found an envelope. Her name was written on the front in his slanted cursive penmanship. She took out the letter and read it.

Dear Veronica,

I'm sure at this point you're ready for me to give up and accept that it's over between us, but I can't allow my mind to relinquish you. You mean too much to me to just walk away as if nothing ever happened between us. That bond is still strong to me, and I can't just forget it. I have a difficult time believing you are able to forget it so easily.

Today I spent all day thinking about you while I was at work. I kept pondering the smell of your hair. I don't know what kind of shampoo you use, but it reminds me of lavender. I searched a drugstore until I found lavender lotion. I hope you like it. When you use it, you'll see how breathtaking your hair smells to me.

You're probably wondering why I would include a bag of rocks in your gift bag. The rocks are really more for me than for you. When you (hopefully) decide to forgive me, please bring these rocks with you when you come to see me. We can take them to the pond on my father's farm, and we'll skip stones until our wrists are sore. I look forward to that day.

I can't seem to express just how sorry I am. Instead of telling you I'm sorry, this time I'll tell you I miss you so much that my heart hurts. You're in my thoughts all day and in my dreams at night. You've become a part of me, and I can't stand the thought of losing you forever.

Please forgive me, Veronica. *Ich liebe dich.*

> Always,
> Jason

Veronica's hand shook as another tear escaped her eyes. Her chest constricted with a mixture of regret and love. She handed the letter to her mother.

Mamm read it, and her eyes misted with tears. "Oh, Veronica. That is so romantic."

Veronica swallowed, hoping to dissolve the stubborn lump in her throat. "I'm so confused," she whispered. "I don't know how to feel about him. He hurt me so deeply, and there's a part of me that can't forget that. Of course I forgive him, but I'm not ready to give him another chance." She cleared her throat while fingering the bag of rocks. "But then there's this other part of me that still loves him and wants to run to him and hug him."

Mamm touched Veronica's cheek. "Follow your heart."

"But I'm so conflicted," Veronica said. "I don't know which part of myself to listen to—the part that wants to forget him or the part that wants things to be the way they were." She lifted the lotion and turned the bottle over in her hands. He'd put so much thought into these gifts. He loved her, but she wasn't sure she was ready to love him completely. She was better off without him instead of risking her heart again. She met her mother's warm, supportive expression. "Have you ever felt this baffled?"

Mamm nodded. "I have felt very similar to the way you're feeling now."

"How did you handle it? What did you do?"

"I took my time before I made my decision," *Mamm* said. "You don't need to feel rushed, but you should pay attention to how you're feeling. Do what feels right and comfortable. Listen to that little voice in your head."

The sound of an engine alerted Veronica that another customer was arriving. She had to get herself together before they walked over to the bake stand. Veronica placed the lotion, rocks, and letter back into the gift bag, then brushed her cheeks with her fingertips.

"Do you want me to talk to the customers for you?" *Mamm* asked.

"No, *danki*." Veronica turned to her mother. "I can handle this. Would you please take my gifts into the *haus*?"

"Of course," *Mamm* said as she lifted the bag. "Call me if you need me."

"I will, *Mamm*." She faced her mother. "And *danki* for listening to me."

Her mother nodded. "I'll always listen to you. That's what I'm here for."

Mamm strode toward the house, and Veronica thanked God for her mother's love and concern.

She turned her attention to two middle-aged *English* women as they approached her bake stand. One lady had short brown hair. She was tall and thin and dressed in jeans and a T-shirt featuring a picture of a man wearing a cowboy hat. Veronica assumed the man on her shirt was a country singer. The other woman was short and plump, and her bright-red hair seemed to have an artificial hue. She wore jeans and a T-shirt that was a swirl of primary colors, which Veronica assumed was tie-dyed. Each of the women had a large leather purse slung over her shoulder.

"Good morning," Veronica said. "Thank you for stopping by my bake stand."

"We heard you have the best raspberry pies in Lancaster County," the tall woman said. "Do you have any pies left today?"

"Oh, *ya*." Veronica pulled two pies from her cooler. "How many would you like to purchase?"

"Two," the short woman said. "Wait." She looked at her friend. "What do you think, Phyllis? Should we get five instead? You said your sons like raspberries."

"That's true." Phyllis touched her lip with her fingertip. "I suppose I should get three. Do you have five?"

"I do." Veronica removed the pies from the cooler.

"Oh, look at these jams, Louise." Phyllis clicked her tongue. "We need to get these too."

While the women tried to decide which jam flavors to buy, Veronica looked toward the back of the house. She wondered if Jason was still talking to her father. He had to be in the store. What was he discussing with her father? What was her father saying about her?

Veronica gnawed her lower lip as her thoughts turned to his sweet, loving letter. Why was Jason still holding on to Veronica so tightly when she was pushing him away? It seemed as if he was positive they belonged together. If he was right, then why was this so difficult for Veronica?

"Miss?" Louise asked. "Are you all right?"

Veronica forced a smile. "*Ya*, I am. I'm sorry. I just have a lot on my mind." She turned her attention to her customers, but her thoughts were still absorbed with Jason. He had lodged himself in her heart, and now she just needed to figure out if he belonged there permanently.

CHAPTER 21

JASON STOOD OUTSIDE THE HARNESS SHOP AND STUFFED his hands into the pockets of his trousers. He was sure Veronica's father could help him figure out how to convince her he loved her. He mustered all the courage he could find and walked up the rock path leading to the front door. The bells hanging from the doorknob chimed, announcing his entrance.

Emily stood at the register, helping an *English* customer who was buying a saddle. She met Jason's stare and smiled at him. He was stunned by her warm welcome. "How are you, Jason?" she asked.

"I'm okay." He gestured toward the workroom beyond the store. "I was wondering if your *dat* is available."

"*Ya*, he's here," she said. "You can go on back."

"*Danki.*" Jason walked through the store and stepped into the workroom, where he found Hank and Leroy working at the benches. Jason cleared his throat, and they both turned toward him. He nodded a greeting.

"Jason." Leroy gave him a surprised expression. "It's *gut* to see you."

"Hi, Leroy. I was wondering if I could talk to you." He wanted to talk to Leroy in private, but he didn't want Hank to feel as if he had to leave his shop.

"Of course." Leroy stood and retrieved his hat from the peg on the wall. "Let's walk outside."

"That would be perfect." Jason followed Leroy out the back door, which led to the fenced pasture on Hank's property. The dark, foreboding clouds in the sky mirrored Jason's mood. The air was cool and smelled like rain. Autumn was teasing the late-summer day. He fell into step with Leroy as they moved to the pasture fence.

"How have you been?" Leroy asked.

Jason considered the question and found it difficult to answer. "To be honest, I'm frustrated." He leaned against the split-rail fence. "I need your advice."

Leroy nodded and placed his hand on a fence post. "I assume this has to do with Veronica."

"*Ya*, it does." Jason shook his head. "I have a feeling you already know what happened between us."

"I believe I do. Mattie tells me she's upset because she found out you knew Seth and didn't tell her. She feels you deliberately withheld that information to manipulate her somehow, and she's hurt."

"That's exactly right. I can't seem to find a way to make her understand that I'm sorry I made the mistake of not telling her the truth, but my intentions were pure, and I want to make things right again." Jason rubbed his chin with the back of his knuckles while reaching deep inside of himself for the emotional strength to put his feelings into words.

"Leroy, I love your *dochder* with my whole heart. In fact, I can see myself spending the rest of my life with her. I think she feels the same way about me, but she's too stubborn to allow herself to admit it."

Leroy smiled. "That sounds like my Veronica."

"If she truly didn't love me and didn't want to be with me, then I would drop this," Jason explained. "I don't want to force someone who doesn't love me to be with me, but it's not like that. I know she feels the connection we have. I know she feels something deep and powerful for me. I can see it in her eyes when I talk to her."

The older man nodded. "*Ya*, I think you're right. She's been moping around ever since she argued with you. I know her *schweschdere* and Mattie have talked to her, but it doesn't seem to have done any *gut*."

Jason scowled as vexation gripped him. "I've tried to get through to her. I came to see her, even brought flowers. But she wouldn't see me. Today I brought her more gifts. She just argued with me and told me to leave. She said it's time for us to move on, but I disagree. I love her too much to move on."

The compassion in Leroy's eyes surprised Jason. "I understand."

"*Danki*. I made a mistake, I've apologized over and over again, and she says she's forgiven me. But she won't give us another chance." He paused and took a deep, shuddering breath. "I'm desperate, and I'm at the end of my rope. I don't know what else to do. Would you please help me?"

Leroy rubbed his forehead and then nodded. "*Ya*, I will. I'll try to think of something that will help you." He paused, contemplating the situation. "I have a few ideas, and I'll see what I can do."

"I don't know how to thank you." Jason shook Leroy's hand as hope sparked within him.

"If you want to thank me, then just make my Veronica *froh*. I've seen her *bedauerlich* for way too long."

"If I could only get her to try again, I would make it my life's goal to make her happy," Jason admitted.

"Just don't give up. If Veronica is anything like her *mamm*, she'll eventually realize that what she wants has been right in front of her eyes all along." Leroy nodded. "You take care, son."

"*Danki*. You too." Jason shuffled around to the front of the store and down the path leading to Leroy's house.

With Leroy's help, Jason hoped he could regain Veronica's friendship. It was time for Jason to back off and allow Veronica the space she'd asked him to give her. As much as the idea stung, Jason planned to leave the Fisher place today and not come back again until Veronica invited him.

Jason rounded the front of the house and noticed the gift bag was gone. He hoped Veronica had retrieved it and opened it. He prayed she had read his letter and it had touched her deeply. The idea made him smile. Jason ambled down the driveway toward his buggy. He stopped in front of the bake stand where Veronica was helping two middle-aged *English* women.

Veronica's glance shifted to him, and her smile crumpled as her eyes locked with his. She studied him, and the intensity in her blue eyes caused his heartbeat to accelerate. It wasn't hatred that he found there; it was something else entirely. He hoped the heat glowing in her eyes was love. Had she read the letter? He longed to read her mysterious thoughts.

One of the customers said something to Veronica, and her attention snapped back to her. She answered the woman and smiled again.

Oh, how Jason missed seeing Veronica smile at him. One of the women examined a pie, and an idea took root in Jason's mind. He knew Veronica would never be rude to him in front of a customer. Jason took the opportunity to talk to Veronica one last time.

The two customers turned toward him as he neared the stand and grinned as if they'd never seen an Amish man before.

Jason smiled at the ladies. "Are you here to purchase her raspberry pies?"

"Oh, yes!" one of the ladies gushed. "We heard they are the best in Lancaster County."

"They are." Jason glanced at Veronica, and her eyes widened with shock and confusion. "I usually come here every Saturday to get one or two. My parents and my brother enjoy them too."

"It seems like you have some frequent customers," the other said.

Veronica nodded slowly, but she kept her questioning expression trained on Jason.

"I'd like to buy two pies please, Veronica," Jason said, keeping his voice calm and his smile wide.

Veronica eyed him and then pulled two pies from her cooler. "These are my last two," she said, her voice tight.

He pulled his wallet from his back pocket as she put the pies in a shopping bag.

"No charge," she said, pushing the pies toward him.

Jason looked at her, longing to see her smile the same sweet, warm smile that had always seemed to be only for him. Instead, she was frowning. "No," he insisted. "I want to pay you."

"Just take them," she said. "You're a frequent customer."

"Right." His mouth formed a thin line. So he was only a customer now. *"Danki."*

"Gern gschehne," Veronica said softly before turning her attention back to the *English* women. "Is there anything else you'd like today?"

Jason made his way to the buggy and placed the pies on the bench seat before climbing in. He glanced back toward the bake stand once more, hoping to catch Veronica's gaze, but she was focusing on her customers. He knew where he stood with her, but he clung to the hope that her father could help him. Surely

Leroy would know how to get through to the independent, stubborn daughter who had stolen Jason's heart.

As soon as the customers left, Veronica put up the Closed sign and then stalked over to her father's harness shop to see what *Dat* had said to Jason. He had seemed so different when he returned, almost serene when he'd come to buy the pies. It was as if all the tension she'd seen in his shoulders earlier had left. What had *Dat* told him?

Concern consumed her as she picked up her pace and moved up the path leading to the shop's front door.

Veronica found Emily sitting behind the register and working on the store's accounting log.

"Hi, Veronica." Emily frowned. *"Was iss letz?"*

"Is *Dat* here?" Veronica asked, ignoring her sister's question. "I need to speak to him."

"Ya, he's in the back." Emily studied her. "You look upset."

"I am upset." Veronica walked through the store and into the workroom where her father and Hank were busy making harnesses and leashes to sell. *"Dat,* what did you say to Jason?" The question burst from her lips before she had a chance to stop it.

Dat turned toward her and raised his eyebrows.

"Hi, Veronica." Hank smiled. "How are you today?"

Veronica fingered the hem of her apron. "Hi, Hank." She cleared her throat. "I didn't mean to ignore you."

Hank stood. "I'll give you two some privacy. I need to take a break anyway." He made his way into the store.

Veronica rubbed her temples where a headache brewed. "It's been a really stressful day."

"Have a seat, *mei liewe,"* *Dat* said, patting a stool beside him. "Tell me what's on your mind."

Veronica folded her arms over her apron in an effort to quell her trembling body. "Did Jason come to see you earlier?"

Dat nodded. "He did."

"What did you say to him?"

"We talked."

Dat handed her a bottle of water from the small refrigerator next to her. "He didn't stay long." He opened a bottle and took a long drink.

She tried to temper her frustration. Why was *Dat* holding back information? He was evading the question, and she was ready to scream with irritation, but she was certain her father would completely shut down if she yelled at him. She had to force herself to remain calm despite her growing resentment.

Veronica leveled her eyes at him. "*Dat*, please tell me what you discussed."

Dat took another drink and then moved the back of his hand across his mouth. "He told me he loves you, and he asked for my help showing you how much he's sorry and wants to make things right."

Veronica blinked. She'd had a feeling Jason had asked her father for help, but hearing her father say those words out loud touched something deep in her soul.

"I told him I would try to help him," *Dat* said simply. "I think his feelings for you are genuine."

Veronica nodded, speechless. Jason was so desperate to convince her he loved her that he'd asked her father for help. Emotions warred inside of her. She took a long drink of water as her body continued to quake.

Dat was looking at her intently. "Are you all right?"

"*Ya.*" Veronica stood. "*Danki* for the water."

She made her way back through the store, where Emily and Hank were talking at the cashier desk. Veronica nodded at them and continued out the door toward the house. She walked up the back porch steps and through the mudroom into the kitchen as the events of the day threatened to overwhelm her.

Her focus settled on the shelf Jason had given her the night he told her he loved her. Despite her efforts to forget him, he continued to make his way into her thoughts and her heart. Did this mean she still loved him?

The question settled deep inside of her, and she closed her eyes. No, she couldn't love him. They weren't meant to be together. She had to fight this silly notion. Jason just needed to get over her, and she needed to let go of her feelings for him.

Veronica opened the pantry door and pulled out an armful of jars of relish and then made her way back to the bake stand. She would keep herself busy until she forgot her feelings for Jason. She would look for more recipes and make more pies— just maybe not raspberry pies. She was glad all the raspberries were gone now. She wanted to forget how that recipe from her grandmother had brought Jason into her life.

That's all she could do right now. She couldn't waste time thinking about Jason. He wasn't right for her.

For the first time since she'd broken up with Jason, Veronica took the lid off the vanilla candle and lit it. She placed the candle on her nightstand and watched the flame dance in the dark silence of her bedroom. Sitting on the bed with her legs tucked under her body, she pulled out the lavender lotion. She pressed the pump and rubbed the smooth lotion on her arms, breathing in the sweet fragrance.

Veronica retrieved the letter from the gift bag and contemplated the words again. She touched the bag of rocks, imagining herself walking with Jason while they made their way around the pond where they'd had the picnic. Was this what she wanted? Did she want to make everything right with Jason? She didn't know what she wanted.

All she knew for sure was that she was bewildered, so bewildered that her vision blurred with tears. She pulled out her grandmother's letter and reread it. Did her grandmother feel this befuddled before she accepted her grandfather's proposal? She longed to talk to *Mammi* and ask her how she managed to move past her grief after losing her brother. How did she know when she was ready to move on?

"If only *Mammi* was still here," Veronica whispered.

She turned off her Coleman lantern and snuggled under her sheet. She pulled Seth's quilt to her and watched the candle's flame as it continued to flicker and dance, casting shadows on her ceiling. She rolled onto her side, closed her eyes, and opened her heart to God.

God, I'm so baffled by my feelings for Jason. In my heart, I know I love him, but I'm afraid to open my heart to him only for him to hurt me again. Please show me the way, God. Show me where I belong. Should I give Jason a second chance, or should I allow myself time to heal before I love someone else? I just don't know what the right path is for me. Please, God, show me the way. Amen.

And then she blew out the candle and drifted off to sleep.

CHAPTER 22

JASON SAT BETWEEN HIS BROTHER AND FATHER WHILE THEY ate lunch after the church service at the Zook farm the next day. The fragrance of animals and hay surrounded Jason as he sat at the long table with the other men in the large barn.

He'd spent most of the service thinking about Veronica and wondering if his efforts yesterday had made any impact on her feelings for him. But in the end he was positive to the bottom of his soul that he'd wasted more of his fragile emotions on her. Veronica had made it clear that she didn't love him anymore and that he should move on with his life. So why was it so difficult for him to accept that it was over?

"You've been awfully quiet," Stephen remarked while smothering a piece of bread with peanut butter spread. "What's going on?"

"Nothing," Jason muttered. He lifted a small pretzel to his mouth, but he wasn't truly hungry. He was exhausted and tired of trying to think of another way to prove his love to Veronica. He was burned out and had exhausted all of his ideas. All he could do now was wait for Leroy to try to get through to her. Was Veronica worth all this emotional pain?

Yes, she is worth it because I love her to the very depth of my soul.

"*Ya*, something is wrong. It's written all over your face." Stephen lifted his cup of coffee and sipped. "Did you go to see Veronica yesterday?"

"*Ya*, I did." Jason sighed and pushed the peanut butter spread around on his plate with another pretzel. "It didn't go the way I'd hoped."

"What happened?" *Dat* asked.

Jason told him the whole story. "I'm out of ideas. I'm just emotionally drained."

Stephen shook his head. "I'm sorry. I thought she would've realized by now that you're a genuine guy."

Dat's face reflected the same sympathetic expression as his brother's. "She's missing out by not giving you another chance."

Dat and Stephen shared knowing looks, and it infuriated Jason to be the object of their pity. He was tired of everyone's sympathy. He was tired of pining over a *maedel* who'd rejected him. He was just plain tired of feeling sorry for himself.

Jason needed to get out of there. Being inside the barn was suffocating. He threw down the pretzel he'd been holding and climbed off the bench.

Dat looked over his shoulder at Jason, and his face clouded in question. "Where are you going?"

"I'm not hungry. I'm going for a walk." Jason weaved past the women delivering dessert and stepped out into the midday sun.

The air was crisp, a clear sign that fall was quickly sneaking up on Lancaster County. He closed his eyes and breathed in the fresh scent of grass and earth. He took a step and walked right into Mary, who stumbled while grasping a tray of apple pies that started to slide from her hands. Jason grabbed the tray and righted it before the pies tumbled to the ground.

"Whew," Jason said with an embarrassed chuckle. "That was close. I'm so sorry. I didn't see you there."

"It's okay." Her cheeks flushed bright pink. "It's a *gut* thing you have quick reflexes. No wonder you're *gut* at playing volleyball."

Mary smiled, and Jason recalled Veronica's suggestion to pursue her. Mary was pretty, sweet, and eager to get to know him. Maybe Veronica was right. Maybe he belonged with someone else.

But I love Veronica.

"Do you want to go for a walk?" he asked, pushing the thoughts away.

"You want to go for a walk now?" Mary looked surprised.

He looked at the pies. "Oh, right. You're busy. Never mind." He pointed toward the pasture. "I'm going to walk out there and get some air. I'll see you later."

"No, wait for me," she said quickly. "Let me hand these pies to someone, and I'll join you." She rushed into the barn and then reappeared a few moments later. "Leah said she'd deliver them for me."

"Great." Jason started toward the pasture, and Mary walked quickly to keep up with his long strides. "I had to get out of there for a bit."

"Are you feeling all right?" Mary asked, her voice full of worry. "Is your stomach upset?"

"I'm feeling okay, *danki*. I just needed some time to clear my head." He toyed with the idea of telling Mary about his issues with Veronica, but why would Mary want to hear about another *maedel*? "I haven't seen you in a while. How have you been?" he asked, hoping to steer the focus away from himself.

"I'm doing fine." She smiled again. "Last week was busy, but it was *gut*. How about you?"

"It wasn't a *gut* week. I was hoping I had figured out a solution to a complicated situation, but I only managed to make it worse." He followed the fence line, and she walked beside him.

When he came to a bench located under a big tree, he sat down, and she sank down beside him.

"Do you want to talk about it?" Mary offered.

Jason smiled at her enthusiastic expression. "I don't think you would want to hear about it."

Her smile faded. "It's about Veronica Fisher, isn't it?"

Jason paused and looked into Mary's brown eyes. He didn't want to hurt her feelings, but he also couldn't lie to her.

"You can be honest with me, Jason," she said. "I know you have feelings for Veronica. I've known since that time you were talking to her by the pond at the youth gathering. I'm not as naive as most people think I am."

"I never thought you were naive," Jason told her. "You've always gone out of your way to be nice to me, and I appreciate that."

"You're my *freind*, right?" Her smile returned, and he nodded. "I know it will never work between us. We're not attracted to each other, and that's okay. We can still be *freinden*. I'm actually sort of seeing someone. He lives in Lititz and works with one of my cousins at a carriage shop. We haven't officially started dating, but we've been talking a lot. He's really nice, and he told me he likes me."

"That's fantastic. I'm so *froh* for you." Relief flooded Jason. He was thankful to no longer feel pressured to date Mary, and he was also grateful to have her friendship.

"Thanks." Mary rested her elbow on the bench's armrest. "I know Leah and Stephen were trying to set us up. I was disappointed at first when it didn't work out, but then I realized you had feelings for Veronica. When I met Tim, I knew you and I were only meant to be *freinden*." Her expression showed concern. "So what's going on with Veronica? You can trust me."

"I appreciate that." Jason shared a brief version of everything that had happened between him and Veronica. Mary listened with interest, and he appreciated that her eyes weren't full of pity. "Now I don't know what to do. I keep feeling that I need to just stop worrying about her and wait to see what her father can do to help me. What do you think?" He held his breath, awaiting Mary's assessment.

"From what you've told me, I think she cares for you. She's dealing with a lot of emotions after losing her fiancé." Mary pushed the ribbons from her prayer covering behind her shoulders. "Like I said, I could tell you were attracted to each other that night at the youth gathering, so I'm positive she cares for you. I have a feeling she'll contact you soon. Just give her some time to sort through everything."

Even though Mary hadn't told him anything he hadn't heard before, Jason appreciated her thoughts. It was a relief to hear another *maedel*'s point of view.

"Jason, you're a really sweet guy," Mary continued. "You made a mistake, but you didn't do anything unforgivable. Veronica will eventually come to that conclusion on her own."

"*Danki.*" His thoughts turned to the apple pies she'd been carrying. "Would you like to share a piece of that apple pie?"

"That sounds *appeditlich.*" They walked back toward the barn together.

"Are you coming to the youth gathering tonight, Jason?"

"No, probably not," he said as he rubbed the back of his neck. "I think I'm going to go home and relax this evening."

"Oh, I was hoping you could meet Tim. He and his cousin are coming tonight. The gathering is in Bird-in-Hand."

Jason's stomach tightened when she mentioned Bird-in-Hand. Would Veronica be there? If he went, would she even talk to him?

"You'll have to come another time," Mary continued. "You'd really like him."

"I'm sure I would." He smiled at her. "*Danki* for taking a walk with me and giving me some advice."

"It was fun." She picked up speed and made her way toward the barn ahead of him. "I'll grab us a piece of pie."

Jason considered Mary's words about Veronica and hoped she was right. He prayed that Veronica would soon realize he only wanted to make her happy.

"I DON'T WANT TO GO," VERONICA REPEATED FOR THE FOURTH time. "You two go on and have a *gut* time, but I'd rather stay here."

"No. You're coming with us." Rachel enunciated the words while they stood in the driveway. David's horse and buggy sat nearby with David at the reins looking impatient.

"We're tired of seeing you mope," Emily chimed in.

"In that case, I'll go mope in the privacy of my own room." Veronica appreciated her sisters' concern for her mental health, but she had no interest in going to the youth gathering tonight. She would rather be alone.

Her sisters exchanged annoyed looks before each took one of her wrists and pulled her.

"Hey!" Veronica protested while trying to free her wrists from their grip. "I'm the oldest, so you're both supposed to listen to me. I give the orders!"

"Today we're giving them, and you're going to do what we say," Rachel repeated.

"That's right," Emily said. "*Mamm* told us to get you out of the *haus*, and we're doing it."

They dragged her to the buggy.

"Get in," they sang in unison.

"Fine," Veronica acquiesced. "But I won't smile."

"We don't care if you don't smile," Emily said with exasperation. "Just get in the buggy."

Veronica climbed into the back, and Emily sank down beside her. With her chin in her palm, Veronica stared out the back of the buggy during the ride to the farm where the youth gathering was going to be held. Rachel sat in front with David and seemed to be trying her best to keep a conversation with him going.

What is going on with David?

"It's not so bad, you know," Emily said, leaning over to talk to Veronica. "I'll keep you company at the gathering, and Malinda said she'll be there too."

"That's right," Rachel said, turning to face them. "Malinda told me she wants to talk to us. She got a new job teaching at a special school for *kinner* who need some extra help."

"Really?" Veronica sat up with interest. She hadn't heard this news about their favorite cousin. "When did she start teaching there?"

For the remainder of the ride, Rachel filled them in about Malinda's new job and training. Soon they were at the farm, and David guided the horse toward the barn.

Veronica climbed out and walked with Emily toward a group of young women who were watching a volleyball game. Rachel and David walked in the other direction toward another group.

Veronica scanned the crowd in front of her, mentally picking out familiar faces. There were many unfamiliar faces, and she wondered if this youth gathering had been combined with a few other youth groups. The thought caused her stomach to tighten. Why hadn't she made her sisters tell her if this was another combined group?

"I don't think he's here," Emily said, reading her mind. "And if he is, then you should talk to him."

Veronica eyed her sister. "How did you know I was—"

Emily's very unladylike snort interrupted Veronica's words. "Please, Veronica. It's so obvious that you're trying to ignore how you feel about Jason, but you're in love with him. When are you going to stop torturing yourself and accept that you want to be with him?"

Veronica was speechless. Her youngest sister was right, and the truth of her words had struck Veronica right in the gut like a stray volleyball.

"Do you want to play volleyball?" Emily asked.

"No thanks. I think I'd rather watch." Veronica sank onto the ground and smoothed her dress over her legs.

"Suit yourself." Emily trotted off to join a team.

Veronica picked at a stray dandelion while her sister laughed and talked with other volleyball players. She recalled what it was like to be that outgoing and secure with herself when she was nineteen. Now that she was older and had weathered two heartbreaks, Veronica was much more guarded with her emotions.

"Veronica?"

She tented her hand over her eyes and glanced up, finding Stephen Huyard smiling down at her. "Stephen. How are you?" So Jason's youth group was here.

"I'm fine, thanks." He pointed toward the grass beside her. "May I join you?"

"Sure." She sat up straight.

Stephen sat down, stretching his long legs in front of him.

"Are you here alone?" she asked, her stomach clenching again.

"No," he said, pointing toward the volleyball games. "My girlfriend is playing on the same team as your *schweschder*."

"Oh." Veronica picked at another dandelion.

"Jason isn't here," Stephen said. "I couldn't convince him to come with Leah and me. He said he wanted to stay home and be alone."

"Oh," she repeated. *I know the feeling.* "How is he?" The question sprang from her lips before she could stop it.

"He's stricken," Stephen said. "Over you."

The sincerity in Stephen's eyes cut Veronica to the bone. She blinked, unable to speak.

"Look, Veronica," Stephen began, "it's really none of my business, but I feel compelled to tell you something. I was with Jason when he saw you at the visitation."

"You were there too?" she asked, her voice thin as emotion swelled inside her.

"*Ya*, I was, and you might remember I was also there the day we first came to your bake stand." He paused, gathering his thoughts. "Jay honestly planned to tell you the truth from the start. In fact, I warned him that if he didn't tell you we worked with Seth that he'd lose you, and that's exactly what happened."

"You worked with Seth too?" she asked, astonishment wafting over her.

"I did." He nodded. "Seth was a great guy, and we miss him. I'm really sorry for your loss."

"*Danki*," Veronica whispered as more emotion drenched her.

"Jay messed up by not telling you when he originally went to see you to express his condolences," Stephen continued while absently pulling up blades of grass. "The truth is that he took one look at you and was completely mesmerized. He already had feelings for you the first time you spoke to him."

Veronica's eyes widened, and she eyed him with bewilderment. "Did he really?"

"*Ya*, he did. My *bruder* is a lot of things, but he's not a liar. He's very impulsive, almost to a fault. He wanted to find you after he saw you at the visitation, and he made it his business to learn where you lived. I cautioned him from the beginning that it was a little strange to search for you, but Jay was determined to see you and tell you he was sorry he couldn't save Seth. He blames himself for Seth's accident, even though it wasn't his fault at all."

Veronica sniffed as her eyes stung with tears. This news was almost too much for her to bear. She took a deep breath and willed herself not to cry. She'd already shed too many tears.

"Then before he could find out where you lived, he was surprised to find you were the *maedel* selling the raspberry pies my mother wanted us to buy for her. When Jay met you," Stephen continued, "he forgot his original plan. He just wanted to get to know you. It wasn't his intention to mislead you, but he was so worried about losing you that he couldn't bring himself to tell you the truth, afraid he would only remind you of Seth." He flicked a blade of grass and then brushed his hands on his trousers. "And now that he's lost you, he's a complete mess."

I am too. Veronica looked out toward the volleyball game as her sister served the ball with the grace of a professional player. She tried to avoid Stephen's eyes as regret assaulted her soul.

"Jay is crazy about you," Stephen said. "I hope you can find it in your heart to forgive him."

Veronica nodded and attempted to shield her raging emotions from him. "I appreciate your concern."

"You appreciate my concern?" Stephen lifted an eyebrow with a wry smile. "Is that just a polite way for you to tell me to mind my own business?"

Veronica laughed at his outspoken remark. "No, that's not what I meant. I really do appreciate that you're worried about your *bruder.*"

"Of course I am. He's my only sibling. I have a feeling your *schweschdere* take care of you too."

Veronica shook her head. "You have no idea. They literally

dragged me to the buggy tonight. I didn't want to come, but they made me. It was completely against my will."

Stephen eyed her with interest. "So you wanted to stay home alone, too, huh?"

Veronica nodded. "That's right."

"Sounds like you and Jay are both miserable." He smiled. "Something tells me you miss each other."

Veronica turned her attention back to the game as a lump formed in her throat.

"You don't have to say anything," Stephen said. "But please make me one promise."

"What do you want me to promise you?" Veronica asked with suspicion.

"Please don't make him suffer much longer," Stephen said as he stood.

Veronica gave him a small smile. "I'll see what I can do."

"*Danki*. That's all I can ask. See you later." Stephen grinned before running off to the volleyball game.

CHAPTER 23

"I'M GOING TO THE HARDWARE STORE THIS MORNING," *Dat* announced at breakfast the following morning. "I want you to come with me, Veronica."

"You do?" Veronica looked up from her plate of eggs and bacon just as a suspicious look passed between her parents. What were her parents conspiring about?

"*Ya*, I do," *Dat* said. "We don't talk enough. Come with me and I'll take you to lunch."

"Okay." Veronica shrugged. "I need some baking supplies, so I'll run into the grocery store too."

"Great," *Dat* said, lifting his coffee mug.

After Veronica helped her mother and Emily clean the kitchen, she ran upstairs to grab her purse before following her father out to the waiting van. Her father had hired his usual driver, Charlotte Campbell, to take them into the center of town in Bird-in-Hand.

During the ride, *Dat* sat in the front of the van next to Charlotte and discussed the weather, talking about how nice it was to finally have some cooler days after the hot and humid summer they had endured.

Forgetting that her parents had been acting suspiciously at breakfast, Veronica lost herself in her thoughts. She had too much on her mind, and *Dat* and Charlotte's weather discussion was only background noise for her. She mentally considered her conversation with Stephen last night. Jason's brother had unknowingly confirmed everything Jason had told her. She now believed Jason had never meant to hurt her. When she had awoken this morning, she found herself at peace with her feelings for Jason. She had not only forgiven him, but she was ready to start over just as he suggested.

As the van steered onto Highway 340, she opened her purse and peeked inside. She touched the bag of stones, and her heart fluttered. She couldn't wait to give Jason the bag and ask him to take her to his father's pond. She wanted to hold his hand and walk around the pond while they talked about their feelings for each other and their future plans. It made her feel so happy to think about having plans for the future with Jason. After their walk, they would skip stones together until their wrists were sore. The notion caused her insides to warm and her lips to turn up in a smile.

After their shopping, Veronica was going to ask *Dat* if they could stop by the Lancaster Shed Company to see Jason. She was ready. Ready to face a future without Seth, ready to open her heart and let Jason in completely, ready to love again.

Excitement rushed through Veronica. She couldn't wait to see Jason and apologize to him.

"YOU REALLY SAID ALL THAT TO VERONICA?" JASON REGARDED his brother with surprise as they stood in the middle of the shop. "You told her I'm a complete mess since I lost her?"

Hammers banged, saw blades whirled, and air compressors

hummed as the sweet scent of wood and stain surrounded them. But Jason had become oblivious to it all. He was stunned, not sure if he should yell at his brother for interfering or thank Stephen for defending him.

"*Ya*, I did. I also told her you were afraid of losing her. I was only trying to help." Stephen shrugged as if it wasn't a big deal. "I only told her the truth, and she looked stunned. I asked her to forgive you, and she listened intently. Hopefully I made a difference."

"*Danki*." Jason decided to thank him. After all, his brother had told the truth, and it seemed as if it might have worked.

"*Gern gschehne*," Stephen said as he started to go. "I'll be right back. I need to remind *Dat* about the supply order. We're running low on nails."

Jason shook his head and grinned as Stephen disappeared into the office at the front of the shop. Leave it to him to be so nonchalant about emotional turmoil. He could just imagine Stephen telling Veronica about his own brother's feelings so matter-of-factly.

Jason continued to smile as he stuck his hammer in his tool belt, picked up a handful of shingles, and walked toward the ladder to the roof of the large, two-story shed he and Stephen had finished building last Friday. As he walked toward the ladder, his feet slammed into something sturdy. He stumbled, lost his footing, and his feet went up in the air, sending him crashing down with the heavy armful of shingles and the hammer.

His body crashed to the cement floor, and he landed on his right arm. He heard a loud crack as his head slammed against the same unforgiving surface. The wind was knocked out of him, and a searing pain radiated up his arm to his shoulder. He couldn't move. He couldn't exhale. The pain stole his breath, and he lay immobilized on the cold, hard floor in the center of the shop.

"Jason!" Stephen hollered. "Don't move!"

He could just barely hear his brother as he barked orders.

"Call nine-one-one. Someone get my *dat*! *Dummle!*"

Jason tried to speak, but the pain worsened, choking off his words.

Stephen hovered over him. "Don't move. We're getting help."

Jason's eyes started to close as the pain covered him like a thick, smothering fog. The voices swirling around him sounded as if they were in the distance. He wanted to sleep. He wanted the agony that was paralyzing him to go away.

"Jay!" Stephen said, his voice strained with worry. "Stay with me, Jason. Don't close your eyes. Don't fall asleep."

"What happened?" *Dat*'s voice echoed somewhere in the distance.

"Jason tripped over that can of paint," another man called. "He landed on his arm and hit his head pretty hard. I heard his skull smack the cement."

"Has someone called nine-one-one?" Stephen yelled.

"Rufus is calling," *Dat* said. "Jason, stay with us. You're going to be fine." *Dat*'s voice quaked. "Don't fall asleep."

"I-I—" Jason tried to talk, but the burn of the pain in his arm stole his ability to form words. "My arm," he managed to say, his breath coming in short bursts. "Hurts."

"An ambulance is coming!" Rufus hollered. "Hold on, Jason."

Jason closed his eyes, and everything went dark.

"DO YOU WANT TO GO TO THE HARDWARE STORE FIRST?" Veronica asked as she climbed from the back of the van. "Or we could go to the grocery first for my baking supplies. It doesn't matter to me since they're both close by."

She had already glanced over at Lancaster Sheds—a place she had avoided even noticing for months whenever she was in town—but it was too early to mention her plan to stop in there.

"It's up to you," *Dat* said. "I just thought we could do our shopping first and then go to lunch. The truth is, Veronica, your *mamm* and I think you and I should talk some more about Jason over lunch, away from the *haus*." Before she could respond, he leaned into the van. "Do you think you could pick us up in about an hour?"

"I actually need to get a few things from the hardware store, too, so I'll just park here and wait for you," Charlotte said. "Take your time."

"*Danki*, Charlotte. Veronica," *Dat* said as he turned back to her, "where do you want to go first then—"

The blare of a siren interrupted their conversation. As the sound grew louder, Veronica turned around and faced the road. She spotted an ambulance steering into the parking lot behind the Lancaster Shed Company, and her stomach plummeted.

"Jason!" she yelled. "*Dat*, we have to go check on Jason!"

Without awaiting his response, she took off running toward the store. She burst through the front doors and found the showroom empty, then rushed through doors she assumed would lead to the shop where Jason worked. EMTs were gathered around someone who was on the floor.

Veronica's body began to tremble as the memories of learning about Seth's accident consumed her mind. She'd heard about the ambulance coming to the shop and the EMTs finding him already gone. They'd called the coroner and had his body taken to Margaret's, where the bishop had already gone to break the news to her and Ellie. Then when Ellie called the harness shop phone and told her to come . . .

She shivered, hugging her arms to her chest.

A hand clasped her shoulder, and she jumped with a start.

"Calm down," *Dat* told her. "Everything is going to be fine."

Stephen's face emerged from the sea of workers standing close to the EMTs. He crossed the large shop and approached her. "Veronica? What are you doing here?"

"Is Jason okay?" Her voice was shaky and higher than usual, making her sound like someone else. "We saw the ambulance, and I had to check on him."

Stephen grimaced. "Jason tripped over a can of paint, and he took a pretty bad fall. We heard his skull hit the cement floor."

Veronica's knees buckled as more memories from the aftermath of Seth's accident assaulted her mind. Just as he had done then, her *dat*'s strong hands grabbed her arms and steadied her.

"No, no, no!" she cried. She could feel the blood draining from her face, and fear overpowered her. "I can't lose him. Not now!" She could hear her voice growing shrill.

"Calm down," *Dat* repeated. "It's going to be okay."

"He's awake now and he's talking, but we think he may have broken his right arm." Stephen pointed toward the EMTs. "They're taking his vital signs before they move him to a backboard."

Veronica cupped her hand to her mouth, and *Dat* gently squeezed her shoulder.

"He's going to be fine," *Dat* said. "If he's awake and talking, then he'll be okay."

"Can I see him?" she asked, tears spilling from her eyes. "I want to tell him I'm sorry, and I want to start over. I need to tell him he was right about everything."

"Shh," *Dat* said, consoling her. "You'll have plenty of time to talk to him later. Let the EMTs take care of him now. He's probably in shock and wouldn't recognize you right now."

Jason cried out as the EMTs moved him to a board, and Veronica swallowed a sob. Her heart was pounding so hard she was certain everyone in the shop could hear it. Her father encircled her shoulders with one arm and pulled her close to him. She looked up at Stephen and spotted tears shimmering in his brown eyes.

The EMTs placed the board on a gurney, secured it, and then one of the men pushed it toward the back exit. Veronica rushed over to the gurney as her blood pounded in her ears. Jason was moaning and gnawing his lower lip. His eyes were sealed shut, and his face was twisted in a painful grimace.

Veronica wanted to tell him she loved him and she was sorry. She longed to touch his face and his hands. But an EMT gently pushed her away from the gurney.

"We need to get him to the hospital as soon as possible, miss," the man said. "You can visit him after he's stabilized."

Veronica's heart was lodged in her throat as the EMTs pushed the gurney out to the ambulance. She closed her eyes and prayed, begging God to place his healing hand on Jason. *I can't lose him. He has to be okay; he just has to!*

A tall man with graying brown hair and a matching beard rushed over to Stephen. He had the same light-brown eyes as Jason and Stephen. "I'm going to ride in the ambulance with him. Will you call your *mamm*?"

"*Ya, Dat.*" Stephen rubbed his eyes. "Go on. I'll find a ride to the hospital."

His father gave him a quick nod and then rushed out of the shop.

"We'll take you," *Dat* said. "We can go pick up your *mamm* too."

Veronica nodded with emphasis. "*Ya*, we'll take you. I'm sure our driver is still just outside."

"Let's go," Stephen said.

Veronica's nerves were raw as they hurried out of the store. She continued to pray silently as they climbed into the van.

JASON'S HEAD WAS FUZZY AS HE SAT PROPPED UP IN THE hospital bed later that afternoon. His right arm was in a cast and a sling, but the pain radiating through it was now a dull throb thanks to heavy painkillers. He also had some bruises. All in all, he was okay. His parents sat nearby, and his mother was still dabbing her eyes with a tissue.

"I was so worried when Stephen came to get me." *Mamm* sniffed. "When he said you'd been in an accident, all I could think of was your *freind* Seth. I just sobbed and sobbed."

"I'm sorry I scared you," Jason muttered with a croak. His voice sounded strange to his own ears. It was as if he had a frog in his throat. "I didn't mean to fall. I'm just a klutz."

"Why didn't you check to make sure there wasn't anything on the floor before you picked up those shingles?" *Dat* asked. "Those shingles are so heavy, Jason. You could've been hurt worse."

"I was just walking to the ladder, *Dat*," Jason said. "We all climb ladders a thousand times every day."

"You're blessed that your worst injury is that broken arm," *Dat* continued, berating him. "When Stephen shouted to call nine-one-one, I had the same fear your *mamm* did."

"I'm sorry," Jason said again. He tried to adjust himself in the lumpy bed, and the sharp pain shooting from his arm stopped him. "This bed is terrible. When can we leave? I really would like to rest in my own bed."

"We have to wait for the doctor to release you," *Dat* said, fingering his suspenders. "He said he wanted to watch for signs of a concussion. You took a really hard fall."

Jason tried to recall the accident. He remembered the sickening sensation of his feet slipping and then the horrific thud of his body hitting the floor. He vaguely recalled his brother talking to him and then the sound of the siren. For some inexplicable reason, he also remembered hearing Veronica's voice and then the sound of her crying. Why would he have heard Veronica? That must've been caused by the thick fog of pain from his injuries. There was no chance Veronica had been there.

Stephen appeared in the doorway with bottles of water. "I brought drinks." He gave their parents each a bottle and then handed one to Jason. "How are you feeling?"

"I think I know what a nail head feels like after it's been pounded into a piece of wood." He tried to smile, but it came out as a grimace.

Stephen blew out a deep sigh. "You scared me to death today, Jay. I think I lost ten years off my life."

"I'm sorry," Jason repeated. "I really didn't mean to trip."

"I know. I'm just glad you're okay." Stephen twisted the top off his bottle. "Are you ready for visitors?"

"I have visitors?" Jason asked. "Who's here to see me? The guys from the shop?"

"No, it's not the guys from the shop. They've been calling for updates, but they're still working. You really have only one visitor, someone who wants to see you as soon as possible," Stephen said with a smile. He turned to his parents. "Do you want to go for a walk for a few minutes?"

"*Ya*," *Mamm* agreed as she stood. "*Dat* and I can go find something to eat. I think I'm ready for a little lunch."

Dat stood and took her hand. "We'll be back in a while to see you. You just relax, Jason."

Stephen smiled at Jason again. "I'll be right back."

"Stephen, what's going on?" Jason scowled. "I'm in no mood for jokes."

"It's not a joke. Just drink your water, and I'll be right back." Stephen moved out of the room.

Jason stared after his brother and parents and wondered what the big secret was. He sipped the cool water and breathed a sigh of relief that he was going to be okay. He could cope with a broken arm, which would heal in time.

VERONICA POPPED UP TO HER FEET WHEN STEPHEN ENTERED the waiting room. She'd spent the past two hours praying for Jason. The pleasant expression on Stephen's face told her Jason was going to be all right, and the tension that had taken hold of her body relaxed slightly.

"How is he?" Veronica asked.

"Jason is okay," Stephen said. "He has a broken arm and some other bruises. He's awake and talking. The doctors just want to watch him to make sure he doesn't have a concussion."

"Praise God!" She clapped. "I'm so thankful he's okay."

"He's ready to see you," Stephen said. "I haven't told him you're here, but I told him someone wants to see him."

Veronica's heart pounded against her rib cage as she turned to her father. "Do you want to come with me?"

"No. You go on alone," *Dat* said, patting her shoulder. "Stephen, would you show me where the cafeteria is?"

"*Ya*, my parents just went down there. We can have lunch with them." Stephen started toward the door. "I'll take you to Jason's room, and then I'll take your *dat* to lunch."

Veronica's hands continued to tremble as she followed Stephen through the winding hospital hallway to a room at the end of a long corridor. Stephen gave her an encouraging look and then led her father away. Veronica took a deep breath in an attempt to settle her shredded nerves and then knocked on the door.

"Come in." Jason's voice was soft and hoarse on the other side of the door.

Veronica pushed open the door, and her eyes prickled with tears when she found Jason propped up in bed with a sling covering the cast on his right arm. His expression brightened, and his eyes widened.

"Hi," Jason said.

"Hi," she whispered with a sniff. She closed the gap between them and stood at the bed on his left side. "I thought I'd lost you." Tears slid down her cheeks as the emotions she'd tried to keep in check since they'd left Lancaster Sheds came bubbling out. "I was close to the store with my *dat* when we saw the ambulance pull in there, and I immediately feared you'd been in an accident. When I saw the EMTs working on you, I thought you were gone. It was just like how I imagined it was when I lost Seth." She dissolved in sobs and sank into the chair next to the bed.

"Veronica," he whispered, and despite his thin voice, it sounded like a sweet melody to her ears. He reached over and touched her cheek with his left arm. "I'm right here. I'm just a little banged up, but I'll be okay."

She grabbed a tissue from the table by the bed and rubbed her eyes and nose. "I'm so sorry. I'm sorry for pushing you away. I had no right to treat you so badly. I know you never meant to hurt me. Please forgive me."

Jason shook his head. "You don't have to apologize."

"*Ya*, I do need to apologize," Veronica insisted as guilt

washed over her like a tidal wave. "I was cruel to you. I said horrible things. I didn't mean it when I said it was over and I told you to forget me. I don't want you to date Mary."

Jason smiled as he took her hand in his. "You don't need to worry about that. She already has a boyfriend. I never wanted her anyway. I only wanted to be with you."

"*Danki*. I know you only wanted to be with me." Veronica sniffed, enjoying the feel of his warm hand on hers. "I was so determined to protect Seth's memory that I lost sight of my own emotions. I liked you from the moment I met you, but I was afraid of getting hurt. Instead of getting to know you, I shut you out when I needed you most."

"It's okay," Jason said. "You don't have to explain yourself." His eyes were warm, reminding her of caramel, and her heart swelled with love for him.

"I do need to explain myself." She squeezed his hand. "I realized after talking to my *schweschdere* and also to your *bruder* that I was wrong. I was so determined to guard my heart that I missed what I needed, and that was you. You were right in front of me all along, Jason. I'm so sorry."

"Veronica—" he began.

"Please, let me finish," she said, interrupting him. "I've been doing a lot of thinking. We both lost Seth, and we both miss him. Rachel made me realize you were hurting just as much as I was. I had no right to deny you the right to grieve. I was only focused on the fact that you didn't tell me you were Seth's *freind* when I first met you. I understand now that you were afraid of losing me, and that makes sense. I should've respected your grief instead of blaming you for my grief."

Jason nodded. "I understand why you were upset. I should have been honest with you the first day I met you."

"Stephen explained to me why you were nervous to tell me

the truth from the beginning." Veronica paused to gather her thoughts. "I realized last night that you tried to tell me a few times. When we were walking by the pond after the picnic, you started to tell me you had lost someone close to you and you understood how I felt. You were talking about Seth, weren't you?"

He nodded, frowning. "*Ya*, I was."

"And you tried again the night you gave me the shelf. You started to tell me something, and then you stopped. You didn't want to scare me away."

"Exactly." Jason sighed. He shifted slightly in the bed and then grimaced.

"Are you okay?" Panic shot through her, and she stood and reached for him, not sure what to do to help him. "Do you want me to call the nurse?"

"I'm all right," he said, his voice breathless. "My arm is killing me, but I'm thankful I didn't break my back." He cleared his throat. "What were you saying? Oh, right. You were talking about the night I realized I had to tell you about Seth. I had already told you I loved you, and I knew my feelings for you were growing. I decided I had to be brave and finally admit the truth."

"Well, the truth is that I love you," Veronica said as more tears trickled down her warm cheeks.

His eyes widened and he smiled. "I love you too, Veronica."

"I'm sorry I pushed you away." Veronica looked down at the bedrail, and her thoughts fell into place. "After you told me the truth about knowing Seth, I went up into the attic looking for more recipes. I was trying to find a way to channel my grief, and cooking has always been the best way for me to cope. I didn't find any other recipes, but I found a letter my *mammi* had written to my *daadi* when they were dating."

She explained that her great-uncle had died in an accident, and he had been her grandfather's best friend. She also shared about the letter her grandmother had written after her grandparents' argument.

"In the letter, my *mammi* told my *daadi* that she realized she would always keep her *bruder* in her heart. She'd been afraid of moving on with her life because she didn't want to disrespect her *bruder*'s memory. She also said her *bruder* would want her to be *froh*." She met Jason's gaze and found him watching her intently. "I think the letter applies to us." She took his hand in hers. "I don't have to put my life on hold because I lost Seth. I'll always keep my memories of Seth alive in my heart, but you and I will make new memories together. We both loved Seth, and we'll never forget him. And Seth would want us to be *froh*."

He squeezed her hand. "I agree," he whispered, his voice straining with emotion.

"Jason, I want to start over." She pulled a plastic zip-up bag from her purse and looked at him with a smile. "Hi. My name is Veronica Fisher, and I'd like to teach you how to skip stones. Word around the community is that I'm the expert and you need some help."

Jason chuckled and then winced before saying, "Well, Veronica Fisher, my name is Jason Huyard, and I'd love to have you teach me how to skip stones. I think we'll have to wait until after my arm heals for you to give me lessons, but I'll be *froh* to watch you skip them."

"That sounds like a *gut* plan." Veronica grinned. "I love you, Jason."

"I love you too, Veronica."

She leaned down and rested her head on his left shoulder and closed her eyes. She was thankful God had given her a second chance at love.

EPILOGUE

VERONICA HELD JASON'S HAND AS THEY STOOD BY THE pond on the Huyard farm two months later. She shivered as the early November wind seeped through her coat, and she hugged her arms to her chest while Jason chose a rock from a bag and flicked it out over the pond.

"Look at that!" Jason said, clapping his hands. "That was six skips before the rock fell into the pond. Can you beat that?"

"That's great." She smiled as her teeth chattered. "Can we go in now? I'll make some hot chocolate, and we can sit by the fire and warm up."

"Hang on." He chose the last rock from the bag. "I've waited two long months to do this. I'm glad the break wasn't as bad as it could have been. But, still, I thought that cast would never come off and therapy would never end."

"*Buwe*," Veronica muttered with an eye roll.

"I heard that." He flashed his adorable crooked grin, and her pulse galloped through her veins. He flicked the last rock, and it skipped seven times before plopping into the water. "Did you see that one?"

"*Ya*, I saw it." She tried her best to sound enthusiastic, but the cold was seeping into her bones. "Now can we go?"

"What's the rush?" He took her hands in his. "We just got out here."

"In case you haven't noticed, it's cold. You're the weatherman, so you should've already known that." She smiled up at him, taking in his handsome face.

The past two months had been wonderful as she and Jason had enjoyed getting to know each other better. Jason's arm had taken two long months to heal, and he spent that time working in his father's office instead of building sheds. His cast, however, didn't hinder Jason from visiting Veronica. They spent as much time as possible together—taking long walks, going on picnics, and sitting on each other's porches late into the night while talking about everything from their memories of Seth to their feelings for each other. Veronica enjoyed every moment with Jason, and she found herself falling deeper and deeper in love with him every time they were together.

"I'm not ready to go in yet," he said before touching her nose.

"But you ran out of rocks." She held up the empty bag. "See? No rocks left. We can skip stones again next spring, when it's not freezing outside." She stuffed the bag into her coat pocket, took his hand, and started to tug him toward the house. "Let's go have hot chocolate with marshmallows."

"No." He gently pulled her toward him. "Let's go this way."

"Why?" Veronica asked with an exaggerated moan. "I told you, I'm cold."

"Just walk and quit whining." Jason grinned at her, and she complied. He squeezed her hand. "I want to show you something."

"What is it?" she asked. "More dead grass?"

Jason shook his head. "No, it's more than that. At least it will be." He pointed toward the far pasture, beyond the pond. "Do you see that big tree out there?"

"*Ya*, I see it." Veronica shivered again and leaned against him, hoping some of his body heat would seep into her coat and warm her to above frigid temperatures.

"That's where I want to build our *haus*." He kept his focus trained on the far pasture. "I've envisioned it would have two stories, a wraparound porch, and three bedrooms, but we can have more bedrooms if you want."

Veronica blinked, and she was suddenly dizzy with excitement. Did he just say he wanted to build her a house? Had she heard him correctly? "What did you say?"

Jason gave her a warm smile and touched her cheek. "I want to build you a *haus*, but I need to ask you something first." He cleared his throat and looked into her eyes as if they held all the answers he needed.

"I love you, Veronica. I've loved you since that first time I met you at your bake stand and you looked at me as if I were a lunatic. I want to spend the rest of my life with you. I want to have a family with you, and I want to grow old with you. I've already gotten your father's blessing, but I have to ask you something. Will you marry me and let me build you a *haus* on my father's farm?"

"Yes," she whispered as sudden tears flooded her eyes. "Yes, I will marry you."

He placed his hands on her cheeks, leaned down, and brushed his lips across hers, sending her stomach into a wild swirl. She closed her eyes and savored the feeling of his lips against hers. All her dreams had come true.

"I can't wait until next season to get married," he said. "Let's get married a week or two after Christmas."

"A week or two after Christmas?" she asked, her thoughts swirling with anxiety. "That's barely two months away. There's so much to plan, and I need to make dresses for my *schweschdere* and for me. And all of the baking." She looked up at him and shook her head. "I don't know, Jason."

"Veronica, my accident taught me that life is fleeting. I can't wait to start my life with you, and I don't want to wait if I don't have to." He took her hand and led her back toward his parents' house. "If you want to wait a year, then we'll wait. It's up to you."

As they climbed the porch steps, Veronica could sense the disappointment in his voice. Excitement rushed through her as she thought of being Jason's wife before spring set into Lancaster County.

"Wait," she said when they reached the top step. "I don't want to wait to get married next year either, but I don't think two months is enough time to get ready. How about February?"

"February?" His eyes flickered with excitement.

"*Ya*, that will give me enough time to prepare."

"Yes!" Jason lifted her up and spun her around. "You've made me the happiest man on the planet." He kissed her again, this kiss lingering longer than the first. Warmth swept through her body, and she suddenly forgot that it was November.

She took his hand and led him to the house. "Let's go have some hot chocolate. We have some plans to make. I want to hear more about this *haus* you're going to build for me."

WHEN VERONICA TOLD HER FAMILY THE EXCITING NEWS, they were overjoyed, but her mother and sisters also agreed that they had a lot to do before the wedding. They began making lists of everything they needed to make and buy in preparation. Veronica was so thankful to have her sisters to help her plan her wedding and share in her excitement.

After supper Veronica helped her mother wash and dry the dishes while Emily spent some time in the store and Rachel and David talked on the porch. Veronica wanted to tell her mother about all the plans she and Jason had already made.

"Jason is going to build a *haus* for us on his parents' property," she told her mother while drying a pot. "He said he's going to build a bake stand for me, too, so I can keep making pies. I think he wants me to make them for him, but he says I can sell them as well."

"I'm so *froh* for you, Veronica." *Mamm* smiled as she scrubbed a pan. "I had a feeling Jason was the one for you, but I wanted you to feel that way in your heart."

"I do, *Mamm*. I'm so very happy. *Danki*." Veronica stowed the pot in the cabinet. "You know, *Mamm*, I'm already thinking about what pies I'm going to bake for the bake stand next year—besides raspberry pies, of course. That is, if you'll let us buy raspberries from you. Do you have more of *Mammi*'s pie recipes? I know she made several different kinds."

"Veronica, you can help yourself to the raspberries. But I'm not sure if I have any more of *Mammi*'s pie recipes," *Mamm* said.

"When we were looking for more recipes together in the attic, we got sidetracked with *Mammi*'s letter." Veronica wasn't sure she should mention the hope chest. "Would you help me look around up there some more?"

Her mother seemed to hesitate for a moment, but then said, "*Ya*. I'll help you."

Later, when *Mamm* said she was ready, Veronica grabbed flashlights and followed her mother up the spiral staircase to the third floor.

As she hummed to herself, she flipped open boxes and sifted through some books and papers. *Mamm* looked in some old dresser drawers.

Eventually Veronica found her way to the back of the attic and spotted her mother's hope chest again, where she'd found both the forgotten, but all-important, raspberry pie recipe and her *mammi*'s letter. She glanced at her mother, remembering

294

Mamm had locked it the last time they had been in the attic together. Would she allow her to look in the hope chest once more? There could be more recipes in there.

"*Mamm*? May we look in your hope chest one more time?"

Mamm nodded. "*Ya*. I brought the key up with me in case you asked." She pulled the key from her apron pocket, unlocked the chest, and then slipped the key back into her pocket. "I'll check for you."

Mamm opened the lid and moved some items around, this time digging a little deeper. When she lifted a small, flat box near the bottom of one side a little too quickly, the lid fell off, and a brand-new, blue, newborn-size onesie spilled out onto the floor.

Veronica immediately picked it up and examined it, noticing a faded price tag hanging from the arm. She heard her mother gasp, and when she looked up, *Mamm's* eyes had widened.

In an instant, questions swirled through Veronica's mind. Why would her mother, who had given birth to three girls, have a *blue* onesie? Had the onesie belonged to another baby? But whose baby could it have been? Why was *Mamm* so shocked to find this? Didn't she know it was in the chest?

She craved answers.

"*Mamm*," Veronica began, "why did you—"

"Please give that to me." *Mamm* snatched the onesie from Veronica's hand.

"Where did it come from?"

"It's just something I was saving." *Mamm* stood, bent to fetch the box, and her fingers scrambled to place the onsie back inside and replace the lid.

Veronica stood beside her. "Why were you saving that?"

"I told you, I just was." *Mamm* was obviously evading the question. "Let me put it back, and then we can talk some more about your wedding." She returned the box to the bottom of the hope chest, locked it, pocketed the key again, and started for the stairs. "I don't think there are any more recipes up here anyway." Behind her, Veronica could see her shoulders rise and fall as she took a deep breath.

"I was going over your lists earlier, Veronica, and I thought we could go to the fabric store tomorrow to pick up material."

As Veronica drew up beside her mother and tried to look into her eyes, she could tell *Mamm* was avoiding her gaze. She had no idea why she wouldn't discuss the small garment. Was *Mamm* hiding something? Was she saving it for someone else? But *Mamm* had made it clear the subject was closed.

"I think blue will look lovely on you and your *schweschdere*," Mamm said as they descended the stairs.

"*Danki, Mamm.* I agree, and Jason likes blue too." Veronica followed her mother and pushed the confusion about the onesie and the locked hope chest away. Turning her thoughts to her wedding made her smile. She couldn't wait to get started on all their plans, and she couldn't wait to start her life with Jason.

ACKNOWLEDGMENTS

AS ALWAYS, I'M THANKFUL FOR MY LOVING FAMILY, INCLUD-
ing my mother, Lola Goebelbecker; my husband, Joe; and my
sons, Zac and Matt. I'm blessed to have such an awesome and
amazing family.

I'm more grateful than words can express to Janet Pecorella,
Lauran Rodriguez, and also my mother for proofreading for me.
I truly appreciate the time you take out of your busy lives to
help me polish my books. Special thanks to my Amish friends
who patiently answer my endless stream of questions. Thank
you also to Stacey Barbalace for her research assistance. You're a
blessing in my life.

Thank you to my wonderful church family at Morning Star
Lutheran in Matthews, North Carolina, for your encourage-
ment, prayers, love, and friendship. You all mean so much to my
family and me.

To my agent, Sue Brower—you are my own personal super-
hero! I can't thank you enough for your guidance, advice, and
friendship. I'm thankful that our paths have crossed and our
partnership will continue long into the future. You are a tremendous blessing in my life.

Thank you to my amazing editor, Becky Philpott, for your

friendship and guidance. I'm grateful to Jean Bloom, who helped me polish and refine the story. I also would like to thank Katie Bond and Kristen Golden for tirelessly working to promote my books. I'm grateful to each and every person at HarperCollins Christian Publishing who helped make this book a reality.

To my readers—thank you for choosing my novels. My books are a blessing in my life for many reasons, including the special friendships I've formed with you. Thank you for your e-mail messages, Facebook notes, and letters.

Thank you most of all to God—for giving me the inspiration and the words to glorify you. I'm grateful and humbled that you've chosen this path for me.

Special thanks to Cathy and Dennis Zimmermann for their hospitality and research assistance in Lancaster County, Pennsylvania.

Cathy & Dennis Zimmermann, Innkeepers
The Creekside Inn
44 Leacock Road
PO Box 435
Paradise, PA 17562
Toll Free: (866) 604-2574
Local Phone: (717) 687-0333

The author and publisher gratefully acknowledge the following resource that was used to research information for this book:

C. Richard Beam, *Revised Pennsylvania German Dictionary* (Lancaster, PA: Brookshire, 1991).

DISCUSSION QUESTIONS

1. Jason is distraught when his friend Seth is killed in a work accident. When he sees Veronica at the visitation at Seth's mother's house, he feels compelled to share his grief with her. Have you faced a difficult loss? What Bible verses helped you? Share this with the group.

2. Veronica feels God is giving her a second chance when she falls in love with Jason. Have you ever experienced a second chance? What was it?

3. Emily quotes Psalm 46:10: "Be still, and know that I am God." What does this verse mean to you?

4. Veronica busies herself with baking raspberry pies as a way to deal with losing her fiancé. Think of a time when you felt lost and alone. Where did you find your strength? What Bible verses helped?

5. Jason believes he's shielding Veronica from hurt when he fails to tell her he was friends with Seth. In the end, it's still painful when Veronica finds out the truth. Do you think Jason's intentions were justified? Have you ever found yourself in a similar situation? If so, how did it turn out? Share this with the group.

6. Near the end of the book, Stephen feels compelled to talk to Veronica about Jason to try to convince her Jason never meant to hurt her. Have you ever tried to defend someone who had hurt someone else? How did this situation turn out for you?

7. Veronica is afraid of opening her heart to Jason. By the end of the book, she realizes she is ready to love again and then agrees to marry him. What do you think causes her to change her point of view on love throughout the story?

8. Which character can you identify with the most? Which character seems to carry the most emotional stake in the story? Is it Jason, Veronica, Stephen, or someone else?

9. After his accident, Jason is eager to get married. He feels life is fleeting, and he doesn't want to waste another day. Have you ever had a life-changing experience? If so, share this with the group.

10. What did you know about the Amish before reading this book? What did you learn?

THE SECOND INSTALLMENT OF
THE AMISH HEIRLOOM SERIES
–COMING JULY 2016!

The Courtship Basket

The *Kauffman*

Amish Bakery Series

The
GIFT
of
GRACE

AMY CLIPSTON

A
SEASON
of
LOVE

AMY CLIPSTON

A
PLACE
of
PEACE

AMY CLIPSTON

A
PROMISE
of
HOPE

AMY CLIPSTON

A
LIFE
of
JOY

AMY CLIPSTON

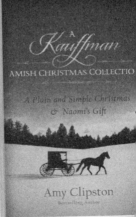

A Kauffman
AMISH CHRISTMAS COLLECTIO

A Plain and Simple Christmas
& Naomi's Gift

Amy Clipston
Bestselling Author

ABOUT THE AUTHOR

Photo by Dan Davis Photography

AMY CLIPSTON IS THE AWARD-WINNING AND BESTSELLING author of more than a dozen novels, including the Kauffman Amish Bakery series and the Hearts of the Lancaster Grand Hotel series. Her novels have hit multiple bestseller lists including CBD, CBA, and ECPA. Amy holds a degree in communication from Virginia Wesleyan College and works full-time for the City of Charlotte, North Carolina. Amy lives in North Carolina with her husband, two sons, and four spoiled rotten cats.

Visit her website: amyclipston.com
Facebook: Amy Clipston
Twitter: @AmyClipston